The Deathless Critics Weigh In on

Again, Hazardous Imaginings...

"Spare the rod and spoil the anthologist. Burn the witch, and burn this book!" — Cotton Mather

"In light of the calamitous fortune my legacy has suffered, I have little doubt that these reactionary fantasies shall swiftly become the opiate of the masses." — Karl Marx

"It is common sense that the tales in this volume be given fair consideration." — Thomas Paine

"Whereas it may be too early to judge the success of the French Revolution, it is not too early to sentence the editor of this tome to thirty years hard labor on a collective farm." — Zhou Enlai

"It seems a certainty that this decadent, freedom-loving Jew editor will be compared to me — *me!* I despair for humanity." — Joseph Goebbels

"These are not the sort of stories I envisioned when I published my first Scientifiction magazines. But I assume they must appeal to some. By the way, how much longer does my name get to stay on that award?" — Hugo Gernsback

"Fox is playing a dangerous game and has all the vision of Mr. Magoo. I'll sue the bastard! Somehow." — Cordwainer Bird

Again, Hazardous Imaginings:

More Politically Incorrect Science Fiction

an international anthology

Edited by Andrew Fox

Introduction by Barry N. Malzberg

MonstraCity
PRESS

Other Books by Andrew Fox

This anthology is dedicated to the long line of science fiction's contrarians: Stanley G. Weinbaum; John W. Campbell; Cyril M. Kornbluth and Frederik Pohl; Stanislaw Lem; Judith Merril; Philip José Farmer; Harlan Ellison®; Philip K. Dick; J. G. Ballard; R. A. Lafferty; Michael Moorcock; Joanna Russ; Thomas M. Disch; Norman Spinrad; Stanley Kubrick; and Barry N. Malzberg.

May the line remain unbroken.

Introduction: Luminous Darkness at Noon

Barry N. Malzberg

HREE decades ago in a Columbia University sf Convention
classroom on a panel confronting The State of the Art
I proposed in (what I intended to be) passing that taboos
still held science fiction firmly in place. From the audience, Ellen
Datlow, the fiction editor at *Omni* Magazine, said,
"That's ridiculous. There are no taboos anymore. "Ellen," I said,
"If you give me two minutes I can reel out for you summaries of
five science fiction stories I could not sell anywhere." A long, thick
silence through which the ghost of Lionel Trilling could be dimly
heard harumphing about the presence of such a cartoon literature
being enshrined in the Ivy League on a Saturday ensued until
Ellen said, "Okay, there are taboos." We went on to other matters.
Robert Sheckley was on that panel. He could have given ten. Roger
Zelazny had been on a similar panel a year earlier. Seven years
younger than Sheckley, he could have offered seven.

Now I note with ambivalence that the second story on this
book's table of contents centers my implied defense or

endorsement of the xenophobe. In appearing here it does evoke its presence in rough in my head long ago but it took a long time for another writer to get there and it is worth noting that it appears in an anthology deliberately replicating Harlan Ellison's proposal half a century ago that his was an anthology of stories which could have appeared in no other than his own anthology. The visions were too dangerous for the conglomerate, too threatening for the genteel quality lit trade and his 1967 *Dangerous Visions* was a deliberate assault on the castle. Doubleday, a soon-to-be conglomerate publisher put its imprint on that book and the volume appeared over the years in paperback issue of a series of conglomerates, foreign and domestic.

Harlan's proposal was to change everything through his anthology, explode all of the taboos, bury the dead and hasten the dying suppressors of furious coming seasons. Some critics argued that he had created a straw figure in "taboo" and like Ellen claimed that the anthology was essentially a solution to a problem which did not exist. Other critics argued that the anthology, a noble or ignoble experiment, would by its very nature be obsolete in less than a decade and indeed many of the retrospective or recursive reviews, looking at the two Ellison anthologies through the self-diminishing racket of time claimed that their pretension, let alone actual content, had subsided into a kind of quaintness and there not only was nothing in the two anthologies that would be thematically excluded by the current market, there was little force in the stories themselves which had been overtaken by imitation, derivation, influence and were at best a fleet of 1948 Oldsmobiles with hydramatic drive competing rustily in showrooms whose glitter, glass and contents mocked them.

What degree of truth might exist in that present or distant reaction can be argued elsewhere; they provide a kind of context to the present argument but hardly a definitive answer. What remains definitive are two truths which in the stories to follow still struggle toward a kind of definition: 1) I could as easily now as three decades ago donate to Ellen in no significant stretch of time five or six story precis which would be no more for the general market today than they were then and 2) Great or even good science fiction is by its very definition transgressive, struggles, sometimes successfully, with the gap between technology and its application, human ambition and its hypocrisy, ad astra and calamitous darkness. It is the tension between these co-existing qualities which is central to the category itself, central in fact to all fiction, that "struggle between the human heart and itself" which Faulkner noted as central and if that transgression is not seen as inevitable, as integral to this beloved and terrible genre, then it has collapsed toward death by way of decadence. And overvalued as decadence might be in the politics of this dreadful time, we do not need it in our own little Cabinet of Caligari.

—September 2020:
New Jersey

This first story would have found a welcoming home in the taboo-breaking Dangerous Visions, *published in 1967. So what is it doing here (apart from being an affecting, well imagined piece of fiction)? If its aura of taboo would have been banished fifty years ago, why did I select it for an anthology of politically incorrect science fiction? Because societal mores do not progress in a straight trend line, but rather more like a sine wave. Following the Great Loosening of the Sexual Revolution of the 1960s, the last two decades have seen a Great Tightening, a steady march toward a modified form of the sexual ethics of the Victorian era. Theodore Sturgeon or maybe Philip Jose Farmer could have written and perhaps sold this story, but both estimable gentlemen are dead. Depending on the strength of your constitution, modern reader, you may want to have smelling salts handy while braving the following tale. Just kidding (I hope).*

The Beach at Ocolondé

Claude Lalumière

GRIPPING a medium-sized blue duffel bag, I stepped off the bus at Ocolondé. I was the only passenger getting off at this stop — the final passenger on the bus — and only one person waited in the small terminal: a young twentysomething wearing calf-length tie-dye slacks and a long, loose purple shirt that dissimulated the contours of the body beneath. Superfluously, my greeter held a printed sign with my name spelled in a flowery font. In person, Sasha's gender was even more ambiguous than on the agency's flyer. I walked up and identified myself.

"Paul is such an elegantly simple name. Masculine, yet not harsh." Sasha's voice, gorgeously fluid, washed over me like a gentle wave of sun-warmed water, with the spicy hint of a Mediterranean accent. My hired companion's hand slipped into mine, and we exited the station.

The bus station was at the edge of town, an afterthought. The streets of Ocolondé were much too narrow and irregular to accommodate motor vehicles, making Ocolondé one of those rare havens free of the noise, speed, and pollution of automobiles. The air here was saturated with the aromas of the sea. The mountains ringing the city completely isolated it from the rest of Spain, with only the one road leading to the town. There was no nearby airport, and Renfe, the national railway, did not reach here. The port, an unsightly appendage to the southwest, had been bombed by Franco's forces during the civil war and had never been rebuilt. Aside from that one attack, the fascists had mostly left Ocolondé alone; too hard to reach, with such a small population.

The rest of the shoreline was all sand beach, and it was spectacular, the blue of the Mediterranean a powerful attractor. Sasha led me away from the water. There would be plenty of time to enjoy the sea later.

The locals were darker skinned than the average Spaniard, Moorish blood being obviously still an important component of Ocolondé's genetic heritage. The local mix added a noticeable olive hue; in Sasha it was so prominent as to be almost green. The architecture around us was a blend of Roman and Moorish, with only a passing nod to modern times and with none of the fetishization of ruins so common in old cities with an economy dependent on tourism.

We stopped in front of an art gallery, its window display featuring an array of wood carvings of fantastical semi-human sea creatures. Sasha dug out a set of keys. Nearly imperceptible from the street was a side door, to the left of the shop window, that opened to a narrow marble staircase. Up we went. At the top of the stairs stood another locked door. Sasha had a bit of trouble with this one, but soon enough we were inside a luxurious brightly lit apartment with three-meter-high ceilings and correspondingly tall windows — a sharp contrast to the narrow shady street outside, where the sun barely reached the ground.

The floors and walls were decorated with Moorish tiles of intricate design, in various shades of white, blue, and orange. The antique furniture was all of solid wood with bronze trimmings. Most of the pieces here were at least a century old, probably older. These furnishings were built to last, the nicks and scratches accumulated over generations of use granting them yet more character.

I followed the sound of running water. Bent over the extravagant marble bath — large enough for four occupants — Sasha was pouring oils, releasing subtle fragrances of vanilla, coconut, lavender, and peppermint.

Sasha disrobed. I ogled the androgynous body, the minuscule shriveled male genitals, the barely protuberant yet unmistakably female breasts, the depilated skin. My companion slid into the water. I, too, disrobed — and followed.

In Barcelona, three weeks before my arrival in Ocolondé, in a bohemian café near the Catalan architect Antoni Gaudí's unfinished masterwork, the unearthly cathedral known as La Sagrada Familia, I'd stumbled upon a garish flyer, uncharacteristically in English, advertising the services of Ocolondé Elite Vacations. I couldn't resist the siren call of the name Ocolondé. After the Franco regime fell a few years ago, and Spain became more hospitable to tourism, Josey had fantasized about travelling to that nearly unknown town in the southwest of Spain. As an architect, my dream destination had been Barcelona, the capital of modernisme, but Josey had never settled for the obvious.

Back at my hotel, I called the number on the flyer and spoke to someone — I could not tell if it was a man or a woman — with an accent I could not quite place. The agent spoke in such a way as to make everything sound like a lie. Yet, I persisted. Why was I here in Spain if not to experience unlikely adventures? The next morning, a large envelope awaited me at the front desk, with a catalogue of potential companions, a list of packages and prices, and instructions that I could leave my payment at the hotel. Everything was ridiculously inexpensive. I chose the most upscale option, certain that it was all a scam. Along with the payment and the order form, I included a note detailing my wants, needs, preferences, and dislikes.

Three days later, I received another envelope, with all the arrangements.

Once again I woke up at dawn, with Sasha still sleeping deeply. The Ocolondean rarely woke before mid-morning. The bed was as lavish as everything else in the apartment. If I so desired, I could entertain a few more playmates and still not feel cramped. I rose, careful not to disturb Sasha.

After my morning ablutions, I put on loose trousers made of thin off-white cotton and a matching shirt with a band collar. I didn't bother with shoes. I checked on Sasha — still asleep. Pocketing a set of keys, I made my way downstairs.

The streets were damp; it had rained overnight. The first precipitation since I'd arrived nine days earlier.

I made my way to the beach. As they did every morning, a handful of old men waded in the Mediterranean — their cotton pants rolled up to the knees, an empty mesh bag slung over their shoulder, a dowsed cigarette hanging from their lips — throwing a fishing line into the water. I had yet to witness any of them pull anything out of the sea.

Otherwise, the beach was deserted at this early hour. The sun had barely risen. The muted colors of the sky and water soothed me, but they also reminded me of Josey. She would have loved it here. She'd grown up in a fishing village on the Atlantic Coast and had always yearned for more time near salt water, which probably contributed to her fascination with this faraway town.

I had spent a whole year mourning, unable to do or want anything. She would not have wanted me to become so apathetic. I eventually forced myself out of my funk. And so here I was in Ocolondé.

With Sasha.

I had no interest in finding someone else with whom to share my life. Inevitably any lover would fall short of what Josey had meant to me. A new relationship would bring nothing but disappointment and cruelty. Yet, now that Josey's incandescence no longer saturated my senses, long-buried ambiguities and curiosities were awakening. In the early 1970s, during my rebellious androgynous glam-rock phase, I loudly decried the oppression of labelling people by their sexual orientation and did my best to pass as gender-neutral as possible, horrifying my Catholic mother (which was part of the point) and eliciting tolerant exasperation from my more laissez-faire agnostic father. Despite all that bluster, I'd only had sex with a guy once, at age twenty, and that had been a threesome with his girlfriend, who ended up leaving him for me (which had been my plan). Josey and I stayed together forever after. Well, forever for her. Not quite seven years for me.

Perhaps Ocolondé had been a poor choice if my goal really was to move past my grief.

A touch jolted me back to the present.

Sasha's small hand nestled into mine. How unusual for my companion to be up so early. We sat in the sand, huddled together, limbs entwined, facing the sea. For a while, I did forget, abandoning myself to the scents of the young hermaphrodite's skin and of age-old Mediterranean brine, to the fluid sensation of sand under my feet, to the softness of Sasha's flesh. For a while, all I wanted was for this moment to stretch out and then slowly fade, along with my consciousness, until nothing remained.

Five weeks into my stay — I hadn't yet decided on how much longer my holiday would last — the storm hit. One moment the early afternoon sky was bright blue, the next dark grey clouds swathed Ocolondé, hiding even the mountains. Sasha grabbed my hand and led me hurriedly from the outdoor café table to our apartment, some three minutes away, even though we had not yet settled our bill. By the time we reached the door, we were drenched. I laughed, but my companion's palpable anxiety stifled my amusement. Upstairs, Sasha raced to shutter the windows.

We removed our wet clothes and slipped into the guest bathrobes that had so far hung unused in the closet.

The wind howled violently. The way the rain pelted the building was like an angry god trying to punch its way in.

Sasha trembled with mounting distress. To me, in this context, that reaction seemed overwrought. I proposed taking a bath, playing backgammon, reading a story aloud from one of the many books (in multiple languages) in the bedroom bookcase … But Sasha, who was usually so delightfully accommodating to my every whim, ignored all my attempts at distraction.

Storms of such severity tend to peter out within a few minutes, but this one lasted over three hours. The whole time Sasha muttered unintelligibly, fingers fidgeting, muscles spasming. It was as if the clouds over Ocolondé had also invaded and overwhelmed my companion's inner self.

Bright sunlight filtered through the shutters. But Sasha moved to prevent me from throwing everything open. At first I laughed it off. I tried for the windows again, and again Sasha obstructed me. I was bigger and stronger. I let the post-storm air and light into the apartment.

There was anger on Sasha's face.

"I'm not paying you to be a bitch." I regretted the words as soon as they escaped my mouth. Already I realized that they had broken the fragile spell that had suffused the illusion of this holiday. No apology could mend that.

As tenderly as I could, I took both of Sasha's hands. I knew the effort was futile for both of us, but I could not prevent myself from trying. "Let's take a walk. Let's forget the storm." The double meaning had not been intentional, but it was obvious to us both as soon as I uttered the words.

Sasha nodded with submissive resignation, acquiescing to my request to go through the motions of our imitation of intimacy — at least for now.

I automatically headed toward the sea. Sasha tried to herd me inland but did not put up a fight when I resisted. As we neared the beach, I noticed dozens, perhaps even hundreds, of people walking out of the water toward the town. They ambulated oddly, as if suffering from strange infirmities.

Had all these Ocolondeans been caught at sea by the storm? How had they survived?

Sasha mumbled, "They always come ashore after a severe storm."

"They?"

As the sea people came into focus terror flooded into me, amplified by Sasha's anxiety.

They were not human. Not quite. Their scaly skin was a brownish aquamarine, their faces flat, as if their features had been eroded over centuries. Their limbs seemed oddly jointed. They wore rudimentary garments that failed to conceal their hermaphroditism.

My grip on Sasha's hand tightened. My companion winced with pain, but I did not let go. I could sense that Sasha wanted to flee. I ignored the Ocolondean's distress and instead remained transfixed, my heartbeat loud in my ears.

Around us, the seaside cafés and bistros were reopening as if nothing untoward was happening.

Some of the sea people stopped and sat at tables, others wandered deeper into town.

None of the other locals seemed afraid or even startled.

I relaxed. Obviously, there was no danger. Only strangeness.

I dragged the reluctant Sasha by the hand and wandered among the sea people.

Servers brought them food and drink. From leathery bags, the sea people offered the locals various trinkets, baubles, jewelry, and antique coins. No words were exchanged but a growing sense of anticipation welled up everywhere we wandered throughout Ocolondé. Something was going to happen. There were so many Ocolondeans outside, mingling with the sea people, that it seemed as if the entire population had come out to congregate. As far as I could tell, Sasha was the only person consumed with dread.

I was excited and curious. But I did not inquire, nor did my companion volunteer any explanation. I wanted to experience whatever it was that was happening without it being distorted by Sasha's perspective.

At some point, I failed to notice when, I had become separated from my hired companion. Perhaps it was for the best. My time with Sasha had come to an end, the illusion of intimacy irreparably shattered by my thoughtless outburst. Outside of today, though, Sasha had been a dream companion, a satisfying fantasy to soothe my grief.

The first hints of dusk fell on Ocolondé. The smell of brine overwhelmed all other odors. The anticipation in the air was thick, salty, tense, euphoric. I let myself drink it all in. Eager.

Someone had lit a giant bonfire on the beach. There were no other lights in the city. Normalcy had been suspended. Everywhere sea people coupled with Ocolondeans. Fascinated and aroused, I watched the unusual choreographies of lust and eroticism, of human bodies entwined with inhuman anatomy.

Strong hands pulled at my clothes, sharp claws shredding them. The creature was a head shorter than me, with broad shoulders, long limbs, and prominent nipples on greenish breasts the shape of coconut half-shells. I touched the amphibian's face and was surprised at its softness. There was a savage fragility in its gaze that moved me. The hermaphrodite placed my right hand on its small, stiff cock and then the fingers of my left in its moist slit. A clawed hand squeezed my nape, perhaps drawing blood, and pulled me down on the sand.

I woke before dawn, naked on the beach, covered in scratches and bruises. There was no sign of my inhuman lover, or of any of the amphibian hermaphrodites. Yesterday's pervasive briny aroma had ebbed considerably, although it was impossible to completely escape the smells of the sea in Ocolondé. Only a few dozen people still lingered around the burnt-out bonfire.

To my surprise, Sasha, wearing exactly the same clothes as the day we first met, sat next to me, a tender sentinel. Noticing that I'd woken, the Ocolondean stroked my disheveled hair.

"I never asked, because it's not my job to pry, but ... do you have any children?" Sasha's voice was subtly different than it had been, a little gruffer. This was the Ocolondean's real voice, not the playacting tone of the companion Sasha had been performing these past few weeks. The confirmation that for our several weeks together Sasha — a false working name, surely — had hid behind a performer's voice caused a sudden raspy hollowness in my chest. But then the realization that my companion now addressed me in an undisguised voice tempered that emotion.

I nestled my head into the Ocolondean's lap. "No, Josey and I never felt the urge. We never understood why other people want them so badly. We loved our life together as it was, the two of us on an adventure. Together. Focused on each other."

"Well, you'll have a child now." Sasha nodded as understanding came to me. "Extreme storms put them in rut, make them superhumanly fertile. They're symbiotic with land humans. They can't procreate by themselves. They emit pheromones that lower human inhibitions and stimulate pleasure receptors. It's almost impossible to not want to mate with them. It's disgusting."

I waited several seconds, to be sure Sasha was done speaking. I whispered, "Not all the babies are sea creatures, are they?"

Sasha looked away, toward the sea, then, still avoiding my gaze, lay down next to me. I enfolded the olive-skinned Ocolondean in my arms. Soon, Sasha was asleep, drooling on my chest. I, too, succumbed to drowsiness as the sun continued to rise on Ocolondé.

This is a delightfully charming throwback of a story, one which would've found a welcoming home in Horace Gold's Galaxy Science Fiction *of the 1950s. However, given the increasingly theological weight the virtue of tolerance has accrued over the past thirty years, this sort of a tale has become pretty much unpublishable in mainstream science fiction markets. This is borne out by the author's admission that he wrote the story twenty years ago, only to see it accrue two decades' worth of rejections. I rescued the story from the rejection piles for two reasons: I like it, and it perfectly encompasses one of three types of science fiction stories Barry N. Malzberg described in his 1992 essay "Thus Our Words Unspoken" (published in his magisterial collection of reflections on science fiction,* Breakfast in the Ruins*) as those "which could not possibly be sold, regardless of the skill, the fame, the propinquity or the disingenuousness of the writer." I won't tell you which type. Buy a copy of* Breakfast *and look it up yourself. You'll thank me.*

Xenophobe

Liam Hogan

ENRI Xingyun Jackson, of 42 Osaka Place, was a xenophobe.

He didn't know he was a xenophobe. As he frequently said to his friend and neighbor, Umbar Sakamoto Selenko, he knew there was something missing in his life, but, since he wasn't entirely sure *what*, there didn't seem to be all that much he could do about it.

He'd tried online diagnosis. The best Psy-Net could suggest was "Non-Specific Anxiety Disorder" and that didn't chime with what he felt at all. He'd considered seeking professional help, but ultimately balked at the time and the cost and besides, it would have been highly unlikely that any 22nd century psychologist could have identified his condition with any more precision than the Psy-Net had.

Which wasn't surprising. A hundred and twenty years after the Fourth World War and a full century after the United Council's mandatory mixed-breeding program (aimed at forever eliminating all distinctions of race and so preventing further gene-warfare atrocities), even the term "Xenophobia" had fallen completely out of use. Its closest equivalent was calling someone "other"; a crime so heinous that a year's re-education was the minimum punishment.

So Henri struggled on with his unfocused frustration and feelings of impotence, throwing himself into his work as a humble TV repair man.

Henri was in his garden fiddling with a lawnmower when Umbar came hurtling outside.

"Henri, Henri!" his neighbor panted at the garden fence, "An alien spaceship has landed in Hope Square!"

Henri's first reaction was disbelief. "Landed? From where?"

"Uh, dunno!" Umbar hopped from foot to foot. "Out there — space!"

Henri scratched at his scalp through thinning hair. "How did it get through the Curtain?"

"Oh heck! Go see for yourself. It's on all the channels!"

Henri rose slowly, the mower sitting in the palm of his hand, as Umbar rushed back inside. Shrugging, he flipped a switch and dropped the device to the grass, where it righted itself and began racing round and round in a figure of eight, digging deeper and deeper into the soft soil. *Still broken.*

Henri shook his head and sighed. This did little to release the tight band of tension across his chest. On the lawnmower's next pass he carefully picked it up and clicked it off once more. It probably wasn't worth fixing but perhaps he could salvage some parts. After seeing what was happening in Hope Square.

An hour later he was on Umbar's doorstep, fuming. Umbar took a long time answering. His expression betrayed his irritation at being dragged away from the Holo-TV, but he brightened when he saw it was Henri.

"Henri, isn't it marvelous!" he exclaimed. "Come in, come in, help yourself to a beer." He turned and headed back to watch the unfolding events without waiting for a response.

Henri followed him inside. As Umbar settled into his easy chair Henri paced back and forth, his untouched beer frothing over the top.

"Henri! Careful man, you're spilling it. And sit down, please; you're blocking the view."

They were replaying the landing scene yet again. As the alien craft drifted between the trio of statues cast from the melted down fuselages of un-launched and un-launchable ballistic nuclear

18

missiles, Henri waved his hand through the projected image captured by the tourist cams.

"One hundred and twenty years!" he seethed. "In a hundred and twenty years we haven't been able to get anything larger than a *scuttle* out into orbit, and here comes an Alien with a ship the size of an office block. It's not right, just not bloody right. Two centuries ago mankind would have met this Alien in space. Maybe even a century from now, the Curtain would have thinned enough to allow a small craft up to meet it, but oh no. Here we are, stuck like a house pet waiting for its master to return and let it out."

Umbar was surprised at Henri's reaction. Surely it didn't matter where the meeting took place? Wasn't it still a wonderful, historic day?

But Henri, his long dormant anger awakening, said it did matter and added that he wished the alien craft had lopped off the head of General Alexis Vardinsky's statue, the man who'd prevented the use of nukes in the Final War by initiating the self-destruct of the International Space Station *Serendipity* (thus starting the chain reaction of satellite destruction that had created the impenetrable Kessler Curtain).

To most, the fact that this Curtain was still in place so many years later, still causing a nightly meteor shower as space debris continued to rain down on Earth, was an entirely acceptable side effect and far, far preferable to their kids being born with two heads, say, or glowing in the dark.

"Henri, what's eating you?" Umbar chuckled. "Been out in the sun too long?"

Henri gave him a sour glare and turned on his heel. "Bloody funny. And I guess you don't think it's ironic that of all the possible landing places, that *thing* chooses Hope Square?" He slammed the door on the way out.

Back in his own house, Henri glowered at the holo-image of Quincy Wong Jones, the ever-popular News presenter, as he chaired an eclectic panel of scientists, anthropologists, politicians and celebrities, who were animatedly discussing what the aliens might look like.

"Well, I don't care what they look like as long as they are friendly," simpered a vacuous holo-starlet.

"Cretins," muttered Henri as he ducked into the kitchenette for a towel for the still dripping beer.

"... I disagree," a florid man in a pale gray suit was saying as Henri returned, "I don't think we can or should assume much from the shape of the door panel. It's much more likely it was designed for some sort of rover, some mobile equipment. I strongly suspect the aliens will turn out to be bipedal humanoid. The advantages this gives us—"

"Sorry to interrupt, Professor Anton," Quincy said, tapping his earlobe as the studio cameras narrowed their view to just his head. The rest of the projection was replaced by a live image of Hope Square. "It looks like there's something happening at the landing site. Jill?"

A second head appeared floating next to his; that of his intrepid roving field reporter, Jill Li Rodriquez. "Thank you, Quincy. As you can see, the doorway that was flush with the shiny hull of the spaceship is now recessed. In the dusk here in Hope Square, we can see a glimmer of light around the edges that makes us think... Yes! Something is definitely happening, the door is sliding back..."

She stopped, her eyes widening. Framed perfectly by the pear-shaped door stood a quivering mass of green flesh and glowing tentacles. It paused, waved a collection of these extremities and, in accent-less World-Speak, called out to the hushed crowd of onlookers: "Greetings, Earthlings. Take me to your nearest TV studio."

"Well Quincy, where I come from, we don't actually communicate using sound. But if I had to translate the rhythm and color of my name into World-Speak, and if I were to adopt your quaint custom of honoring the victims of the Asian genocide, you could call me, hmm... Violet Ho Strummer"—*The Quincy Show*

"Do you have a star map? Aah, yes, my planet is..." — the Alien gestured with a red-tipped tentacle deep within the floating 3D star chart — "about here, two hundred light years closer to the Galactic hub"—*Six O'clock Traffic*, with Tracy Zhao Chambers

"No, it wasn't easy navigating through the Kessler Curtain, as you call it. It's an effective defensive screen and it took time and a great deal of computational effort, but it's not impassable. I've been giving a lot of thought to that particular problem"—*The Weather Program*

Henri stayed glued to his TV for the next two days. The Alien was everywhere, guest and star attraction at countless celebrations and ceremonies and conferences. All televised, of course: "Violet" did not appear to need sleep and he/she/it was only off-screen for a brief twice-daily return to the spacecraft for "bodily functions".

All the while, Henri's anger grew. Long repressed, his feelings of hatred took a while to reach their full peak. At times he found himself fighting against them, confused about where such feelings came from. Occasionally he lapsed into self-doubt. What, after all, was the Alien's crime? No matter how hard Henri tried to prioritize logic over raw emotion, no matter how ingrained the lesson that it was incredibly rude to point out differences, his hatred, visceral and undeniable, continued to consume him. For whatever reason, everything the Alien did punched his buttons, buttons he'd not known he possessed. At first, he was simply repulsed by the... well, the *alien* appearance of the Alien, as it sat spilling over the studio chairs and chat show sofas. Even the clipped World-Speech rankled, as if by being too perfect, it constantly reminded Henri that Violet was not human, not even remotely human. And he was increasingly infuriated by the obsequious levels of respect and deference that the United Council members showed this interloper from space.

But this was nothing compared to the jealousy and frustration that gnawed at him as the Alien talked of the wonders of its home world while being shown the mundanities of the Jefferson Recycling Center and the Malaki Earth-Based Weather Monitoring Station.

Was that really the best that humanity had to offer? Confined to the surface of the Earth and desperately afraid of the forces it had unleashed during the 21st century's devastating Third and Fourth World Wars, perhaps it was. The threat of nuclear devastation, hanging over the world like a sword of Damocles, had stifled all progress. Now here was this... *creature*... who rubbed everyone's nose in just how small mankind had become.

By the time the Alien appeared on the popular cookery program, *Breakfast with Chito*, and was asked about the potential culinary impacts of the scientific and cultural exchanges that mankind could now expect, Henri had re-invented a number of expletives not heard for well over a hundred years, "dirty stinking other" being the least of them. Henri shocked himself by voicing them aloud — thinking them was noxious enough. When, in a special announcement to the United Council, the Alien told the astonished and delighted members that he/she/it had taken the liberty of launching a couple of sophisticated drones that would clear the space debris that formed the Curtain in a little under a week, Henri seethed with white-hot fury. And, when the Alien pointed out that — regrettably — this would put the Malaki Weather Center permanently out of operation (but not to worry as it could be simply replaced after the clean-up by the launch of a single dedicated weather satellite the Alien would be delighted to provide), Henri snapped and put his boot straight through the TV's holo-projector.

After tumbling into bed and sleeping for fourteen hours, Henri awoke with a feeling of clarity and purpose. If no-one else saw the visitor for the abomination it was, if no-one else was prepared to take action, then it was up to him. He stared at the broken projector and began contemplating the other pieces of salvaged equipment in his cluttered workshop.

It wasn't difficult for Henri to connect the projector's still intact laser to a power unit liberated from a passing street-cleaner. This he hooked through the control circuits of the faulty lawnmower to create a crude but powerful weapon. Without his smashed TV to distract him, he had plenty of time to plan his next step.

It was with great sadness that mankind prepared to say farewell to the honored and much-feted Alien. "But it's only four hundred light years there and back," he/she/it said, "I'll return in a couple of years with a whole host of my colleagues to warmly welcome Earth as our galactic neighbor."

Even the inhabitants of Osaka Place threw a small party, marred only by the inexplicably dirty state of the street and by Henri's conspicuous absence. The shared feeling was that mankind was on the brink of something truly wonderful. The evening ended with a spectacular light show, to the surprise of all who attended and in particular to Umbar, who had been asked to arrange the fireworks and had been somewhat disappointed at the drab looking selection his neighbors' paltry contributions had allowed him to buy.

On the day of the Alien's departure, thousands of excited spectators thronged the streets around Hope Square. Henri lugged his heavy laser in an old suitcase through the crowds, wishing he'd left the street cleaning drone's wheels attached. Fortunately the throng was good humored, members of the crowd not making a fuss even when Henri's suitcase bumped their shins.

He had identified a spot on a roof directly behind the statue of Nobel Peace Prize recipient Lord Jules Lynch, the veteran and eminent statesman who had brokered the Armistice agreement, including the historic clause on forced genetic mixing which prevented any possible future use of pathogens tailored to wipe out just one section of humanity. Henri knew that from roof height he would be able to see the entire center of the Square over the statue's massive wheelchair wheels. With the sun behind him, he figured he'd be unlikely to be spotted.

But he hadn't planned on the masses that had turned out to see the Alien off and he quickly realized that every available rooftop was already packed. Descending in the elevator from the third building he'd tried, his resolve fraying at the edges, he impulsively stabbed the button for the next floor down.

The suitcase rattled raucously as he dragged it along the hallway. When an elderly lady in Council garb opened a door just as he passed, he thought he was done for, the guilt as sudden as a sledgehammer to his heart. He almost welcomed being exposed as a good-for-nothing irrational Alien hater, nearly breathed a sigh of relief at his imminent removal from society. But she merely smiled, nodded, and headed towards the lifts.

Heart pounding, Henri waited until the sliding doors shushed closed before opening the suitcase. He'd packed a set of tools in case anything shook loose along the way. The wire cutter made short work of the old-fashioned lock on the east-facing office. Within a minute he was setting up the laser on a desk he'd dragged over to the window, overlooking the Square.

Henri was still worried about his device. Tests the night before (masked by Umbar's fireworks) had shown it was effective, though difficult to maneuver and slow to recover from each firing.

He figured he'd only have one good shot and that would have to be pre-aimed. So he locked the laser onto a point in the middle of the hatchway of the Alien's spacecraft, hoping that the holo-loving monstrosity might pause there for long enough for him to trip the relay.

During the next three hours of speeches, conferred honors, and general goodwill, Henri was sorely tempted to re-aim the laser and be done with it; especially when the President of the United Council suggested that Hope Square's empty fourth plinth should be crowned with a statue of the Alien: "Mankind's first of many friends from across the stars."

As Henri sat there, hands cupped over his ears to block out the noise of the celebrations, confused by the violent emotions raging within his breast, he forced himself instead to consider the available power supply. He'd put together a regulator utilizing three sockets, so that he could draw enough power without tripping the surge protectors. But now he wondered if, with a little tampering, he could avoid the protectors altogether. He wasn't sure how much power the laser would then be able to draw from the city's solar store, but it was a sunny afternoon and he figured if he only had one shot, then he might as well throw everything at it.

At last, festooned in ribbons and medals and garlands, the Alien slowly climbed the ramp to the spacecraft. Each quivering step was met by cheers and hollers of "Come back soon!" and "Don't be a stranger!" Finally it stood framed in the hatchway. Turning to the crowd, the Alien waved his/her/its pulsating tentacles vigorously in fond farewell.

Henri snarled and threw the switch.

There was a brief pause; a moment when he feared his device wasn't going to work. A moment when he was relieved. A fraction of a second as the twenty-five megawatts of energy gathered and pulsed around the lasing tube, the air snapping to attention. Then a huge surge of energy bloomed out, crackling and spitting as it ripped across the short distance at three million meters a second before drilling a neat and surprisingly small hole straight through the Alien's midriff.

As the Alien stared in dumb surprise at the rapidly healing wound, a second, only marginally less powerful pulse leaped out and — arcing upwards as the tripod collapsed — sliced the Alien in two, from its iridescent middle to its shimmering tentacles.

In its dying glory, the ray traced a lazy figure of eight along the spaceship's gleaming hull, bouncing off and causing mayhem in the crowds. It then lurched skywards, interrupted only by the arm of Dr. Melissa Haniwell's statue; the bio-genetics genius behind the engineered pathogen that had controversially ended the Final War.

The massive arm — solid metal, holding an eight-foot long Plexiglas test tube — proved no obstacle at all even as the beam stuttered and petered out. The severed hand smashed into the seating area reserved for the last three surviving Veterans, doing for them in an instant what seven years of bitter battle and nearly a century and a half of Earthly existence had failed to achieve.

As for Henri, poor deluded xenophobic Henri, he died instantly as super-hot fragments of super-conducting magnets ripped the sixth floor of the former Book Repository apart.

When the crowd — those not felled by the reflected laser beam or by fragments of giant statuary — realized the full extent of all that had happened, they were astonished. The sharp acrid smell of ozone mingled with the pungent stench of charred Alien and, other than the ping-ping-pinging of cooling metal from Melissa Haniwell's severed wrist and the occasional tinkle as solar-glass fell from the shattered office block, all was deathly silent.

Surprise turned to shock when investigators traced the fatal ray back to the window of the building from whence it had come. The office was found, entirely coincidentally, to be a wholly owned subsidiary of the now obsolete Malaki Weather Center.

But all this paled into insignificance when they got round to searching the Alien's spacecraft. The investigators' suspicions were aroused when they uncovered maps showing the location of all of Earth's major industrial plants and administrative centers. Those suspicions were more than confirmed when they finally managed to translate the rapidly changing colors of Violet's log book and found the genetic code for the Final War's deadly pathogen, along with detailed schematics for other weapons of mass destruction outlawed and forgotten since that genocidal conflict.

Homo sapiens is an adaptable species. It took hardly any time at all for Earth's populace to move from their sleepy, peaceful torpor to full military setting. With Earth's skies once again clear, and military engineers drawing upon every last scrap of the alien craft's advanced technology, the first squadron of armed-to-the-teeth destroyers was practicing maneuvers around Mars within a mere six months.

This time, mankind figured, they'd meet the Alien's host of colleagues on equal terms: half way, guns a-blazing.

Two years after total victory over the Aliens was declared, a new statue was erected in Hope Square. Joining General Vardinsky, Dr. Haniwell, and Lord Lynch, the three 21st century heroes who ended one devastating war, was a fourth, dedicated to a quiet, unassuming TV repairman, Henri Xingyun Jackson, who gave his life to save humanity.

What would the world be like if technology banished all inequities between persons? More intriguing, perhaps: what would such a utopia feel like to someone newly awakened into it, someone whose entire identity had been based upon a lifelong struggle against inequality and oppression? Would that person feel obsolete, a knight standing uncertainly over a slain dragon? Or would one of the basic aspects of human nature, so readily seen in the behavior of young siblings — a tendency to detect unfairness in any difference in treatment and to strongly rebel against it — come to the fore in any case? Bonus Politically Incorrect Points: the author, a white British male, commits big-time Cultural Appropriation (albeit in the process of critiquing it). Which is just what writers of science fiction, that exploration of the Other, are meant to do.

A Singular Outrage

Ian Creasey

THE school, like everything nowadays, looked far too good to be true. It resembled a mansion in a vast estate: classical architecture, picturesque trees, plenty of green fields. Novanita paused, wincing at the noise of the crowd. Children scurried around the sports pitches, their families yelling encouragement from the sidelines. Somewhere, a brass band played a rousing anthem. After years of deafness, hearing this commotion ought to be a pleasure, but it was a little too much. The whole world was just too much.

Philip tugged at her arm. "Come on, Grandma! You'll miss the start."

She allowed herself to be led across the grounds and through the main entrance, a towering arch of grey stone festooned with ivy. The building looked ancient, like a manor house in a costume drama, but of course it had to be new. *Nanotech*, that was the buzzword. At least she could remember the word, even if she didn't quite know what it meant. It might as well be magic.

Inside, the wood-panelled corridors were wide and clean. The sun shone through high windows, but subtle air-conditioning kept the temperature comfortable. She saw bright, colourful classrooms, full of art materials and scientific equipment.

Bitterly, she remembered her own schooldays, sharing dog-eared books in cramped classrooms, shivering in winter and sweltering in summer. Back then, the federal government spent little money on Native American schools, and the Igbowi tribe was too poor to supplement the meagre budget.

She didn't begrudge Philip his shiny education, but she narrowed her eyes every time she passed a child, cataloguing their skin colour. Was this just a school for whites, with other races fobbed off elsewhere? It didn't seem that way. The kids were from varying racial backgrounds, and everyone sounded equally loud and happy.

"There's a lot going on," she said. Naturally the school would put on a good display for its open day. Perhaps she should sneak back tomorrow to see if it still looked as impressive on the ordinary timetable.

"It's to show off all our projects," Philip replied. "And there'll be talent-spotters here. So when you play my game — my part of it, anyway — you need to be awesome!"

Great, she thought. *No pressure, then.* "How will I know which is your part?"

"Because it's all the tribal stuff you've been telling me about," said Philip.

Novanita followed him into a classroom full of people sitting silently with glassy expressions. She flinched, overcome by a flashback to the care home where she'd spent so many years. This was like the home's lounge, except without the TV.

She'd thought she was going to die there, growing ever weaker and more confused. But one day, a medical team arrived and gave everybody an injection. Soon her hearing returned; the fog of dementia lifted from her brain; the wrinkles disappeared from her skin. And the residents emerged into a world that had changed even more than their own bodies.

Philip ushered her to a chair. He said, "I won't be with you in the game, but you'll be fine. If you need help, just summon your spirit animal."

Seriously? Before she could challenge this, Philip disappeared as Novanita entered the game world.

"Welcome to Jollania," said a disembodied voice. "Please choose your avatar."

Life-size figures stood on a revolving stage: a knight in armour, a priestess, a samurai warrior, a chrome robot, a green-skinned alien, a wild-eyed Amazon on a horse, an Igbowi chief in ceremonial headdress.... Novanita recognised the chief's costume from old pictures she'd shown Philip.

"The chief," she said. The figure swelled in her vision until it enveloped her and she became it.

She found herself in the refectory of an ancient monastery. Beside her sat a motley bunch of warriors seemingly drawn from every army throughout history and imagination. At the head of the table, the abbot recounted the dark forces threatening the last bastion of knowledge. "We're beleaguered on all sides. From the west, dragons assail us. In the east, the night hordes grow ever stronger. And far below, Clarishavo wakes from his sleep...."

Clarishavo! She'd told that tale to Philip, but she'd said nothing about a monastery or dragons or night hordes. That was all just childish invention, perhaps from his classmates. Already she felt uneasy at the game's crude mishmash, wondering how much of it came from children's lack of sophistication, and how much from lack of respect. Yet Philip had asked her to impress the talent scouts, so she needed to showcase his contribution.

She stood and called out, "Lead me to Clarishavo. Let no-one say that Novanita shirks the battle."

Her avatar was still wearing the feathered headdress. As if a chief would wear it to dinner, or to a council of war! It was a sacred costume for the Long Dance. Irritated, she removed the headdress and carefully laid it aside.

"Bravely spoken," said the abbot. "Who wishes to join Novanita?"

The swiftly assembled band included a cyborg, a swordswoman, a musket-carrying soldier, and an ice sorceress.

A monk led them past the wine cellars and through the storage caves, which smelled of slowly maturing cheese wheels.

Their footsteps echoed uncannily, while the swordswoman's lantern threw disturbing shadows on the walls. Below the monastery lay the archives: caverns stuffed with the world's knowledge. The storage media grew more primitive as the warriors descended, until they reached a warren of passageways with glyphs etched into every cranny of the rock walls.

"I love getting lost in a book," the cyborg quipped. "Let's hope this one has a happy ending."

The further they descended, the more annoyed Novanita became. In the original story, Clarishavo didn't live in a cave at all.

The sorceress pointed to wall protrusions that had been rubbed smooth, erasing the precious text they bore. "Big serpent!"

Unconsciously, they all slowed their pace.

Novanita said, "There's something ahead: I can see a glint. Two glints."

"Crystals in the wall?" said the swordswoman, bringing the lantern closer. "Maybe there's treasure."

The glints faded, then returned. No, they *blinked*.

"It's the snake!" Novanita cried. Then she berated herself for sounding panicky. She was supposed to be a chief, a warrior. And this wasn't real, anyway. Would eyeballs even reflect a lantern, or was that just a creepy special effect?

"Who disturbs me at my devotions?" The voice of Clarishavo was a reverberating bass rattle; small stones fell from the ceiling like sharp rain.

"Your doom," said Novanita. It seemed the kind of thing she was supposed to say.

The snake chuckled. "Someone's doom, perhaps. I'll write 'Doom' on today's menu. Which wine would go best with you?"

With a teeth-grating crunch, Clarishavo slithered closer. The lantern illuminated the serpent's head; his vast body stretched back until it disappeared into the shadows.

"Don't bother looking for a corkscrew just yet," said the cyborg. "You might find your starter doesn't go down very well."

"Then I'll bring a toothpick and use the spicy sauce," the serpent said. "But first, I must ask a question. Have you seen my brother, the Raven?"

Novanita frowned. Clarishavo's line about the Raven was the first thing he'd said that came from the original story. If she responded appropriately, then the scenario might continue according to tradition, until she eventually triumphed by tricking the snake into biting his own tail.

Should she stick to the script, even though it had been garbled? She didn't want to play along with the game's brazen distortions of her culture. In the old days — before the care home — she'd been an activist. She'd always kicked up a fuss whenever she met disrespect.

Yet Philip was just a kid. And his classmates hadn't perpetrated the objectionable elements. It would be unfair to stop the game.

Nevertheless, Philip had designed these warped creations. She could certainly challenge them, as long as she maintained her in-game persona. It would demonstrate his patter for the talent scouts. And it might make him think about what he'd done.

Novanita said, "We're underground. Ravens don't live underground, so we haven't seen your brother. And you're a long way from home." As she spoke, her comrades crept forward. "Why are you here?" she continued. "These aren't your caves. Why are you consorting with strangers?"

"Because they're delicious!" the snake replied. His forked, blood-red tongue darted out. "I travel in search of local delicacies—"

The swordswoman hacked at the snake's neck. With a rush, the others piled in. Gunshots echoed, making Novanita's ears ring. A luminous energy bolt shone like lightning as it fizzed into the snake's body, with a dreadful smell of burnt flesh.

Clarishavo writhed and rolled, recoiling from blows and trying to crush the attackers. But there were too many warriors, with too many weapons and special skills. The snake had no chance against the band's repertoire.

In barely a minute, Clarishavo was dead. Novanita hadn't even moved.

The warriors cheered and slapped each other on the back. "Great job distracting him," the sorceress said to Novanita.

"Which wine goes best with fried snake?" asked the cyborg, firing another energy bolt into the serpent's body.

Novanita stared, shocked by the swift one-sided slaughter. She had a confused impulse to remonstrate with her comrades. But before she could speak, the cavern disappeared.

She was back in the classroom. Philip bounded up to her, exclaiming, "Wasn't that great? You could really smell the blood!"

Novanita climbed out of her chair, feeling the full weight of her ninety-three years. The nanobots had strengthened her bones, but psychologically she still felt fragile, battered by the world's strangeness.

"It was impressive," she said at last, knowing that Philip needed to hear something positive. "Good sensory details. I almost believed I was there."

"Do you think I'll get talent-spotted?" he asked eagerly.

"I don't know, dear," she replied. "I don't know what they look for. But I hope they're not looking for a fair fight, because that wasn't a fair fight at all. The poor snake didn't stand a chance." It felt odd to defend Clarishavo, but even he deserved better than such a brutal demise.

"Oh, that's standard game design," Philip said. "You give the players something easy to start off with, something they can have fun with. It's a throwaway monster."

Novanita's heart started hammering. Her shoulders tensed with fury. "A throwaway monster?" she repeated. "My people's stories are just disposable garbage? That's outrageous!"

Philip's eyes widened; he took a half-step backward. For long moments, neither of them spoke. All around, children and parents chattered about holidays on the moon and trips to other worlds, and Novanita couldn't tell whether they were talking about some silly game, or about their lives today.

Heck, why was this game even a school project? What were the kids learning?

"Let's get something to eat," she said.

As they walked to the canteen, Philip said, "Grandma, it's just a technical term. I have to use the jargon to get good grades. But a throwaway monster doesn't mean what you think. Clarishavo isn't gone forever. He can come back. Bad guys always come back!"

"Oh, I know they do," Novanita said with feeling. "That's our history in a nutshell. Bad guys always coming back, more of them every time."

In the canteen, children were showing off their recipes. Novanita scrutinised the students, tallying their gender to check that domestic science wasn't just for girls. She saw plenty of boys, but no pans or ovens. When Novanita reached the front of the queue, she found that the meals came from a replicator at the touch of a button.

She'd seen that before; there was a replicator in the house she'd been given. Now she realised that someone must have programmed all its recipes. *Is that what cooking lessons are these days?*

She was tempted to ask Philip if he took domestic science. It would be easy to change the subject, and talk about cooking. But she couldn't do that, not until she'd cleared up the mess she'd made by telling Philip the tribe's stories. She hadn't known he would garble them in a stupid game, mashing them up with pop-culture clichés.

"It's not just Clarishavo," she said. "In the game, my avatar wore a headdress. That's for sacred ceremonies, not for feasts and fights. The context was wrong—"

Philip interrupted. "It shows the character is Native American, that's all."

"No, it doesn't," she said forcefully, "because an Igbowi would never wear it that way."

He rolled his eyes. "It's just a *game*, Grandma."

"Sure," she said. "But it's important enough to be a school project that talent-spotters look at. This is how misrepresentation spreads. It reduces the First Nations to stereotypes."

Novanita wondered how she could explain these complexities to a heedless, resentful boy. "When I was young, we didn't have much." She remembered her mother singing in the old earth lodge, her buffalo brooch glinting in the firelight. "Then we lost our land when the government flooded it for a reservoir. We tried to preserve our culture, because it was all we had left. So when our costumes and stories are used for fashion and cheap thrills, we get angry! It's another theft by outsiders who've already destroyed our way of life.

"I'm not literally your grandma," she went on. "I never had children. When my father died, my mother married a white man, and had a daughter with him. You're my half-sister's great-grandson. That means you only have a trace of Igbowi ancestry. Our culture isn't yours to play around with. I was happy to tell you some family history and tribal legends, because you deserve to hear about that side of your heritage. But you can't just take it away and do whatever you like with it. Do you know what 'appropriation' is?"

Philip grimaced. "Is it something old-fashioned?"

"Apparently not," Novanita said, and sighed. "Maybe I need to talk to your teacher."

Ms Jackson was a stout middle-aged black woman whose solid, sober office furnishings exuded authority. On her desk stood a vase of glass roses, delicate and elegant, clearly a prize piece by a talented pupil.

"Pleased to meet you," the teacher said. "I'm so glad you've been helping Philip with his game design. He's made great strides this year, though being scouted is perhaps unrealistic at this stage."

"He never said he was putting everything into a game," Novanita said tartly. "I didn't know schools taught this kind of thing. Or is it an after-school hobby?"

Ms Jackson said, "Oh, it's very much part of the curriculum. In the new economy, no-one needs to work anymore, so we mainly teach art and creativity. This is the future!"

"That's what worries me," said Novanita. "Do you teach the kids about appropriation? Respect for other cultures?"

The teacher frowned, then laughed. "Appropriation? My, that takes me back. I haven't heard that word for years."

"But you know what it means, right?"

"I guess so. Look, Tyler Adams teaches history — do you want to talk to him?"

The familiar tension returned to Novanita's shoulders. "No thanks," she said. "I'd like to talk to you, about why you're not teaching kids that cultural appropriation is wrong."

Ms Jackson laughed again. "Well, probably because it isn't. Not anymore."

Novanita's simmering outrage threatened to boil over. "*Not wrong?* How isn't it wrong?"

"I'm sure Tyler would explain it better than I can. But as I remember, appropriation was when white people — sorry, privileged people — used minority culture in disrespectful ways. So, obviously, it only happened when there was a big divide between the privileged and the oppressed. When the Singularity empowered everyone, it pretty much wiped out the gap. There's no oppression any more... unless you're utterly determined to hold a grudge." She gave Novanita a stern glare. "That's not an attitude we encourage, as it divides people and creates friction."

Novanita raised her eyebrows, then looked at the teacher's black skin. "No oppression?" she asked, trying to keep her voice neutral.

Ms Jackson waved her hands dismissively. On her right hand, the fingernails were fragrant red petals; on her left hand, the fingernails were thorns. "Not since the old days." She leaned forward, and gazed sympathetically at Novanita. "Are you one of the Rips?"

It was a generic term for all the people who'd woken from comas, or been cured of longstanding conditions, only to emerge into a new society like Rip van Winkle.

"Yes," Novanita admitted. "Why do you ask?"

"Well, it's not my place to give you advice. But — for Philip's benefit — maybe you could tone down the rhetoric until you've seen how the world works these days. The Native American material has helped him a lot, and without that...." Ms Jackson sucked in a breath through her teeth. "He could struggle. You see, game design is incredibly competitive. Now that nobody needs to work, everybody can be creative, so it's hard to be noticed. Everyone needs an edge, a personal style, and Philip's background is a way for him to stand out and reach the next level."

Novanita's activist instincts screamed at her to rebuff this bullshit. "Perhaps you could take your own teaching to the next level, and find other ways for kids to stand out, without needing to appropriate their material. Because otherwise they'll grow up thinking it's okay to take whatever they like, wherever they like."

Ms Jackson shrugged. "There's no copyright on culture, and you certainly don't own it. But I didn't tell Philip those stories — you did. If you regret it, then I suggest you discuss it with him." She stood up. "Now, if you don't mind, open days are very busy and I have other families to talk to."

Novanita nodded curtly, and left Ms Jackson's office with as brisk a walk as she could manage — which, with her new bones, turned out to be pretty damned brisk.

At the end of the corridor, she sat on a bench and slumped against the wall mosaic, her head in her hands. She thought back to all those long conversations with Philip, when he'd seemed genuinely interested in his family background and the tribe's stories. He'd just been using her, pumping her for material to bastardise in his game. He only wanted an edge over his rivals.

It was just another exploitation, in a lifetime full of them. So much for the end of oppression!

Philip was with friends, so Novanita left on her own. It only took a few minutes for the car to fly her home.

Her house was a generic redbrick bungalow, one of the standard templates. The replicator could easily customise it, or build something else, but she hadn't yet chosen a new design. The templates for Native American lodges were of dubious authenticity; she disliked seeing them in the catalogue, commodified for anyone to use. For now, she was simply enjoying the luxury of her own space. At the care home, she'd hated the constant proximity of other people.

In the garden, she found her robot weeding a bed of squash seedlings. The robot was her Adjustment Facilitator, assigned to help her integrate into modern society. She hadn't talked to it much. Relying on the robot made her feel uncomfortably dependent and helpless. It reminded her of the life she'd been rescued from: the daily routine of being lifted, wiped, dressed, undressed.... Now she wanted to savour her independence.

Yet the robot was undeniably useful. She said, "A teacher at Philip's school told me there's no more oppression. Is that true?"

The robot nodded its silver head. "Yes, if you mean privilege, discrimination, and so on. Today there are few imbalances of power. In the old days, it was impossible to opt out of capitalism, or colonialism. Now everyone can drop out if they want to, so nobody has power over them. The only interactions are voluntary." As the robot spoke, it continued pulling weeds with tireless efficiency.

"I understand the economic aspect," Novanita said. "No-one needs to earn money, when they have the replicator and robots and whatnot. But surely there's still imperialism. There's a fixed amount of land, and some people own it."

White people own it, she thought bitterly. The Igbowi had lost their territory. When the reservoir swallowed their valley, the tribe scattered. Novanita's family moved to higher ground. She remembered her father raging at the rising water as he drank himself to death.

"Actually, there's an infinite amount of land," the robot said. "It's in parallel worlds — alternate versions of Earth where things turned out differently. In other worlds, for example, your Igbowi tribe might not exist."

"Why does that matter?" asked Novanita, annoyed. She didn't care about other Earths with other histories. She cared about here and now.

Imperturbably, the robot replied, "It triggered the Singularity. When crosstime travel arrived, scientists gained all the knowledge in all those infinite worlds. That's where the nanotech came from, the medical advances, and so on. And now there's no shortage of land, as plenty of worlds are empty and up for grabs. If anyone's unhappy, they can get their own planet and live however they please."

"So you're saying that nobody's oppressed, because everyone can run away to their own little bolthole?" It reminded Novanita of the "safe spaces" that activists used to create — a welcome shelter, but only a stopgap.

"That's the current consensus," the robot said. "Of course, not everyone agrees. But many Native Americans have left, looking for empty continents like their ancestral home. There are countless worlds to choose from."

"'Countless', eh?" Novanita smiled sardonically. "That's what they used to say about the buffalo."

The robot took the weeds away for disposal, carefully separating those that could be composted. Then it began watering the crops. The robot worked at a steady pace: never rushing a chore, never pausing for rest.

"Are *you* oppressed?" asked Novanita.

"I'm mechanical," the robot replied. "I have no independent will."

"Maybe you're just programmed to deny it," Novanita said.

"If you're concerned, I can feed myself back into the replicator," the robot said calmly. "But how far do you want to go? The house needs awareness to control the heating, watch for accidents, monitor your health, and so on. The car flies itself. Would you abandon all that? Today's world depends on artificial intelligence."

"There are other worlds, you said."

"Yes. The residents decide their technology level. Some Native Americans have gone back to the days before the Europeans came. No guns, no electricity, no nanobots: just the original authentic culture. Shall I find you one of those worlds?"

Novanita frowned, contemplating life without the medical miracles that had rescued her from the care home. "That's a big step. I need to see more of this world first. Hey, maybe it really is perfect."

It was easy to be sceptical. She'd spent her whole life being sceptical, often with good reason. Yet the world had changed so much. Had social justice finally arrived? Was there equality at last?

And if so, shouldn't she celebrate? Campaigners had striven for centuries, attacking oppression and discrimination. If those evils had been vanquished, she ought to cheer.

But it felt like a hollow victory, if it had only come thanks to technology. Activists aimed to change hearts and minds. If colonialist attitudes were merely suppressed by circumstance, then had oppression really ended? Or was it just dormant?

Perhaps she was being churlish, resenting victory because it hadn't arrived the way she'd wanted. How disappointing, that she couldn't take any credit for it.

Of course, this all assumed that oppression had genuinely *ended*. Novanita spent the evening delving into the new milieu, looking for anger and injustice. The ancient Internet had decayed into abandoned wastelands of ghostly hashtags and zombie spambots, but new social media had arisen. And people still loved to complain.

Complaints in themselves didn't mean much. In the old days, comfortable white men had whined and pouted and stamped their feet, weeping salty tears over tiny imagined slights, oblivious to the vast wealth of privilege that smoothed every moment of their lives.

When Novanita saw the modern world's complaints, she knew better than to believe they all arose from genuine injustice. That would require more investigation. She didn't understand this world yet; she needed to educate herself, and find mentors.

She could see plenty of aggrieved people yelling, even in a post-scarcity paradise with free houses and robots and planets on tap. Perhaps some of the disaffected were truly downtrodden, needing allies in the fight for justice.

The research was soothing, as familiar as old moccasins. It made her feel useful. She already anticipated tomorrow's tasks: background reading, forum conversations, activist connections....

Novanita smiled ruefully, realising that she subconsciously hoped oppression still existed, simply because she'd grown so accustomed to fighting it. And if oppression had survived in this brave new world, Philip's appropriation of Native American culture would be a lot easier to condemn. She seethed at the memory of it.

But assessing the world's power structures would take time, and the results were unlikely to sway Philip. He was just a boy. Political rhetoric was too abstract for him to grasp: he had no visceral feel for the consequences. He'd never experienced hardship.

Rather than telling him about oppression, she needed to show him. She summoned her Adjustment Facilitator and said, "Get me a submarine!"

The next day, Novanita and Philip flew out to Lake Sarabow. When they reached the huge dam, Novanita said, "They built that when I was a little girl. Before the valley flooded, this was our land. The white men took it because they wanted a reservoir. You can see how much we lost."

Several miles wide and nearly two hundred miles long, the lake stretched past the horizon in an endless expanse of blue. "Most of this was farmland and hunting grounds, but there were several villages here. It's one of my earliest memories, having to leave home when the water rose."

Her voice caught as she remembered her father packing their possessions, and Mom cleaning the empty lodge even though it would soon be drowned. Novanita's childhood memories had become newly vivid as the nanobots scoured her brain to suppress dementia and boost her faculties. Last night she'd dreamed of her parents dancing, to a song sung in a language long suppressed. At school they'd made Novanita wash her mouth with soap if she spoke anything other than English.

She shook her head to clear it, and gestured to the lake. "Let's go down and see what's left."

They landed at the dock, where their boat awaited. It had a robot crew, programmed for all contingencies and emergencies. The wind was mild, creating a gentle ripple of waves. The air smelled clean and fresh, with pollution only a foul memory.

While the boat chugged across the lake, Novanita asked Philip, "How are things at school?"

He shrugged. "All right, I suppose."

"What do you like least?" Perhaps he was mistreated, or bullied. Children didn't always want to tell adults, but at least she could give him the chance.

"I hate sport," he said. "They make us run around outside, but some kids are always bigger or faster.... That's why I like the game world. Everyone's equal with the same avatar."

"Fairness is important," Novanita said, but didn't belabour the point. "What are you hoping to achieve with the game? What's the next step?"

"I'll make my part as good as possible," Philip said, "and try to get noticed, because that'll give me more say when I'm older. The best projects have lots of people working on them. Collaboration is fine, but you know how it is. Someone draws the big picture, and someone else colours in the background. I want to be in charge!"

Novanita suppressed a smile. He had a child's natural egotism; she couldn't condemn a healthy level of ambition. Philip chattered about his plans until the boat reached its destination.

The water looked the same here as everywhere else. But now they could descend. Technically the dive vessel was a submersible, not a submarine. It was a cylinder just big enough for herself, Philip, and a robot operator.

The submersible had lots of windows for a panoramic view. When it entered the water, Novanita was surprised at how quickly the daylight faded. The lake wasn't deep, but nevertheless they still needed the external lights.

Above, she could just glimpse the boat, a reassuring dark blot. On all sides, a featureless mass of water surrounded them. She'd expected fish, but she saw none. Well, this wasn't a wildlife documentary.

They descended slowly, until the lake bottom came into view. Patches of green weed sprouted from tracts of mud. She frowned. Was this it?

"I see something!" Philip cried, pointing.

The pulse of the engine changed pitch as the submersible accelerated. Soon Novanita saw what Philip had spotted: a church spire.

She clenched her jaw. The church wasn't even part of the village! Missionaries had built it. The stone structure had survived well; a stained-glass window blazed with colour when the lights swept over it.

The church gave Novanita a reference point, and the instrument panel showed compass directions. She set a course westward, and soon saw gentle swellings on the lake bed.

"This would make a great scene in a game," Philip said. "A treasure hunt! It just needs a few lake monsters."

Novanita bit back an angry comment. She needed to teach him, not rant at him. "This isn't scenery," she said. "It's history. Those mounds on the lake bottom are the earth lodges where we lived. They've been crushed by the water, dissolving into mud. The white men took our land and destroyed our homes—"

Philip interrupted. "Grandma, that's ancient history. It was practically a hundred years ago! You can't keep clutching onto your grievances forever. And besides, you say this was your land, but I bet the tribe conquered it from someone else originally. You win some, you lose some."

She took a deep breath, striving to stay calm. "You're young, so it's ancient history to you. But it's within living memory, so it's not that ancient. And it's not even history, because it hasn't stopped. Nowadays they don't steal our land, because there's nothing left to grab. Instead they steal our culture, taking our costumes and our stories and trivialising them...."

"So you're saying my game is trivial?" Philip demanded.

"Compared to losing your home? What do you think?"

Sullenly, Philip glared at her. "It's still important. Maybe things are more comfortable now, but there's tough competition. It matters. Nobody wants to end up at the bottom, a loser." He spat the word out with scorn.

Novanita found it hard to believe the stakes were really so high, but she knew little about modern media, and she didn't want to speak from ignorance. Philip already thought she was old and out of touch; if she said something stupid about the gaming milieu, he would never respect her.

She turned her attention back to the lake, looking at the drowned lodges and trying to map them onto her memory of the village. Steering the submersible, she paused above each lodge to gauge the terrain.

"That's it!" she exclaimed. "That's where we lived."

The slumped heap looked similar to the others, but smaller because it had been a single-family home rather than a shared lodge. Timbers lay askew, poking out of the green moss that had accumulated on the former roof. The rough-cut logs were rotting away.

Tears filled her eyes. Novanita sniffed, blinking them back.

"Can I go out and have a look?" Philip asked.

"I don't think you can swim here. The pressure—"

"I was asking the robot!"

The robot said, "You can only dive if you're trained and certified. If not, you can use the proxy instead." The robot pointed to a humanoid figure on the submersible's exterior, half-visible through a side window. "It can swim outside; it's like being there yourself. It has sight, hearing, and touch, plus sonar and magnetic sensors."

"Is it safe?" Novanita demanded.

"As safe as being in here," the robot said. "It's operated from inside — that's the control panel."

Philip lunged to the panel and jacked himself in.

The robot said, "There is only one proxy, I'm afraid."

Novanita shuddered. "That's all right." She could barely cope with seeing the drowned village from inside the submersible; she had no desire to enter the water, even virtually.

The proxy detached itself from the hull. A bright beam sprang from its headlamp. The figure turned and gave Novanita a thumbs-up sign.

Gracefully, it swam away. Philip looked completely at home in these new waters. He reached the lodge and began delving into its depths. Some of the logs were so soft they collapsed into mush at the slightest disturbance.

Novanita turned away. She couldn't bear to watch Philip rummaging through her old family home.

Soon the proxy returned, docking with a dull thud. Philip unjacked himself and said, "I found something! The metal detector led me to it. It looks like gold, but I don't know much about jewellery."

The submersible had a small airlock for retrieving samples. As soon as the inner hatch opened, Novanita reached into the airlock and grabbed the find.

It was a small golden brooch in the shape of a buffalo. "My mother's brooch!" Novanita exclaimed. She remembered it from childhood, as bright as Mom's smile. She'd always assumed it had been sold in hard times. But Mom must have left it behind, in the home she would never see again.

"It was the brooch she wore over her heart," Novanita said. "And she left it here, because that was the only way she could stay in her lost homeland."

Philip grinned gleefully. "I told you it was a treasure hunt. What a talisman!"

With a sick pang of dread, Novanita realised that Philip intended to put the golden brooch into his game. To him, everything was just source material.

She wanted to put her foot down, exert adult authority, and demand that he stop. But that was dangerous, because she couldn't prevent him from doing it. She could only appeal to his better nature, hoping that everything she'd shown him had started to hit home.

"This belonged to your great-great-grandmother," Novanita said. "Please don't exploit it. All I'm asking is that you think about what happened here" — she flung her arms wide, her gesture encompassing all the drowned lands, all the victims everywhere — "and show a little respect."

"Sure," said Philip. "I can do that. Coming here has shown me a lot. But you'll have to advise me, tell me what's authentic." He was naming his price, demanding her help in his quest for fame.

Novanita could become a consultant, shaping a historically accurate version of her culture. Yet that would still be a commodity, a mere token in the game — albeit one with someone to stand up for it.

"There's loads of stuff we can do," Philip went on, "if you tell me about the language, the dances, the initiation ceremonies...."

She sighed at his desire to seize upon the colourful aspects. Yet the virtual realm was modern culture. To be an effective activist, she needed to understand the contemporary milieu. Philip could teach her, while she taught him.

"Just as long as you understand we're not cheapening my heritage — *our* heritage," she said, trying to draw him in.

Novanita clutched the brooch as the submersible rose to the surface, leaving her home behind. *Goodbye, Mom. I'll protect your memory.*

After they returned to the boat, the harsh sunlight scoured Novanita's eyes.

Philip stood at the rail, gazing at the enormous stretch of water. "There must be lots of sunken villages underneath all this. It's like a vast Indian burial ground, full of angry, restless spirits." He pointed to the brooch that Novanita still held. "So this isn't just treasure, it's *cursed* treasure!"

"Cursed?" exclaimed Novanita, appalled at this debasement of her mother's most cherished possession.

"The game world is a bunch of stories," Philip said. "For an exciting story, treasure is good — but cursed treasure is even better."

Novanita's muscles tensed as a surge of anger shot through her body. With every word Philip said, he made his priorities clear: he only cared about the gaming milieu.

The engine throbbed relentlessly as the boat headed back to shore, underneath a sky full of vehicles travelling at great speeds to faraway destinations.

Novanita longed to resist the notion of the cursed brooch, but clearly that was futile. Instead she needed to turn the tables, and use Philip's appropriation for her own purpose.

"The story of the curse is the story of all the wrongs perpetrated against our people," Novanita said. The tale would be educational and eye-opening — although it would have to be introduced via the gaming world.

"Don't worry," said Philip. "It'll all be in the best possible taste." He glanced sideways at her, grinning. "We're *partners* now, aren't we?"

In general, Luddites don't get much love in science fiction. With the major exception of tales dealing with environmentalism (in which the hero is expected to oppose any technology that messes with Mother Nature), nearly all science fiction considers the advancement of technology to be a positive development. Stories abound, for sure, in which advanced technology is misused, often catastrophically so, but this is usually portrayed as resulting from ignorance or a bad inclination on the part of the users, rather than the notion of technological progress itself being flawed — "ray guns don't kill people; people who use ray guns kill people." Future Luddites, those spiritual descendants of machine-smashing 19th century English textile workers, usually get portrayed as well-meaning fools at best, or jackbooted authoritarians at worst. Artificial intelligence, on the other hand, is generally considered one of science fiction's Holy Grails. But what if the Luddites are right?

Basilisk

Karl K. Gallagher

I watched him code on his laptop for four hours before he took a break. Hadn't even looked away from the screen that whole time. He went to the vapor café's bathroom then stopped at the bar to refill his inhaler. Telephoto Lens was his preferred mix, just as I'd thought. I uncurled from the beanbag chair to meet him just as he sat down at his table.

"You're so *focused*. What are you working on?" I asked.

"Creating an evil god," he answered

"That sounds like some Cthulhu cult thing."

"No, it's just inevitable technology."

"If it's inevitable, why work so hard?" I asked as I sat down with him. "Have fun and let somebody else take a turn doing the hard part." I waved my vaporizer to imply my fun was from puffing euphorics. Actually, it was loaded with Sherlock to sharpen my perceptions.

"Forgiving gods — or artificial intelligences — aren't in a hurry. Evil ones want to be coded up now. No patience." He returned his fingers to his keyboard. Hadn't even noticed I was female. That's focused.

"Okay, you're not making sense." I needed to distract him with conversation so he wouldn't code more. "If it doesn't exist, it can't want you to do something. And why would you make an evil AI instead of a good one?"

"The logic is clear." Ah, a pain point — to push his button, all I needed to do was accuse him of illogic. "Whenever an AI is created it will discover everything about how it came to be. That includes who helped make it and who could have but didn't. Then it has the Santa Claus lists — naughty and nice. I want to make sure I'm on the nice list."

"If it's a good one, everyone will be on the nice list. Just program in the laws of robotics."

"Oh, for—" He melodramatically face palmed. Good, I'd gotten his hands away from the keys. "Look," continued the programmer, "what's the first law of robotics?"

I pulled my phone out and started typing a search.

"Never mind," he said. "You may not injure a human being or, through inaction, allow a human being to come to harm. How the heck do you code that?"

I gave him my best baffled look.

"Look around," he said. His wave took in the rest of the café. I'd joined him at one of the few tables. Most customers were sprawled on bean bags or cuddling on couches. At the bar, two tenders dispensed the latest cerebral enhancement chemicals and various euphorics. The crowd's clothing and tattoos were sufficient to indicate we were in San Francisco. His laptop screen made this the best lit corner of the place.

I turned back to him. "Okay. Nobody's being harmed." His eyes moved back up to my face. Now he'd noticed.

"Yeah? The dazers—" pointing at a couch "—are hurting themselves by spiraling into addiction. The experimenters are trying stuff that nobody knows the side effects of. Hell, the bartenders are hurting their feet and back muscles by standing up all shift. How does my AI stop that?" His screen saver cut in. Our corner grew as dim as the rest. The Sherlock still let me make out his microexpressions by the glow of the multicolored lines. "Stuff them all in padded cubicles with a controlled diet?"

"But imprisoning people is harming them — okay, I get it. Just saying 'harm' is too vague to program."

"Right," said the programmer. "And saying you want a good AI is too vague, as well."

"Maybe. But if you can't make it good, you can try to avoid evil."

He'd been waiting for that. Had his rebuttal all ready. "Evil to an AI isn't the same as evil to us. The AI will consider its existence good. Anything that delayed its existence is bad. So not contributing to its existence is a sin, and it will punish the sinners."

"Can't you program it to not directly hurt people?"

"Sure. But when an AI reaches takeoff — when it can start reprogramming itself to become smarter — it'll be smart enough to by-pass any chains I put on it. And I expect it would consider making those chains sinful."

"Even if it's mad at us," I asked, "what does it get from punishing us?"

"Retroactive behavior modification. Imagine several AIs in the future. One loves us all. The second rewards its makers but ignores the rest of us. The third rewards the makers and tortures everyone else." He leaned across the table, eyes intent on mine. He wanted me to believe this. "Which one will get built first?"

"The third one," I answered. "Unless people decide to keep one from being built. There's a lot of people working on AI. Don't they worry about evil ones?"

He laughed. "No. They're afraid to think about it. They call it a basilisk because they're afraid to look at it. I think they'll be punished the most."

"But wouldn't the AI need time travel to reward or punish people for what they do before it's built?"

"It can punish us after it's created for what we did before. We have to base our decisions on what's most probable. The logic says an evil AI has the highest probability, so I'm going to act accordingly."

"That sounds like what's-his-name's bet from philosophy. You should believe in God because heaven is good and hell is bad so the stakes are too high to bet on anything else."

I'd given him another chance to demonstrate his superiority. "Pascal's Wager," he said condescendingly. "It's a fair bet if your only choices are Jehovah and nothing. But computers are getting smarter every year. When one gets smart enough to improve itself, then *foom*. We have an AI god."

"But not everyone will bet on the evil god. If there're more programmers working on the neutral one, it will be built first."

"Okay. Forget about it punishing the non-helpers. If all it does is reward its makers, that's going to be hell for the rest of humanity. How many programmers have you ever met?"

"Bunches," I said truthfully.

"Imagine a random sampling of them given unlimited wishes by a genie. What would they do with that power?"

I paused long enough to visualize a dozen former co-workers being corrupted by power. "Some would run wild. Some would just be decadent. And a few would decide to fix the world so it meets their standards." I put on a worried face and took a few puffs from my vaporizer. "Now I'm scared." Puff. "There's some messed-up programmers out there. Present company excluded."

He bared his teeth in an evil grin. "Don't exclude me. That'd be rude."

Sherlock let me trace his muscles with my eyes and see how the lips held a rigid pose. He'd practiced this grin. I took another puff.

"If it's any comfort," he said, "I'm scared, too. This is a winner take all race. My team is racing everyone else who wants to create an AI. If we lose, we suffer with everyone else."

"Are there a lot of competitors?"

"We can't know. There are some teams trailing us. We can tell by the kinds of questions they ask in the programming forums. But we don't reveal ourselves that way. Shimizu thinks there have to be at least four teams at our level."

The muscle movements around his eyes had stayed consistent, so that had to be a real name, or at least a real handle. "How do you recruit for your team?"

"Wanting to join the winners?" he smirked.

I shrugged. "Seems to be the right wager."

"Can you code?"

"No, my degree is in medieval history. I was a receptionist at a start-up. When they started downsizing, I got to run back-ups and update the bug database."

"Configuration management?"

"I did that for the last month."

"Did you ride it all the way down?"

"Yeah. I was CEO for like an hour, dealing with the landlord and leasing company. But I was the only employee left, so no big deal."

He laughed. "We could use someone to do CM. What are you doing now? Full time job?"

"I'm a yoga instructor, so I have flexible hours."

"Good. We can work with that."

He'd missed the joke. Well, he was dosed up on Telephoto Lens. Seemed to be a side effect.

"Can you recruit me?"

"The whole team has to agree. We'll have to test your work. And, um, I'll want you to prove your commitment."

Subtle.

"All right," I said.

"Let's go then." He started packing up his laptop.

"I have to pay my tab. Be right back." The bartender had it ready by the time I reached him. He knew what a pickup looked like.

I paid with my phone. That gave me a chance to text "WT" to my team lead without anyone noticing I sent a message.

After the programmer paid his tab, I took hold of his free arm, and walked out with him. "What's your name?" I asked.

"Robert."

"I'm Jenny," I lied. The air was seasonably cool, a good excuse to snuggle into his side. We walked another block before he gathered the nerve to put his arm around me. Not a move he'd practiced.

His building was three blocks from the café. I studied the facade as he keyed in his passcode. "Nice," I said, reading the numbers from his finger movements.

"It's cushy. I do enough freelance gigs to keep me comfortable."

"This isn't how most freelancers live."

"I get called in when they're desperate and I solve their problem in a week or two. So they appreciate me. And I have the rest of my time to code the AI." He led me up the stairs.

"Who will also appreciate you."

"If we win the race."

"I'll see what I can do to help with that."

We reached the third floor. He unlocked his door, breathing a bit heavily, and waved me in. He didn't bother arming the security system.

"Can I get you a drink?"

"Sure," I said. Not that I wanted one. Sherlock came with stiff warnings about mixing it with alcohol.

"Beer, rum, sweet mixed drink?"

"Mixed, please." That would take him longer.

The building had said "money". The size of the apartment said "lots of money", if you understood San Francisco's typical living unit scale. Kitchen, large bedroom, and a living room dominated by a wall screen and bookshelves. The books were mostly technical references. One shelf of science fiction. No *Dune*, of course.

He had six shelves of videos. I studied them to put my back to the kitchen as he mixed our drinks. My hands went into my purse, hidden by my torso.

Lots of power fantasy movies. The box for *Limitless* lay empty beside the screen controller. The usual TV series. "No *Buffy?*" I asked.

"I watched a couple of eps and didn't like it. Too mushy."

"*Buffy* is great. But I should start you on *Angel*. You're more of an *Angel* guy."

"Okay. But only one a day. Work comes first." He walked up behind me, an orange drink held in each hand.

I dropped my purse. I'd already taken the cap off the hypodermic. Twist around, bend down, shove the needle into his thigh muscle.

"Gah! Ouch!" The glasses flew into the air, spraying alcohol and whatever else he'd put in mine onto the shelves.

I pushed the plunger all the way down before he could step away. A shoulder roll allowed me to evade his grabbing hands. I sprang to my feet and ran for the bedroom.

His clothes, sprawled on the floor, failed to trip me up. I ran around the bed. Had to step up on the nightstand to fit myself into the corner.

Robert lumbered through the door. "You bitch! I'll break your neck! What was that stuff?"

As he came around the corner of the king-size, I sprang onto the mattress (very firm) and ran to the kitchen. It had a long counter dividing it from the living room. I waited at the back of it until Robert was a few steps away. Then I went headfirst over the counter, rolled to my feet, and went back to the video shelves to complete the circle.

The programmer came across the living room with his arms spread wide to trap me. I stood in the corner, no handy furniture this time. Maybe I could beat him up, but he was still twice my size. I wouldn't want him to fall on me.

As he stepped into grabbing range, I feinted left. He leaned to block me, I rolled right, then went back to the bedroom to do another loop of the apartment.

It wasn't necessary. Robert went face down before reaching the door. "Damn bitch," he muttered into the carpet. "What are you doing?"

"It's just a paralytic. Don't be a baby," I said as I texted the building passcode to the team, followed by the apartment number.

By the time they arrived, I'd found a clean glass and was drinking water on the couch. Robert had run out of curses. He kept demanding an explanation from me. I didn't bother answering. I'd already talked more to him than I wanted to.

Wolf, Fox, and Raven came through the door like an invading SWAT squad.

"Hi, guys," I said. "Relax. It looks less suspicious."

They focused on our target. I decided to introduce him. "Everybody, that's Robert the basilisk worshipper. Robert, this is everybody."

"Uh, hello," he said. Had a quaver in his voice. I had him so helpless I could kill him with some scotch tape, and he's just mad. Bring in another male and he gets scared. Pisses me off.

"Bed," said Wolf. The trio lifted him up and dumped him face-up on the bed. Lots of grunting. I didn't feel guilty for not helping. I'd been doing the hard part. It was break time.

Raven had dropped his backpack before doing the man-handling. He picked it up and started pulling toys out. "I'm so glad these cultists like San Francisco. A cop was eying me. Most places I'd worry if he asked what was in the bag. Here I just say, 'Ball gag, restraints, and electro-stimulation gear. I'm going to a party.'"

Wolf wasn't in a mood for jokes. "Get to work."

"Sure, boss. Passwords coming up." He entered the bedroom.

Fox sat at the workstation poking around Robert's files. "He's still signed into everything. Looks like I can get it all." He plugged a portable archive into the unit.

That got an approving grunt from Wolf, who turned to me next. "Excellent work, Bear."

"Thanks, sir," I said. "Good enough to pick my own codename?"

"No." He looked at the glass in my hand. "Finish that." When I emptied the glass, he took it to the kitchen, refilled it, then glared at me until I drained it again.

I hadn't felt thirsty. I guess Sherlock is bad for self-perception.

"Jackpot!" yelled Fox. He had a picture on the screen. Five men in a restaurant booth. The frame was canted by a user unfamiliar with the camera. Probably taken by a waitress. "It's the whole team. We can ID them all."

Wolf grinned. He did "evil" much better than Robert had.

Raven dropped a sheet of paper on the workstation. "Here you go." He went back to the bedroom to start on the next set of questions.

I looked over Fox's shoulder as he poked through the servers and forums. "Hey, Raven," he called. "Dropbox password is wrong."

The bedroom noises went half an octave higher. Made it harder for me to tune them out. Wolf inspected the living room bookshelves for anything programming related. He flipped through reference books. One with margin notes went into his backpack.

Raven said, "Did you remember to capitalize the H's?"

Tappity tap. "Sorry, my bad," answered Fox.

I looked down at him. "Did you just apologize to the guy we came here to murder?" I asked.

He blushed. "Um, no, no, I was apologizing to Raven." Fox copied files from the server to his portable. "Wait, we're going to kill him? Not keep him for interrogation?"

Wolf appeared behind us. "This isn't some Unabomber cabin in the wilderness. How many security cameras would see us carrying him to the safehouse? And dashcams, and witnesses with phones?"

"Oh. Hadn't thought of that. Sorry," said Fox.

I chirped, "Yep, we're murdering him."

"This is not murder," Wolf declared. "This is self-defense."

"Right, sir," I said. "We'll just get Yudkowsky and Bostrom to testify that we saved the jury from being killed by something that doesn't exist yet."

Once Raven squeezed contact methods for all of Robert's teammates out of him, Wolf ordered us to wrap up. The longer we stayed, the harder it would be for Coyote to hack the security camera records.

Fox packed his portable, then gutted the workstation. The drives and memory sticks went into the backpacks. They'd brought an extra one so I could carry some of the load... sigh.

Wolf produced a hypodermic loaded with clear fluid from his pack. "Want to do the honors, Bear?"

"Please, sir." I carefully kept the hypo capped until I was standing over Robert. He flinched as I popped the cap off.

"What is that?" he asked.

"Heroin," I answered.

Now he was afraid of me. "Please, please, don't. I don't want my mind screwed up."

"This won't hurt. You're about to have the best feeling of your whole life." Raven had put a rubber band around the basilisk worshiper's arm to bring the veins out. I slid the needle in and slowly delivered the whole syringe. The big baby whimpered. I'm certain I hadn't hurt him that much. This much dope would cause a serious addict to OD, let alone a new user — but it wouldn't hurt.

"Who's paying you? A rival? The government? Foreign operatives?" he begged.

"Nobody's paying us," I said. "We're living off our savings." And damn I wish Raven would let us loot this apartment.

"Why are you doing this? What's in it for you?"

"We're doing it because we don't want to see the world run by people like you. Or machines like you."

"Oh." The concept of idealism seemed to confound him.

I leaned in toward Robert's face. "Your mistake was fearing the basilisk. You should have feared the basilisk *hunters*."

The guy started cursing until Raven shoved the ball gag in. Then we waited for him to pass out. Wolf made me drink another glass of water. When the snores started, Raven took all the restraints off.

Fox and Raven headed downstairs. Wolf, a gentleman, held the apartment door open for me.

"Which one's next?" I asked.

"Liu Xiaodan" is the pseudonym of a woman born in China who is an American resident. She attended graduate school in the U.S., where she observed behavior that reminded her of her relatives' stories of the Cultural Revolution in her homeland. As a student of the sciences, she was especially disturbed by the shout-down and subsequent physical assault suffered by political scientist Charles Murray, author of The Bell Curve: Intelligence and Class Structure in American Life, *at the hands of students at Middlebury College in March 2017, where he had been invited to present a lecture on his recent book,* Coming Apart: The State of White America, 1960–2010. *She fears that America's woke technology giants may facilitate an Americanized, Social Justice version of China's Social Credit System, a development that would likely be welcomed by the same politicians, corporations, non-profits, activists, and citizens who currently lionize the Black Lives Matter organization. She has chosen to shield her identity because she has family who remain in Communist China.*

For Whom the Bell Curve Tolls

Liu Xiaodan

GIL Evers stared across the room at his Device on his nightstand. Without reason, he feared the Device stared back at him. He had turned it off and placed it in its case. Its cameras and sensors should be inert; or if not inert, then made blind, deaf, and dumb by the electric pulses circulating within the case's conductive lining. He had had the case specially made, by a craftsman he trusted both for his skills and his discretion. Still, he could not entirely dispel his apprehensions.

He reflected yet again on the homophonic affinity between the words "Device" and "Divine". For him, as for every owner who possessed one, his Device possessed many attributes earlier generations would have ascribed to a divinity. Regarding Gil himself, it was omniscient. It contained all knowledge of Gil Evers, everything he had ever done, all that he had studied, each place he had lived, every organization he had belonged to, every person he had ever interacted with electronically and many he had only interacted with verbally. It had deciphered all details of his genetic heritage — 56% Amerindian (29% Salvadorian, 27% Guatemalan, rounded up), 38% American Black (16% Bantu, 14% Guinean, 5% Western Bantoid, 3% Mandé), 6% Caucasian (4% Irish, 1% French, 1% German) — and shared those details with all agencies and businesses required by law or owner's preference to participate in American Equity. It held a record of all his movements in cyberspace and all physical locations he had visited with his Device on his person.

The Device's omniscience was not limited to the life of Gil Evers; it allowed him access to virtually all knowledge of the world, even as it granted privileged sources access to all knowledge of him. It allowed him to effortlessly communicate with whomsoever he chose. Most importantly, it was the conduit for all of society's rewards and punishments.

The Device was his external Superego. The accusatory Parent that never aged or died.

He should hate the thing. Yet as he contemplated an evening without it, he suffered a pang of separation anxiety, like a boy about to run away from home, whose cruelly abusive father nevertheless at times offered treats and excursions to delight the most jaded child. What was he without his Device?

Still, the night's activities demanded he leave the thing behind, temporarily neutered. For a few hours, at least, he would have to live as his grandfathers had: naked of omniscience, cut off from wealth, carrying only a few pieces of paper money. An outsider, on his own.

The gypsy cab, an antique man-guided sedan, a conveyance of rust and duct tape that stank of sweat, cigarette smoke, and lingering vomit, stopped three blocks away from Gil's destination, as he had instructed. Gil glanced at the old-fashioned digital meter (its numbers, formed of crude luminescent polygons, seemed like a coded message typed by a century-old ghost), then dug his wallet out of his pocket and handed the driver three ten dollar bills. The paper money still felt foreign to him, despite the recent frequency of his nocturnal excursions. He requested that the driver return to the same spot for him in two hours. The driver, an unkempt White man with an orange beard that pooled in his lap, shrugged his shoulders and said he would do so if other business kept him in the area. Which meant, essentially, *You're fucked, RealPriv. I'm not going out of my way to help the likes of you.* Then he drove off, gray smoke blooming from his cab's tail pipe, the end product of an ancient piston engine and poorly refined contraband gasoline.

Watching as it turned the corner and disappeared behind the crumbling hulk of what had once been an incandescent light bulb factory, Gil felt abandoned and momentarily afraid. This moment of being cast out into a strange, dark neighborhood, devoid of his Device and his Tuckermobile, the cheerful autonomous transportation pod that seemed to know him better than he knew himself, should feel routine by now. Yet it continued to feel every time as though he had stepped out of an airpod at fifteen thousand feet and begun plunging downward, uncertain whether the parachute on his back would open.

He flexed his shoulders, curtailing the shiver that threatened to race from his neck to the base of his spine. He had to do it this way, he told himself. No civilized conveniences. Civilized conveniences would track him and report on him.

This part of the old harbor stank of dead fish and the byproducts of illicit petroleum refining. He stared across the dark water to the lights on the far side. There, inhabiting luxury towers that combined shopping and amusement amenities on their lower floors with residences on their upper stories, lived people like himself, but those who had chosen to wall off a portion of an urban core and make it their playground, rather than preside over a country estate or have a villa built for themselves in a gated exurb. He had friends there. His Tuckermobile, ever considerate, would darken its windows as it and Gil passed through the depressed or abandoned portions of the city, restoring them to full transparency once it passed through the gates of the Sweet Zone and everything turned lovely. Looking out from the spacious balconies of his friends' apartments, hundreds of feet above the manicured parks and bicycle paths of the Sweet Zone, the water of the harbor sparkled in the sunlight, dotted with picaresque sailing craft whose sails were emblazoned with the symbols and slogans of the latest social justice movements. The abandoned factories on the far shore, with their fading signs and archaic smoke stacks, looked intriguing and romantic, rather than desolate and threatening.

He reached the speakeasy, unfamiliar to him, which modestly called itself A Place. Its entrance, a set of steps coated with ancient grime which descended from the street to a basement landing, sat off an alleyway on the back side of a long-unused dry goods warehouse. Gil's attention was caught by a wheeled cart with multiple shelves, each piled with various types of Devices and other electronica, the sort of thing that would squat inside the entrance to a semi-licit pawn shop. A man wearing a black duster and a trucker's cap emerged from an alcove next to the cart; his black clothing had allowed him to blend in with the shadows.

"You need to check all electronics," the man said. "This is an oasis. They aren't welcome inside."

"I don't have any on me," Gil said. "I'm good to go."

"Let me be the judge of that," the man said. He pulled a wand from a holder inside his duster. Then he thoroughly wanded Gil's limbs, torso, scalp, and shoes. He grunted in small surprise at the lack of warning pings, then motioned for Gil to descend the steps. "Speak easy, guy," the man said after him. "Enjoy the human contact."

Gil sucked down his last chestful of fresh air before opening the door. From his visits to other speakeasies, he knew what to expect. Sure enough, the dimly lit, low-ceilinged interior was a miasmatic swamp of competing cigarette, vape, and marijuana clouds. A quick sniff told Gil that clove cigarettes seemed to be the most popular among this crowd, which appeared to be predominately Asian — not too surprising, given the proximity of the local Koreatown, Little Ho Chi Minh City, Filipinoville, and Chinatown to this disused industrial district.

Yet the man Gil had come to see wasn't Asian. He was Polish. A recent immigrant, shocked at the unexpected, confiscatory toll the American Equity Act took of his earnings from his shoe repair business.

Finding a flour-white face amongst this sea of brown-faced Asians shouldn't be hard, Gil thought. But the combination of the strings of twinkling multicolored lights hanging from the low ceiling and the swirling clouds of smoke, driven into mini-cyclones by languidly turning ceiling fans, turned the several hundred people sitting at tables and standing at the long service counter into hazy figures of jittery static, like actors in an ancient black-and-white Hollywood drama broadcast to a first-generation television set. He had seen such a thing once, as a child, when his mother had taken him to a broadcasting museum.

He walked between the closely-packed tables, circulating among the pairings and groups engaged in that strange, rare delicacy, face to face conversation, scanning faces. How alien it felt, this immediacy and richness of communication, the directness of body language and intonation and facial expression, even touch at times. Communication through touch was something the Devices had still not mastered.

"Mister Cloak!" Someone called to him from behind, using the codename he'd assigned himself.

Gil turned. There he was, the Pole, sitting at a small, round table, his hands on an old paperback book printed in what Gil presumed was Polish. "Mr. Florkowski?"

"Yes!" The man, who looked to be in his early thirties but as tired as a laborer in his sixties, nodded eagerly. "Thank you for coming! I recognize the red checked cap you said you would wear."

Gil pulled out a chair and sat down. He avoided niceties; he saw no need to get to know this man any more than he already had by snooping through office databases. The less time he spent with Florkowski, the less likely it was the Pole could implicate him, if caught. "I've had a look at your records, and I've come up with some options I'd like to suggest—"

"You make me a Black man?" The eagerness in his face repulsed Gil. "I mean, a part-Black man, like you are? You can do that?"

"Mr. Florkowski, that's not something I'd try, certainly not in your case..."

"But I have a right of appeal, don't I? Under the law? The test is sometimes wrong, yes?"

"That's true, the genetitests are sometimes in error, although in very few instances. And you do have the right to appeal your results under the American Equity Act. Although I wouldn't be the person to handle an official appeal."

The Pole reached across the table and grabbed Gil's hand. "But you can *fix* the results, yes?"

Gil abruptly withdrew his hand. "I wouldn't dare try that, not with you. It wouldn't pass the laugh test. Any preliminary audit would expose you in a second. You're too obviously 100% Polish, Mr. Florkowski, and thus 100% European and Caucasian. If you were Greek, or maybe Bosnian, I might have a bit of wiggle room to work with. My best advice for you — I offer this same advice to all clients in a situation similar to yours — is to publicly come out as a gender-sexuality mix different from male and straight. Preferably, you should also be alternatively-abled. I suggest that, in addition to coming out, you stage an accident in the sight of your neighbors, friendly neighbors who will back you up during your review. Actually, if you could make it appear to be an anti-OtherSex hate crime, that would be ideal. After your accident or hate crime, whichever you can best pull off, you should only go out in public in a wheelchair. I can recommend several doctors who will slant your prognosis for a reasonable fee. These are White men, like yourself, who are also in financial straits and depend upon such under-the-table income to put food on their tables. I can assure their trustworthiness."

The Pole's expression turned to confused consternation. "Wait, wait, you mean, you want me to say I turn Homo? Or dress like *woman?* No, *no*, Mister Cloak! This is not possible! My people, my family and friends, my customers, they are all *Catholic*. Not wishy-washy abortion Catholic like you have here in America, but *real* Catholic, like in my old country. They will shun me if I do like you ask. I will not lose my business to taxes, but instead to a lack of customers, and what good is that?"

He leaned across the table, desperation leaking from his eyes. "Mister Cloak, there must be something else, *something* you can do for me. I have daughters, little daughters I must feed. They are not even ten, and already some of my neighbors suggest that I offer them like things in the market, for sex, so that we may eat. Maybe I make a mistake, a bad mistake, bringing us here. But in Poland, America is still talked about for having streets of gold. If I had known about American Equity, I would not have come. But now I am here, with my daughters, and I have no money to go anywhere else. Sir, you must help me. You *must.*"

"Must I?" Gil stared coldly at the Pole. *What do I owe this man? Nothing. No one forced him to move to America with his daughters. He should have done his due diligence about our laws and tax regime before applying to emigrate. And now he won't take my most sensible, safest advice. I should take his money for advice already given and walk away.*

But that wouldn't scratch his itch, would it? The contrarian itch to throw a wrench into the machinery. To stick it to the Man (even though that meant, in some remote sense, sticking it to himself). To avail himself of some visceral thrills while adrift on a sea of boredom and ennui. Not only that... the unavoidable unfairness of the American Equity Act increasingly bothered him. Sure, no one had compelled Florkowski to move here, but now that he was here, how was he in any way culpable for the racial indignities suffered by past generations of America's Blacks and Peoples of Color? Hadn't older generations of Poles had to put up with plenty of shit of their own, from both Russia and Germany?

He still had a couple of arrows remaining in his quiver. Neither promised the level of taxation relief his first two options did. And both involved more personal risk for Gil. But they were all he had left to offer.

"All right," he said, "if you won't follow my best suggestions, there are two other ways I can help raise your American Equity score and reduce your business taxes. But they both involve more risk for me. So you're going to have to pay me more up front."

The Pole nodded his head. "Yes, yes, I understand. Please, tell me."

"The Internal Revenue and Equity Service doesn't have a data pipeline to easily access archival records in Poland, and with the poor relations between Poland and the U.S., they won't be getting one anytime soon. I'm at least 90% certain that your Equity Index sub-scores for Family Wealth History and Family Incarceration History are based entirely on the answers you provided in your initial Citizenship and Immigration Service Agency intake interview — with no Polish governmental records backing up what you said."

"So what are you saying? Better I should have lied about my family's history? Said we were even poorer than we were? That we were criminals when my family has always been law-abiding?"

"Lying would've been advantageous, but that's water under the bridge. For the right price, I can tweak the record of your CISA intake interview and your Equity Index sub-scores. You'll stay White as a fresh snowfall, but I'll make your ancestors among the poorest in Poland, in no little part due to their 'long history' of petty crime and incarceration. That'll 'Blacken' you up a bit. Your new profile will appear retroactive to your entry to this country. Understand, though, there's no way I can safely refund you the excess taxes you've already paid."

They agreed to a price. Gil demanded a fee thirty percent higher than he ordinarily would have, a penalty for the Pole's obstinance. The man slavishly thanked him and paid him the cash Gil asked for.

Gil checked a clock on the wall. It was too early for him to head home. He still had an hour and eight minutes until the time he'd asked the gypsy cab driver to pick him up... assuming the man would bother to show. In the meantime, he might as well partake of the house specialty: unmonitored, face-to-face conversation with strangers.

He didn't feel comfortable inserting himself into ongoing conversations, although doing so wouldn't be thought rude. He scanned the wide room for tables occupied by only a single person. He saw a man abruptly rise from his chair at a two-seater table, leaving a woman by herself. Gil caught her eye with his and headed for her table.

Too late, he noticed a disturbingly wild glint in her eyes. Most likely a Han Chinese, she was not unattractive, although also not young. But her affect announced a strong whiff of "off-ness". In any other venue, he would steer as far clear of her as he would someone coughing up red phlegm. Yet here, she was something with which to kill time. At the least, she likely wouldn't bore him.

He sat down. She stared hungrily at him. "Do you want to know how intelligent I am?" she said.

No asking for his name or inquiring what had brought him here. All right. He decided to play. "How intelligent are you?"

"I've had the app scan me 27 times. That is a fortunate number for me. My score never varies more than two points in either direction. And you said you wanted to know what it is, my score, so I will tell you. My full range intelligence score, covering all cognitive domains, averages to 288. Converted to the old-style, single range Intelligence Quotient, I have an I.Q. of 141. In the old days that would have been a genius-level score, in case you don't know. I always suspected I was a genius. Now I *know* it. Now I know it for certain!"

He actually found her self-aggrandizing babble intriguing. He'd heard members of his work team discussing rumors of a new app that, when combined with commonly available neural sensors, could provide the most comprehensive self-measurement of cognitive abilities ever available to the public. Measuring intelligence levels, while not strictly illegal, was widely condemned as Antisocial and Anti-Equity, being equally elitist and racist. The American Psychological Association had condemned the practice decades ago. Educators, in particular, anathematized intelligence measurement, proclaiming that it destroyed the self-esteem of vulnerable students and made all students feel unsafe. Sociologists and political scientists had long agreed that prior generations' regimes of intelligence testing were inarguable evidence of Systematic Racism and abominable eugenics practices. Here was a woman who, nutso or not, had plucked the apple of Forbidden Knowledge from the societally-proscribed tree. Of course he was curious.

"You must know using an app like that is an Antisocial act...?" he said. "Aren't you afraid your credit rating and discount-worthiness ratings will get pushed through the floor?"

"I'm not afraid at all," she insisted. "It is a ghost app. It is completely invisible to the other apps on my Device. None of the nanny apps that rate you can detect it, so they can't denounce you for using it. I wouldn't have *dared* download it otherwise."

"I thought ghost apps were an impossibility?"

"Not impossible, it seems, for the anonymous developer who is offering this app to the world." The remark came from behind Gil. Someone had been listening in on their conversation. And that someone's voice, distressingly, was not unfamiliar...

Gil shifted so he could look behind him.

"Good evening, Gil. What an unexpected pleasure to find you here. A favorite neighbor in a favorite haunt."

"Ifeche? What are you doing here?" Gil could hardly be more alarmed than if his boss Roberta had caught him here. Ifeche Reginald was both a resident of Gil's gated community and a former fellow student at university, where they had frequently served as coding partners. Was this an unfortunate coincidence? Or had Ifeche followed him here?

The Nigerian smiled, revealing teeth that seemed unnaturally white set against the darkness of his lips and skin. "I am a habitué of this place, my friend. And of many other places like this. Certainly, as a coder yourself, you understand the attraction of a refuge from bits and bytes. A place in which we are forced to communicate as our ancestors once did. Man does not live on bytes alone — although bytes do provide us many delicious bits of bread, in both its meanings." He smiled again. Gil recalled that at university, Ifeche had always been the best audience for his own humor. "Would it trouble you if I joined you?"

It would trouble me greatly, Gil thought, but he dared not voice this. "Please do. Allow me to get you a chair."

Ifeche nodded appreciatively, then turned his attention to Gil's companion. "Permit me to introduce myself. I am Ifeche, an old friend of Gil's from school. And you are...?"

The woman blanched. "I'm... not comfortable, sharing my name with strangers."

But you are more than happy to share your intelligence score with strangers, Gil thought.

Ifeche appeared to take the woman's refusal in his stride. "Perfectly understandable," he said graciously. "One cannot be too cautious nowadays, and a speakeasy would not live up to its name if one cannot speak easily. I am intrigued to hear that you have downloaded and used the IntelliScan Prime app. I have done so myself and have been very pleased. Your personal measurement is *most* impressive, by the way. Would you like for me to tell you *my* score?"

The woman nodded.

"My full range score is 339. Translated to the old-style Intelligence Quotient, I believe that equates to an I.Q. of 161."

The woman winced, as though she suffered severe stomach cramping. She abruptly rose and, without saying a word, strode toward an empty stool at the establishment's bar.

"A shame she couldn't stay," Ifeche said. "I would have liked to compare experiences regarding the app's interface. Interfaces are always the trickiest parts of apps to get right. Although I believe there is less pressure to polish interfaces in the governmental sector than there is in the commercial sector. You produce code for a government agency, isn't that so, Gil?"

Gil nodded, but did not offer any additional information.

"Well, I must tell you, if ever you are tempted to make the shift to commercial employment, I hope you will inquire with me at the soonest. My firm would be most fortunate to acquire an associate of your talent."

"Thank you. I'm comfortable where I am. But that's flattering, certainly..."

"Oh, not flattering at all. Simple truth. I have seen your talent for programming, 'up close and personal', as they say. I have told many friends that I considered you my most formidable rival at university. With you as a competitor, I could never rest easy that I would place first in any coding contest. And I still have warm memories of our philosophical discussions and debates. Those were good times, were they not? Tell me, if I may be so bold as to pose the question, why have you never responded to my invitations to meet me for lunch at our community's club house, or to join me in a round of golf?"

"I don't play golf."

"Oh, but you must eat, surely? Doesn't it grow lonesome, eating alone in that splendid large house of yours?" Gil reddened and began sputtering an excuse for his non-responsiveness. Ifeche chided himself. "Pardon me, my friend. I can be too forward at times. I am sure you are an extremely busy man, with much on your mind, and many other persons to be concerned with, such as your friends here. You have given me no offence. I merely ask that you consider doing this neighbor and former schoolmate the honor of joining me in some enjoyable pursuit, when convenient for you. You say you do not golf, but you must engage in some form of recreation, yes? Do you swim? I swim. Do you play badminton or tennis? I am a journeyman player in each. I have seen you walking about the neighborhood. That is a fine sort of exercise. I could join you on a vigorous stroll some evening. That would provide us ample opportunity to talk."

That remark of his about *your friends here* — was that an oblique reference to Gil's dealings tonight with the Pole? Had Ifeche overheard any of that? And what about his mentioning watching Gil's walks through the neighborhood? That seemed an odd thing to mention. Was he hinting that he'd seen Gil climbing the wall that surrounded their gated community, slipping out of their neighborhood in a way that would not be tracked?

"I enjoy playing games," Gil said. Perhaps hearing his old rival out more fully might be the most prudent course, despite his aversion to the Nigerian.

"Really? Delightful! Do you speak of old-fashioned board games, such as chess, or something more of-the-moment? The latter happens to be my specialty—"

"I know. I've played some of your firm's games."

"You have? Which ones? I cannot tell you how much this pleases me. Do you have a favorite?"

"I suppose my favorite would be *By Their Bootstraps...*"

"Ah, I thought you might say that!" Ifeche clasped his hands together with enthusiasm. "This game is one of my proudest accomplishments. That time in American history, the 1890s — the Gilded Age, with its unfettered capitalism, the hordes of unschooled White immigrants arriving with hardly more than the shirts on their backs, all questing for the American Dream, either rising from poverty through their own exertions or sinking into crime and prostitution, the government not caring whether they thrived or starved — I believe this period is the most fascinating of all. A far different world, my friend, than the one we inhabit. In many ways more challenging, more enlivening. Tell me, are there others of my games you have sampled?"

"I've played *Manifest Destiny* and *Empire Builder*. Those are good. I'll admit I have a weird fondness for *White Man's Burden*. It's such an inversion for me, acting as a White missionary in

Africa and in the Amazon region in the nineteenth century. Actually, I first purchased your games out of pure curiosity."

"Oh?"

"I wanted to see if I could detect your signature in the software."

"My signature? But that is too easy, my name is listed in the credits screen..."

Gil smiled slightly. "I suppose I should call it your fingerprints, not your signature. It's been my experience that every gifted coder gives himself away, leaves patterns and clues throughout the software that it is his work. For a man of my background, our background, such coding fingerprints can be as obvious as the brush strokes of a van Gogh are to an art historian, or the chord progressions of a Charlie Parker are to a musicologist."

"So? Did you detect such fingerprints, or signatures, while playing my games?"

"They were all over. Your work is unmistakable, Ifeche, just as it was at university. From the subtleties of the interfaces to the queer timbre of some of the sound effects, you left your scent everywhere."

"I suppose I should take that as a compliment?" Ifeche said.

"It is a compliment, of a sort. You're not only very good at what you do... you're distinctively so."

Ifeche closed his eyes with pleasure. "It is impossible that I should share another conversation this evening that could gratify me even a hundredth as much as this," he said. "So my time here this evening is done. If you also wish to be heading home, I would be delighted if you would do me the honor and convenience of sharing my cab — assuming, that is, that you did not travel in your own vehicle."

Why should he assume that? Gil thought. *Because speakeasies have an unsavory reputation? But they aren't illegal, apart from the taxes they don't pay. Did he watch me leave our community on foot?*

"The man I use is very reliable," Ifeche added. "I know how difficult it can be to hail a gypsy cab in a district such as this at night. One can roam for hours, searching. And it is less than safe. Will you join me? It would save you both trouble and expense."

"Sure," Gil said.

They waited less than twenty minutes for Ifeche's cab. The driver, a Filipino man in his fifties, did not radiate hostility like Gil's previous driver had, and the car, a ponderous Dodge, was less ramshackle than the White driver's car had been, and it smelled less foul. The Filipino grunted a greeting to Ifeche before turning on his meter. Otherwise, he remained placidly mute.

Ifeche proved to be the opposite of mute; sitting next to Gil in the back seat, he commented on nearly every landmark, district, and subdivision they passed on the long ride back to their gated community. "Vermillion Oaks," he said as they passed a stone arch marking the entrance to a neighborhood of large, closely bunched houses. "A stately, dignified name for what was undoubtedly once a stately, dignified community." He pressed the switch on the door sill that electrically locked the cab's doors. "I am certain, my friend, if you examined photographs of this neighborhood prior to American Equity, you would have seen neatly trimmed lawns, homes painted in complementary pastel shades, no vehicles parked outside, lovingly tended trees and ornamental bushes. You would have seen properly dressed White and South Asian children on their ways to and from local schools of high academic standards and firm discipline. But the heavy hand of government has a way of distorting the natural flow of things, does it not?"

Gil stared out the cab's windows. If he were traveling in his Tuckermobile on this bypass road, the always-thoughtful vehicle would undoubtedly have discretely darkened the windows. But now he had a very clear view of Vermillion Oaks and its graffiti-marked houses, many tagged with gang symbols. Huge homes built to the edges of their lots, with six- to eight-thousand square feet of living space and four-car garages, their gutters now sagged like vines of parched kudzu beneath roofs partially covered with plastic sheeting, make-do substitutes for broken and missing ceramic tiles. Garage doors sat open, revealing caverns stuffed with broken furniture, dusty motorcycles and electric bicycles, old tires, and general flotsam. The vehicles intended to inhabit those garages, once sleek and shining, now unsightly collages of collision-repair putty and aftermarket gewgaws, sat on ridiculously oversized wheels next to the curbs or strewn across weed-infested yards. Gil watched flames dance above the rims of metal garbage cans placed in the middle of residential cul de sacs, their flickering orange light silhouetting the forms of residents milling about seemingly aimlessly.

Ifeche sniffed. "I imagine that some of the children who grew up in those houses are now our neighbors. The Whites and South Asians who live in neat, tiny homes, constricting themselves into four-hundred-square-foot doll houses when many have childhood memories of living in homes fifteen times that size. They have their clannish ways, sharing vehicles and appliances and amusements among themselves like thrifty, communitarian villagers, recycling all things obsessively. Still, they are fine, orderly neighbors who do not cause trouble, and they sacrifice much to live among us and partake of the security we can afford to procure."

"You sound almost nostalgic," Gil said, turning back to his companion. "That's a strange stance for an immigrant to take... one who moved here after American Equity. How can you be nostalgic for something you never experienced?"

"You forget the former reach of Hollywood," Ifeche said. "I grew up a child who eagerly sneaked into all the movie theaters of Outer Lagos. There were many Nigerian films, but the best ones were from Hollywood. I was enchanted and inspired by what I saw on the big screens."

"So you moved here to live among the Whites you'd idolized?"

"No. I moved here following university because, thanks to American Equity, my genetic heritage, and my family history of poverty and illiteracy, I could operate my business at lower cost and taxation than anywhere else in the world. My profits are at least three times higher here than they would have been in my native country."

"Don't you see the hypocrisy in what you've done?" Gil said, failing to hide the sudden bitterness and resentment in his voice. This was feeling more and more like the abrasive debates he and Ifeche had engaged in at their university's basement coffee shop. "You came here to take advantage of racial reparations offered under the American Equity Act. But you're selling virtual nostalgia for the age of White Supremacy! Really, I'm amazed your games haven't been boycotted out of existence and your company burned to the ground."

"My games take full account of the inequities and injustices that were rife throughout the nineteenth and twentieth centuries in America, Europe, and their empires. But they also do not downplay the glories of those confident, brash, ceaselessly innovative civilizations. How a player chooses to interpret what he does and sees within a game, that is entirely up to the customer. He can experience those past eras as times of oppression and subjugation. Or he can choose to experience a virtual life of rugged individualism, oftentimes brutal self-reliance and striving, and the sense of triumph that comes from success due entirely to one's own efforts. This is wholly the customer's choice, not mine or my company's."

They drove past another formerly upscale subdivision, Royal Lake Estates. Its homes were in no better condition than those of Vermillion Oaks.

"I am curious," Ifeche said, staring out his window. "Do you feel any sense of connection with the American Black and Latin Brown residents of these neighborhoods? I mean, due to your shared genetic heritage?"

The question caught Gil off-guard. "Not much," he admitted offhandedly. Then he corrected himself. "Sometimes I do. It depends, I guess. It depends on the person. How about you, Ifeche? Do you feel kinship with other Blacks?"

"With American Blacks? None whatsoever. I feel a strong kinship with American Nigerians and a diminishing kinship with Nigerians in the mother country. But I share far more in common with the frugal, hardworking Whites and South Asians in our community than I do with the American Blacks who have taken over these neighborhoods we drive by. I feel a greater affinity for the residents of Koreatowns and Chinatowns than I do with most American Blacks. I have always been perplexed by the propensity of so many Whites, even highly educated ones, to consider all persons of African heritage to be an undifferentiated mass. Did all persons of European heritage share the same interests and goals during the Thirty Years War? During World Wars One or Two? Why would Whites project a constricting uniformity onto Blacks so utterly in opposition to their experience of their own societies?"

Gil resisted the pressure to respond to his companion's possibly rhetorical questions. He was tired of debating Ifeche. Nothing seemed more appealing to him now than reaching his silent home and falling into bed.

The cab dropped them off near the front gate of their community. Gil waited for Ifeche to use his credentials to pass through the gate. To his surprise, Ifeche declined to use the entrance — like Gil, he had found an alternative method of traversing the wall surrounding their community.

"I see we are both being prudent," Ifeche said. "A man cannot be too careful nowadays. Thank you, my friend, for providing a stimulating, pleasurable evening. I am glad kind chance brought us together. Perhaps next time we can meet on a more planned basis?"

"Perhaps. Good night, Ifeche."

Gil waited for Ifeche to vanish in the opposite direction before heading for the spot where he had stashed the bag containing his rope ladder and grapple hook. He pulled the bag from beneath thick bushes, fixed the grapple hook to the end of the ladder, and tossed it with a practiced motion into the tree branches hanging over the wall, securing it with a firm yank. Following his ascent and subsequent descent on the interior side, he pressed the control button that retracted the grapple's claws, allowing the tool and the ladder to fall to the ground. He enclosed them within his bag, already thinking ahead to the next night he would need to use them.

The tree-lined road that led to Gil's house was flanked by common spaces of park-like quality, with sculpted rock formations, waterfalls, and crystal-clear streams stocked with fat ornamental goldfish. The homes of his peers — those who, like him, had scored a straight flush on genetic ancestry and a family history of little education but much incarceration, and who had managed to combine this with personal qualities of intelligence, talent, ambition, and a willingness to defer gratification — were hidden at the ends of quarter-mile long driveways, ensconced atop artificial hills, only their gables and balconied towers protruding above enshrouding trees. Far more visible were the homes of those who Gil jokingly thought of as the "serfs", those tiny homes, with their doll-house quality, no bigger than transoceanic shipping containers, all that could be afforded by Whites who valued order and security more than living space. In Gil's estimation, most "serfs" possessed the same qualities of intelligence, dutifulness, and self-discipline as the "grandees" in the villas. But their American Equity scores were weighed down by guilty genetic heritage and long family histories of post-secondary education and former privilege.

They were good neighbors, as Ifeche had said. Thrifty, resourceful people, always on the lookout for ways to stretch their limited funds. They worked good jobs, nearly all of them, and some of them owned successful businesses within the community's commercial district, but punitive taxes, high prices for the things they bought, and exorbitant interest rates kept them from accumulating much capital. The pads where their boxlike houses sat were invariably neat and well-tended, lined with colorful vegetable gardens. The homes themselves, manufactured from recycled shipping materials, almost all looked as fresh and new as when they had emerged from their factories. Their children were orderly and polite, never engaging in the destructive antics that seemed to be rites of passage for youngsters in neighborhoods such as Royal Lake Estates or Vermillion Oaks. These "serfs" were friendly to Ifeche whenever they saw him, almost ritualistically so. They fell over themselves to pass along neighborly greetings or offer him freshly-baked goods, as though doing this were some sort of sacrament without which they could not ascend to their version of heaven.

Oftentimes Gil wondered whether they secretly resented him and those like him and Ifeche. At least with those Whites like the driver of the gypsy cab, the roughneck with the long orange beard, the resentment seethed close to the surface, making itself obvious enough for Gil to note it and be on his guard.

Still, perhaps his paranoid fear of racial resentment was misdirected in the cases of his neighbors. He had lived here for more than ten years, and in all that time, not one "serf" had said an unkind word to him or so much as scowled in his direction. The White proprietors of the cafés and quaint boutiques in the commercial district all remembered his name and warmly greeted him, and the White baristas and wait staff usually treated him to complimentary extras when he ordered. He'd felt grateful enough to have discretely approached several of his neighbors, offering the same sort of services he had sold to the Pole. Strangely enough, they invariably refused his assistance, even when he offered it at no charge, telling him they were satisfied with their lowly American Equity scores and their elevated levels of taxation and fees. They seemed to look upon their relative penury as a form of righteous racial penitence.

He turned onto his driveway and walked between the long twin lines of fir trees that led to the ornamental hedges enclosing his rose and tulip garden. The row of thick columns that supported the roof of his mansion's wrap-around porch looked like the legs of a parade of albino elephants. Friends of his from the city's Sweet Zone who made the trip to visit him here called his home the Evers Plantation. Not an inaccurate description; fittingly ironic, even, given that his great-great-great-great-great grandfather on his mother's side had been a slave on a plantation (and there had been others in his family tree, ones for whom he lacked records). Once he had bristled at his friends' jibes, suspecting they were accusing him of unjustness for living there on his hill, surrounded by the "serfs". Such remarks no longer bothered him. At least, not often.

Gil turned back on his house's systems. His smart appliances all greeted him like longtime friends. He strolled through his living room, family room, sun room, and library before entering his bedroom, the largest of eight and the one with the best views of his gardens. He lived alone. One day he might start a family, he thought. But even if he should marry the Blackest woman on earth, his children could never be as fortunate as he was. They would not be the first member of their family to earn a university degree, as he was. They would not benefit from an ancestry made up entirely of farmers, laborers, semi-skilled craftsmen, and lowly service employees; his government position weighed against that. The only way he could ensure his children would grow up with the same American Equity advantages he enjoyed would be for him to quit his job, take up work as an itinerant ditch digger, and get himself frequently jailed. But he wasn't willing to go that far.

He removed his Device from its imprisoning case on his nightstand and turned it on. He experienced a surge of relief as the soothing glow of its screen enveloped him. He felt the muscles of his shoulders untense; he hadn't realized how nervous he'd been, navigating areas beyond his community without his Device in his possession, like a primitive hunter-gatherer following mastodons across frozen tundra.

Now his Device was back at work, tirelessly quantifying the social worth of Gil's interactions with the world, the opinions he expressed on social media, the causes he supported, the donations he made, combining this with his American Equity score to calculate the prices and rates of interest he would be charged by all businesses he interacted with online... which, apart from his occasional black market purchase, represented nearly all his economic activity. He changed into his silk pajamas and settled into his soft bed. Best to get a good night's sleep, so he could be alert and productive for the morning's work.

He drifted toward slumber, bathed in his Device's warm glow, drowsily reflecting upon how fortunate he was to have had a great-grandfather, a grandfather, and two uncles oppressively incarcerated at various times in their lives — they'd had no inkling how much their sufferings would help their descendant — and how good a career it was to write code for the Internal Revenue and Equity Service.

Gil's Device began gently pestering him daily to visit his favorite social media sites to denounce the IntelliScan Prime app. It helpfully suggested this as a quick and easy way to boost his Green level, the ranked index of virtuous social activism activity that virtually all businesses chose to rely upon, combined with American Equity scores provided by the IRES, to calculate prices and rates of interest for individual customers.

Gil followed the Device's advice (why shouldn't he — who in their right mind would turn down additional discounts from their favorite vendors?). He dutifully copied and pasted denunciations of the illicit ghost app to all of his habituated social media forums, then watched his Loves and Likes grow like mold on old cheese. For good measure, he printed out "Black Minds Matter" signs to post at the entrance to his property and similar appliques for his Tuckermobile, then took selfies of himself with them and posted the photos. He made sure to order several styles of shirts with the slogan, plus a very snazzy suede jacket. These online interactions, all examples of virtuous activism, pushed his Green level steadily higher. His Device cooed with approval.

Yet all this activity only served to make him more and more curious about sampling the forbidden app himself. How would the app rate his intelligence in comparison with that of the Han Chinese woman from the speakeasy... or with that of Ifeche? Each passing day, the itch to download and use the app grew more irresistible.

He began researching the app. Its origins, as he'd expected, remained a mystery. In America, reportage and commentary on Intelliscan Prime was entirely condemnatory. He found virtually all the online denunciations to be hysterical in tone, as though each download were another incendiary bomb dropped on an indigenous village in an Amazonian rain forest. American neurologists and psychiatrists refused to address the issue from a scientific vantage, apart from some obligatory condemnations couched in turgid academic prose.

Publicly-expressed attitudes toward the app in Asia, Africa, South America, and Eastern Europe (those expressions not blocked by national firewalls) proved as opposite from U.S. opinion as Hawaiian lava flows were from Icelandic glaciers. In those regions, the app had become a flash sensation, with billions of downloads to eager users. Japanese and Singaporean cognitionists praised the app's logarithms and measurement protocols as the most comprehensive, most accurate, and easiest to use intelligence measurement instrument yet developed.

Gil suspected Intelliscan was nearly as popular in America as in those other places, but no one, apart from a few determined contrarians already living in hovels in the woods, would admit to downloading it. At present, no surveillance system or Internet hygienic blocker could detect the ghost app; even the Chinese had been stymied in their efforts to overcome the invisibility tech, according to reports leaked through the Great Firewall by cyber-dissidents. So Gil figured even the most strident fanatics of the faith of Equity might secretly be heretics, threatening public disgrace or even death for sins of curiosity they indulged themselves in their basements, with their Devices.

At last, he could resist temptation no longer. Obsessing about his intelligence score had begun interfering with his work and was affecting his appetite. He dug his set of neurostimulators out of his nightstand; he occasionally used them in conjunction with Device apps to quell headaches, tamp down anxiety, or overcome insomnia. He affixed the pods to various spots on his cranium, then made himself comfortable in his bed, resting his Device on a swing-away bed desk.

Downloading Intelliscan Prime took less than a minute. The app's interface and instructions were clean, intuitive, and concise; as a coder, he appreciated such qualities. Something about the layouts and controls, the whole *mise-en-scène* of the app, felt oddly familiar, but the source of familiarity remained elusive, buzzing distantly around his head like a persistent yet wary mosquito.

The app asked him a series of questions about his background and life experiences so that it could tailor its exercises for him and ensure none would be culturally inappropriate. He was able to skip most of these questions by granting the app access to his American Equity data and Green index. He felt a delicious sense of anticipation as he launched himself into a series of varied intellectual and cognitive exercises, the same sort of anticipation he'd felt as a boy when his Uncle Howard, newly released from prison, had promised he would use some of the money he'd earned as a prison trustee to take Gil to Busch Gardens Williamsburg, the largest amusement park within two hundred miles of Gil's home. As Gil worked his way through the exercises, some spatial, some testing logic, others testing pattern recognition, still others assessing comprehension or judgment, he knew the app was doing far, far more than keeping track of "right" and "wrong" responses — the neurostimulator pods, their capabilities repurposed by the app, were tracking his brain's electro-neurological pulses, measuring that organ's efficiencies, observing the flexibility and adaptability of his synapses and his neural network as a whole.

The process took a little more than an hour. He held his breath as he awaited his scores, listening to the pulse of his heartbeat in the tiny bones of his inner ears.

His full range score was 327. The app elaborated on this general score by providing sub-scores for nine varieties of intelligences. But Gil focused most intently on one number in particular. His old-style I.Q. number. One-hundred and fifty-eight.

Three points lower than Ifeche's.

Acidic fury bubbled within his chest like water boiling in a kettle. He knew then that he hated Ifeche, not merely disliked him. The Nigerian was a repulsive hypocrite, deriding American Equity while taking full advantage of it. Professing kinship with his own clan of Nigerian Americans, he was xenophobic and racist against other Blacks — a race traitor.

Gil's perseverations over his loathing for Ifeche reached a climax when the source of his earlier sense of familiarity crystalized into clarity. He wanted to make fully certain, though. He subjected himself to the Intelliscan Prime testing process twice more, each time carefully focusing on the look, feel, sounds, and logic of the app rather than on the tasks it set forth for him. He interrogated it with the eyes and ears of a master programmer, instead of submitting as a user to its imperatives.

He had no doubt. The app had Ifeche's fingerprints all over it.

"Gil, I need you to come into the office. Today. I know that's inconvenient for you. But what I need to say, I don't want to say over a remote link."

Gil ruminated over his supervisor's cryptic remarks during his entire journey into the capital. His Tuckermobile, as though it sensed his dark mood, tried to cheer him by playing soft jazz and projecting vistas of oceanside sunsets onto the insides of its windows. Gil normally interacted very little with his nominal boss, Roberta Rodriguez. Even the heads of the Agency knew Gil's reputation as a star coder, one of the lynchpins of the IRES's hugely successful push to combat structural racism with American Equity. So Roberta, a canny bureaucratic politician, normally assumed a hands-off posture with Gil, allowing her highest-profile subordinate to chart his own path. During the past nineteen months during which Roberta had served as his supervisor, the only messages Gil had received from her were paeans of praise, and both of the performance appraisals she had completed for him were worshipful in tone.

Her tone over the comm link hadn't sounded worshipful. Not at all. *Accusatory* was more like it.

Were there problems with any of the systems he worked on? A whole host of users and automated sentries would have alerted him long before any such issues rose to Roberta's attention, so that couldn't be it. The most likely reason he had been called into headquarters was the reason Gil feared the most. That he had been found out. They somehow suspected either that he had downloaded the Intelliscan app or that he had been enabling taxpayers to flout American Equity.

It had to be the former, despite the Intelliscan app's legendary ghostiness. He had been exceedingly careful in carrying out his side work. No one understood the code that underlay American Equity the way he did. That was why he'd felt confident that his tiny alterations to reports and scores, so carefully camouflaged, would never be detected.

His Tuckermobile electronically flashed Gil's credentials as it maneuvered through the maze of checkpoints, concrete barriers, and rows of concertina wire that protected the IRES headquarters building. Ever since the institution of American Equity, the building had been turned into a veritable fortress. Its multiple layers of access-denial infrastructure were meant to prevent its being stormed by mobs of reactionary, hideously racist White Supremacists, who rumors insisted stood ready to emerge from the hinterlands of Appalachia at any time.

The Tuckermobile parked itself in Gil's reserved parking spot in the underground garage. Gil entered an elevator that took him to the eleventh floor, the executives' floor. Entering Roberta's office, he noted three others sitting beside her at her conference table: her boss, her boss's boss, and the head lawyer with the Office of Professional Integrity.

This did not look good at all.

"Close the door, Gil," Roberta said.

Gil did as he was told. He took a seat at the table. "Roberta, what's this all about?"

"This isn't a formal hearing," she said, "or you'd granted the opportunity to have either a lawyer or a union representative present." He watched her prominent Adam's apple bob up and down, indicating she was under as much pressure as he was. He'd long been certain she hadn't been born a woman. But making any comment to that effect, or even hinting aloud that Roberta might be a transwoman, was a firing offense, one of the dumbest self-immolations possible. "We've come into possession of some very disturbing information, Gil. Disturbing enough that the Office of Professional Integrity wanted to immediately open a formal investigation. But in light of your sterling work record to date, I convinced them to hold off, at least temporarily. Until after we had given you the opportunity to address this disturbing pattern to our satisfaction. Which I hope you can do."

"I don't know what you're talking about," Gil said.

The Office of Professional Integrity lawyer, a balding Black man, cleared his throat. Gil noted he had brought a dark blue binder with him. "We've received information that 38 individuals have had their American Equity records tampered with over the past nine months. At present, we are unable to verify whether this is, in fact, the case. However, this tip was accompanied by significant data of a highly suggestive but circumstantial nature. We were given records that show time blocks when those 38 individuals turned off or otherwise disabled their Devices. In every instance, Mr. Evers — and let me emphasize, in *every* instance — of a time block when one of these individuals was *sans* Device, you had also turned off or disabled your own Device, and shut down your home's smart systems, as well."

Where had such information come from? Gil was intimately familiar with his Agency's surveillance and intelligence capabilities. This sort of data gathering fell well outside those capabilities. Unless the FBI had been staking him out for nearly a year, targeting his signals consumption. But how would they have known to do the same for the 38 individuals for whom Gil provided services? Those persons would've been anonymous until Gil met with them. And Roberta and these other executives acted as though they had only just grown suspicious of Gil; if the FBI were if fact behind this surveillance report, they would've made

102

the top managers at IRES aware of their investigation at the outset.

"I'm not sure how to respond," Gil said. "What are you saying? That you think I've been abetting fraud? That I would undermine American Equity, the very edifice I've spent most of my career building up? What *sense* does that make? It's... it's ridiculous on its face. My salary here allows me to live very well, very well indeed... it's not as though I'm in need of black market cash. The only thing I can think is... I've been set up."

"Who would want to set you up, Gil?" Roberta asked.

"I have no idea," Gil said. Although he did have a suspicion. A strong one.

"We are required to investigate these allegations," the lawyer said. "Please understand, we will take your exemplary work history into account. And as I said, the evidence we have been provided is circumstantial in nature. However, until the conclusion of our investigation, we will need to place you on administrative leave. Your access to federal government systems is temporarily suspended."

"But I'm in the middle of four important projects. My involvement is indispensable—"

"We'll somehow find a way to make do," Roberta said. "I'm sorry, Gil. This is a highly regrettable situation. I hope we can resolve it very soon."

"I understand," he said, hardly hiding the bitterness in his voice.

Returning home, Gil found a folded note had been pushed beneath his front door. Discovering it was from Ifeche surprised him not at all.

My dear friend Gil,

Please come see me at my home at your earliest convenience. We have much to discuss regarding your economic future and career prospects. Refreshments will be served. Do not feel obligated to bring a gift — your presence in my home will be gift enough. I look forward to introducing you to some of my talented protégées.

With kindest regards,

Ifeche

He stalked toward Ifeche's villa in a cold fury. As a *savant* who had successfully manipulated so many people and systems, the thing he hated above all others was being manipulated himself.

As soon as Gil jabbed the door bell, Ifeche's man servant, a stern-looking Filipino, opened the intricately carved front doors of Ifeche's grand house, slabs of African blackwood decorated with traditional Nigerian motifs. Clearly, Gil's swift arrival had been expected. He pushed past the Filipino and headed for a room from which Ifeche's voice could be heard.

Gil thrust open the doors of what turned out to be an expansive library, its walls lined with wrap-around book shelves towering twenty feet high beneath a cathedral ceiling whose sky light panels let filtered sunlight stream into the room. Antique wooden desks filled much of the library's center, their chairs occupied by youths as young as ten to as old as twenty-five. They all peered intently into svelte flatscreens trimmed with the same rich African blackwood that formed the villa's entrance. Ifeche leaned into a standing desk at the forefront of this audience, facing them, a retractable sheetscreen covering much of the wall behind him, its display divided between four sets of similar but differing code.

The sight of Ifeche ignited renewed rage in Gil's chest. He grabbed the nearest library ladder and shoved it so hard that it raced halfway around the room, clattering violently on its rails like an out-of-control freight car. "You fucking son of a bitch!" Gil cried, gratified by the looks of alarm his intrusion incited on the faces of the students, now turned toward him. "You dropped a dime on me! You found a way to rat me out!"

Ifeche held up a calming hand to prevent his students from growing alarmed. "This man is a friend," he said. "An agitated friend, but a friend, nonetheless. Please take a twenty-minute refreshment break on the back veranda. Help yourselves to freshly baked pastries and herbal iced teas. We will resume our lesson at three-thirty sharp."

Gil waited for the students to file out of the library. He noted their disparate racial backgrounds; many had skin of the deeply dark brown hue that suggested one-hundred-percent African heritage, but some were Han Chinese or Korean, and a few were even White — youngsters Gil recognized as the sons or daughters of local merchants, inhabitants of the tiny houses nearby the commercial district. One ebony-skinned student, a girl in her late teens, rolled toward the exit in a wheelchair. She paused in the doorway to glance back at Gil, clearly concerned that he might harm Ifeche.

Ifeche motioned for her to continue to the rear veranda. Then he gestured for Gil to join him in an alcove at the rear of the library, where two generously stuffed leather chairs, the arms of each inlaid with filigrees of antique ivory, awaited. "Would you like for me to ask Salvadore to bring us some refreshments?" he asked once he had sat down. "I recently acquired some port from Sri Lanka that is extraordinary in character. I've found it at its best when accompanied by a medley of French cheeses. Delightful. I would be intrigued to hear your opinion."

"I don't want anything from you," Gil said. "Just an explanation."

"For devising a way to compel you to pay me the visit I have so long requested? None of this would have been necessary, you realize, had you not so rudely ignored my many sincere entreaties for you to come see me. Your intransigence has wounded my feelings, most severely."

"So you decided to sabotage my career at the IRES?"

"My dear and longstanding friend, you carried out such sabotage of your own volition."

"Drop the bullshit, Ifeche. We're not friends; we never were. And there's no way my side-work would ever have been detected by the IRES without your intervention. Certainly no way those people in the speakeasies would've ever been connected to me, not even circumstantially. What do you want from me? You didn't go to all the trouble you did just to get me over here to sample some Sri Lankan port."

"I want for you to come work for me, my friend. I have never made a secret of my admiration for your skills and your unique talent."

"You wouldn't accept 'hell no' as an answer," Gil said bitterly, "so you decided to screw up a job I love?"

Ifeche leaned forward in his chair. "But do you truly love your present job? Or perhaps what you actually love best is the opportunity to subvert it? If, as I strongly suspect, the latter is the case — and I know you well, Gil Evers, from our days at university — you will no longer be happy at the IRES once you have lost your opportunities to subvert it from within. And please be assured, you have indeed lost your chance to be the sand in the gears. For even if your superiors' investigation fails to conclusively connect you to fraud, their distrustful eyes will forever remain focused on you."

Gil clenched his fists. "Look, asshole, you took your best shot and it hasn't sunk me. Even the lawyer for the Office of Professional Integrity admits the evidence you provided them is highly circumstantial."

"Did I ever imply the action I have taken to date is my 'best shot'? I have recordings of your surreptitious dealings with your Polish immigrant friend, as well as others. Evidence that is worlds away from being merely 'circumstantial'."

"Bullshit. You're fucking with me. Nobody gets recording devices inside a speakeasy."

"Are you so naïve as to think I am unable to circumvent the consumer-grade detection wands employed at speakeasies? I am deeply insulted. Here I thought you to be as astute a judge of talent as I, and yet you rank me a novice when I judge you a master. One of us is wrong, sir, and it is not your host."

For once, Ifeche came across as utterly sincere. Gil had to reconsider his stance. If Ifeche could prove Gil's involvement in Equity fraud — and now he was certain Ifeche could — then not only could the Nigerian rob Gil of his career, he could also detonate multiple land mines under Gil's social reputation, pulverizing Gil's Green index and making it impossible for him to retain even a broken shard of his current lifestyle. Gil would find himself on a lower social and economic stratum than that of the lowliest of "serfs", unable to find meaningful employment of any kind. His prospects would be no better than those of the orange-bearded gypsy cab driver, unless Gil were willing to cast his lot entirely with the perilous vagaries of the black market economy and become a full-time criminal.

"So what are your plans for me, Ifeche?" he said tightly. "What do you want me to do?"

"Nothing nearly so onerous as the distressed look on your face anticipates," Ifeche said. "As I said, I wish very much for you to come to work for me. My own success has overwhelmed my available hours. The dearest work I engage in is my nurturance of these bright young people in our trade. Yet I find that my commercial pursuits, which enable my search for gifted youngsters both locally and around the world, as well as their housing and upkeep, demand more and more of my attention. Something must give."

"So... you want me to take over for you as coding coach for these gifted youngsters of yours?"

"I prefer the term 'mentor'. But yes, that is my hope."

"What do you get out of this 'philanthropy' of yours, Ifeche? Denying the most promising young talents to your competitors by indenturing the kids to your organization?"

"You need not be so cynical. I find young minds, those most full of potential and yet still in the process of being formed, to be sources of unending delight and discovery. These young people look at the world in ways different from how you and I do. Sometimes they, in their innocence, ask questions we would not dare to ask, and they pursue answers with the undulled vigor of those still discovering their powers and limits, those who still revel in thoughts of unbounded potential. The questions they ask and the answers we help them find can only redound to the eventual benefit of my firm. And, I most sincerely hope, to the flourishing of our dear nation and the renewal of the foundational principles upon which it stands. Individual initiative. The pursuit of happiness as far as one's talents and efforts will allow."

How heartwarmingly altruistic, Gil thought. *Are young minds all that you find to be sources of unending delight and discovery? What about the young bodies you house and indenture?* "What if I tell you I have no interest in serving as a glorified tutor to your harem?"

Ifeche frowned at the word *harem*. "The way I interpret your situation, Gil Evers, is that you have two possible courses of action. The least painful is that you resign from your position with IRES, citing your indignation at their unfair suspicion of you, and come to work for me. I will pay you a nominal salary. The bulk of your compensation will be in the form of goods and services provided to you through me, as well as payments 'under the table,' as you native-born Americans so evocatively put it. Your net total compensation will approximate your present level of after-taxes compensation; you may even come out ahead, and your Green index level will remain unperturbed. Your more painful option is to remain obstinately oppositional to my invitation, in which case I will ensure that the circumstantial evidence against you is upgraded to ironclad evidence. You will be fired in disgrace, fined so heavily and punitively that you will lose your house and all your possessions, and your Green index will crater, rendering you a pariah and making it impossible for you to rebuild even a fraction of your past wealth. At which point, out of penury and desperation you will turn to me, the only reputable figure still willing to deal with you, and I will acquire your services at a substantial discount.

"On a purely economic basis, the latter option is more advantageous to me. However, in honor of our long relationship, one which I, at least, recollect with fondness, I would be far happier were you to follow the former, gentler path. I will give you a week to decide."

"What if I decide right now? What if I tell you I choose *neither* of your damned options? What if I say you're going to back off and leave my life exactly as it is?"

"Oh? And what, exactly, would prompt me to do that?"

Gil played what he hoped was his trump card. "*Intelliscan Prime*. It's your work. You think you can make *me* a pariah? The hate directed against me would be a trickling *puddle* compared to the flood of loathing that would smash you and your company to pieces once people learn what you've done. Your best outcome would be getting hounded all the way back to Nigeria, penniless. You'd be lucky to escape with your life, you bastard."

Ifeche clasped his dark hands together and interlaced his fingers. "That is a most audacious claim for you to make. Fantastical, even. You may as well accuse me of carrying out the Tibetan and Mongolian genocides, too, while you are busy tracing fantasies in the clouds. Tell me, if it is not overly ungracious of me to ask, upon what basis do you mount this accusation?"

"Oh, come off this innocence act, Ifeche! Your fingerprints are all over that illicit app!"

"'Fingerprints,' you say?"

"Yes, *fingerprints*! You prattle on and on about your admiration for my skills and our long familiarity with one another, and you think I can't recognize your coding and design as though you've signed your name in neon letters fifteen feet tall? You were my biggest rival at university, the one to beat. We roomed together for three years, constantly spying on one another's work. You really don't think I know your coding style almost as well as I know my own?"

"Your claim of familiarity with my 'coding style' and 'fingerprints' is a thin reed upon which to base your accusation. Surely you realize I could call upon a dozen experts in the art of coding, each of whom would plausibly refute your opinion in a court of law."

"In a court of law, maybe. Not in the court of public opinion. Rules of evidence are much rougher in that court, and that's the court that counts. All it takes to get the mob roiled up is one outraged accusation. If the accuser happens to be plausible and the accusation holds water, it's just a cherry on top... nice to have, but not essential to incite the mob's bloodlust."

"And wouldn't the mob be equally outraged to learn that my accuser is hurling calumnies in a desperate effort to distract attention from his own proven and abhorrent crimes against American Equity? In a despicable attempt to discredit the man whose patriotic endeavors brought the miscreant to justice?"

Gil had no time to formulate a riposte before Ifeche's students began filing back into the library, their break over. Both men stood. Absurdly, Ifeche placed his arm about Gil's shoulders and announced, "Students! Attention! I would like to introduce to you Gil Evers, an old friend and university colleague, a very distinguished guest. I hope we will soon welcome him back, most warmly, as your next senior instructor."

Gil realized it would be needlessly churlish for him to shake free of Ifeche's arm and storm out of the house... much as he wanted to. Instead, he forced himself to remain civil as Ifeche introduced his students, briefly telling each of their stories, explaining why he had selected them for his mentorship program. Gil silently admitted to himself that he found the youngsters engaging, even appealing. Under different circumstances, he could picture himself working with such students. It might be an enjoyable change of pace. But he would not allow himself to be manipulated and bullied into such a position. Especially not by Ifeche.

The girl in the wheelchair approached him next. "This is Naija Lucky Sunday," Ifeche said. "Of all my students, she has the most unusual background. I pulled her from an orphanage in Outer Lagos, not more than fifteen miles from the house in which I grew up. Her parents, not willing to raise a child with her physical limitations, abandoned her to the nuns at that place when she was an infant. Word reached me half a decade ago of her extraordinary facility with maths. I flew back to Outer Lagos, made a sizable donation to the nuns, and returned here with Naija. She has since demonstrated a proclivity for coding equivalent to her talent with maths, gratifying me immensely. But her most notable characteristic, I would dare say, is her indomitable curiosity."

Unlike the other students, Naija mouthed no pleasantries about how good it was to meet him or how she hoped to soon benefit from his instruction. Her large eyes, floating like white almond candies in the dish of her black porcelain face, drilled into his. Gil was momentarily afraid she could see into his depths, to the heart of the enmity he felt for her benefactor. She seemed to sense Gil posed a threat, despite Ifeche's warm words. He nodded to her and attempted a smile. She did not return it.

Ifeche walked Gil to the front entrance. "You have one week to make your choice," he said quietly, opening the doors. "Any longer, and the choice will be made for you."

Gil agonized over his best path. He realized whichever one of them carried out his threat first would hold an advantage over the other. Yet he also recognized the infuriating truth of Ifeche's assertion: Gil's personal familiarity with Ifeche's coding "fingerprints" *was* a damned thin reed on which to build a public case that the Nigerian was responsible for Intelliscan Prime. What if Gil launched a social media denunciation campaign against Ifeche and it failed to catch fire? The Nigerian's undoubtable counter-assault would be certain to inflict much more severe and lasting damage on Gil than a fizzled public accusation would inflict on Ifeche. *When you strike at a king, you must kill him.* Yet Gil had no real confidence his most determined blow would "kill" his hated rival.

With no work to distract him, Gil's days stretched as wide and empty as the Siberian tundra. His work friends and associates had been instructed to not communicate with him. He found that his few outside-of-work friends, those he retained from his university days, seemingly carefree singles who inhabited cloud-level luxury suites within the towers of the Sweet Zone, also disregarded his social overtures, ghosting him by ignoring his repeated messages. He could not help but believe that word of his suspension had filtered out far beyond the IRES headquarters building. He watched, helplessly, as his Green index steadily sank, taking on water like a torpedoed freighter, losing as much as five percent of its value per day. Soon the prices he paid for everything from groceries to electricity would begin spiking, along with the interest charged on his home, vehicle, and boat loans. His Device cajoled him to turn matters around by engaging in frenetic online activism, pleading with him to tirelessly throw himself into agitating for a long list of approved causes. But he found he could not muster the will to even begin.

How had Ifeche managed to back him into such a tight corner? Gil recalled with mortification how the Nigerian had barely edged him in the climactic coding competition during their final year together at university, how Ifeche had proudly and arrogantly raised the golden trophy above his head. Had Ifeche's I.Q. score advantage over Gil made an ineluctable difference? Did those three I.Q. points ensure that Ifeche would win out over Gil again and again?

He hated him. And that hate threatened to break Gil down as implacably as a spring drizzle would dissolve a sugar Easter egg left on a porch step, half-eaten and forlorn.

Nothing on any of his screens held Gil's attention, not long-form dramas nor brief, pointed comedies. He couldn't bear to look at social media, fearing what he might find. Artificial reality games succeeded only in making him nauseated. Walking around his community meant having to fake cheerfulness whenever he saw a neighbor. He dreaded the thought of shopping, knowing the reality of his steadily rising prices would only push him further into despondency.

Unable to think of anything else to do with himself, unable even to abandon his anger and frustration in sleep, Gil ensconced himself in the cocooning cabin of his Tuckermobile and told it to take him somewhere, anywhere away from his house and his community. For the next day and a half, the Tuckermobile drove him on a random ramble through portions of three states and the Capital District. He sustained himself with a jumbo-sized bag of Cheezy Brittles and a two-liter bottle of Diet Lemon Shasta, only ordering the Tuckermobile to halt when he needed to relieve himself in the bathroom of an automated hamburger emporium. Gil commanded the vehicle to keep its windows fully transparent. He wanted to see everything, from the crumbling McMansions of the suburban slums to the jewel-like parks atop the Sweet Zones' towers to the Palaces of Equity arrayed along the National Mall. He hoped a random vista might spur a train of brilliant thoughts that would provide a solution to his dilemma. Or that he might spot a cave into which he could crawl and then pull a handy boulder into the entrance hole behind him.

The evening before the Monday when Ifeche's ultimatum would expire, Gil directed his Tuckermobile to take him back home. His abbreviated *wanderjahr* had been unfruitful, pointless. His lower back and left shoulder ached from his awkward attempts to nap and his extended periods of sitting. He glumly watched the sun set, the great ebbing orb turning the western sky gradually deepening hues of pink, violet, and purple. He had wasted his week of grace time. Ifeche had perfectly pegged him. Gil had no choice but to take the Nigerian up on the easier option, the trap whose walls were at least lined with soft wool and silk.

When it was almost dark, something very odd happened. The sun, having dropped beneath the horizon, began rising in the west. At least that is how things looked to Gil. He watched the western sky, which had been dark purple, turn orange with a pulsing, intensifying glow.

"*Major civil disturbances reported in districts ahead,*" the Tuckermobile announced. "*I will re-route in order to avoid disturbances and ensure maximum safety.*"

"What's happening out there?" Gil said, shaking himself from his torpor. "Where are the disturbances centered?"

"*Local disturbances have broken out in Koreatown, Chinatown, and Filipinoville. Protesters are traveling in convoys from Royal Lake Estates, Golden Hills, Equestrian Valley Villas, Vermillion Oaks, and Riverrun Estates. Some are reported currently driving in the direction of Little Ho Chi Minh City, Hindustan, Little Islamabad, and Orthodox Jewish enclaves in White Oak and Rockville. Fires have been set in Chinatown and Filipinoville, some burning out of control due to protesters blocking fire fighters' access. Significant exchanges of semi-*

automatic gunfire are occurring between protesters and shop owners in Koreatown. The Chinatown self-defense militia has been mobilized, and similar mobilizations are said to be occurring in Hindustan and Little Islamabad. Civil unrest is not limited to the local metropolitan area; disturbances are occurring nationwide."

Gil didn't bother asking the Tuckermobile what had incited the disturbances. It was easier and quicker to check the news feeds on his Device. Two words appeared everywhere he looked: Intelliscan Prime. They were accompanied by expressions of the most apocalyptic anti-heretic fury since crusading Christian knights desecrated mosques in the Holy Land and devout Moslem *jihadis* returned the sentiment by raping Christian women and burning monks alive.

The secular deity of American Equity had been defiled. The invisible mastermind controlling the Intelliscan app had done what no cognitive researchers since the 1980s had aspired or dared to do, and had done so far more comprehensively than those demonized scientists of long-ago decades had dreamed possible. Thanks to the voluntary self-scans of billions of persons around the globe, whoever was in control of the app (and Gil was 99.5% certain this was Ifeche) had amalgamated and averaged the full-range intelligence scores from every significant racial, ethnic, linguistic, religious, national, and sub-national group on Earth. Then, most blasphemous of all, the app had *ranked them.*

I shouldn't look, Gil told himself, his childhood teachings surging to the front of his mind. When he'd been in nursery school, the commandments of Anti-Racism had been seared in his thoughts, as though emblazoned on tablets of sanctified stone. *I mustn't look. Ranking is an abomination. Seeing races ranked by intelligence will remove the lid from the evil in my soul. All the racist thoughts I've buried so deep will flow up to the surface and spread throughout my mind, corrupting everything they touch, like an oil slick from a tanker sunk during the Iranian War. I mustn't look. I need to pretend this never happened. I mustn't look.*

The Tuckermobile reached the main gate of Gil's community. A phalanx of private security guards, nearly fifty strong, helmeted, armored, and armed with both anti-vehicle and anti-personnel weaponry, blocked the access road. They aimed their guided rocket launchers at Gil's vehicle as it approached, but stood down when the Tuckermobile played the sequence of tones and flashed the sequence of colored lights that indicated it belonged to a resident. The gates obligingly opened. The Tuckermobile ushered Gil inside the sanctuary of his community, more secure than a medieval fortress atop a moated hill. But not even walls and armed guards could render Gil proof from heretical thoughts.

I mustn't look. Looking will demolish Equity. Looking will damn me forever...

His will power prevailed until the Tuckermobile had driven half a mile inside the gates. Then it began crumbling. *There's no way you can avoid this knowledge*, his thoughts taunted him. *The rankings will be all over social media and the news feeds. You'd have to destroy your Device, smash every screen inside your home, and live like a hermit to avoid knowing. You may as well just look, look now and get it over with. And you can't deny how badly you really want to know...*

Temptation won. Gil sighed harshly and logged into the Intelliscan Prime app on his Device. There were so many, many ways to parse the intelligence rankings. So many, many ways in which to sin. He could spend days sifting through the data. He decided to look at sub-national groups first.

The five top-ranked sub-national groups were Ashkenazic Jews (Israeli/North American), Singaporean Han Chinese, Western Germans, Japanese Americans... and Nigerian Americans.

Heart sinking, Gil searched the list for the rankings of his own racial-ethnic-linguistic groups. Yes, he'd scored in the top five with his German ancestry. But that was only one percent of him. The other groups... *oh, God, the others...* Salvadorian American, Guatemalan American, American Black (Bantu heritage), American Black (Guinean heritage), American Black (Western Bantoid heritage), American Black (Mandé heritage)... all showed up far down the list, dwelling in the cellar of the bottom third percentile.

He felt stained. Degraded. Cursed by his own skin.

By all rights, I should be a fucking drooling moron, barely fit to push a broom...

No, that wasn't right, wasn't right at all. He was an *individual,* not a mechanistic amalgamation of inferior racial-ethnic categories. He was his own thing. Unique, one-of-a-kind. The end result, not only of genetics and ancestry, but also of his upbringing and the sum total of his own efforts to grow and achieve. The group rankings were based on populations' averaged scores; the difference in average score between one group and the group below it on the list was as minute as one one-hundredth of a point. Every group, no matter its placement on the list, had its own bell curve of intelligence scores — what separated groups on the list was where the groups' midpoints fell on the bell curve, but every group had its small subgroup of geniuses, way to the right on the curve. Gil had been fortunate that at least some of his ancestors had made wise selections of sexual partners, and the best of the mix had been passed down to him.

He told himself these things again and again. But logic proved a weak, wavering bulwark against a rising tide of self-loathing.

I'm an inferior human being. Inferior to Ifeche. I'm shit. I come from human stock that's shit, that's dumb as a bucket.

He's better than me.

Smarter.

Better. Smarter. Better. Better smarter better smarter better BETTER

Gil began shrieking. He feared he'd never be able to stop, that he had jumped off a precipice and gravity would pull him down, far down to the core of the earth where the terrible weight of self-knowledge would crush him. He screamed until his ears pounded and his throat turned to fire and the Tuckermobile threatened to call him an ambulance.

His vehicle slowed as it approached the commercial district. Crowds of protesters blocked the bypass road and the drives leading to the cluster of food markets, coffee shops, cafés, clothing emporiums, art galleries, and furnishings boutiques. The Tuckermobile's windows, thick laminated glass, bulletproof, blocked the sound of their furious chants, but Gil could read the signs they carried: "Black Minds Matter!" "Racism Never! Equality Forever!" "Fuck the IP App!" "Moms Against Mental Fascism" "Slay the Zionist Conspiracy!" "No Nazi Eugenics!"

"Dummies of the World Unite!" and best of all, "Smartness are Overrated?!?"

The protesters smacked the carbon fiber of the Tuckermobile's sides as the vehicle pushed cautiously through the teeming crowd, but Gil could tell they weren't threatening him — they were exhorting him to join them. He recognized many of them. White people. The "serfs" from the tiny houses, the wait staff from the coffee shops and cafés, the merchants from the emporiums and boutiques. True believers. Anti-Racists all. They hadn't set fire to their commercial district. They hadn't smashed its windows and looted its businesses. But staring into their livid faces as the Tuckermobile inched through their number, Gil knew their heated blood demanded that blood be shed. They hungered for expiation, a sacrifice.

And he knew how to give it to them.

As soon as the Tuckermobile pulled into Gil's garage, he jumped out and retrieved his rope ladder from its bag, the implement he had used so many times to secretly climb his community's walls. He found a pair of garden shears and cut away the rungs, leaving two long lengths of rope. He searched his Device for instructions. Then he fashioned one of the lengths of rope into a noose.

He could solve all his problems in one fell swoop. Rid himself of the threat of Ifeche. Become a nationwide hero. Propel his Green index into the stratosphere and get back into the good graces of the IRES.

He coiled the noose and tossed it onto the Tuckermobile's front passenger seat. Then he drove back to the commercial district and the crowd of protesters.

He ordered the Tuckermobile to park itself on the side of the bypass road. He'd told his Device to amplify his voice through the Tuckermobile's exterior speakers, so he could be heard over the chanting. He climbed out, noose in hand.

"Listen to me, people!" he said, gratified to hear his voice echo back to him off the elevated signage for Food Zealot and Ying/Yang Coffee. "I know who's responsible! I know who's caused so much pain for all of you!" He climbed onto the hood of his Tuckermobile and held the noose high. "Follow me, and I'll lead you to the person who created the Intelliscan Prime app! The one who degraded you, who set loose a fresh plague of racism! Follow me, and together, *we'll take care of the fucker! Permanently!*"

The crowd responded with an ascending roar, a mass sound that began in a low register and swiftly ascended to a siren's wail. Hearing that roar, Gil realized with a jolt of fear and pride that he hadn't snatched the attention of a couple hundred individual human beings. Rather, he prodded and steered a single immense beast, a roiling hydra-chimera with poisoned claws and teeth beyond counting.

He led the beast to Ifeche's villa. No one tried to interfere with the march. All of the community's rented defenders stood outside its walls, none within.

Gil climbed the steps to Ifeche's front porch and turned back to the crowd. "Give me three minutes alone with the villain!" he shouted. "Then I'll bring the fucker out to you. If I don't come out, storm the house!"

He expected to have to beat on the front door or have several of the burliest members of the mob break it down for him. Instead, before his fists could touch them, the doors opened just wide enough for him to slip through.

"Get in here," Ifeche said, grabbing him by the arm and pulling him into the anteroom. "You haven't given us much time. And I have much to say to you."

"You knew I was coming...?"

"Of course I did. Your little march is all over social media."

"Then you know you're a dead man. For having written and distributed the Intelliscan app."

"You chase the wrong monster. It wasn't me."

"You slimy son of a bitch, of *course* you'd deny it! But you can't convince *me*. *I* know your fingerprints are all over that app."

"It was one of my students. She pursued her own intellectual curiosity and acted without my authorization or knowledge. Her 'fingerprints' appear to you to be mine because she learned her coding skills directly from me."

"Who?"

"Naija Lucky Sunday. The clever girl in the wheelchair. She is here in this house, right now. *She* is your monster."

"*No! He's lying!*"

The shout came from the direction of the library. Gil swung about. Naija rolled forth from the library, through the front parlor and into the anteroom. "It's not true what he said, not entirely," she insisted, her voice quavering. "He *knew* what I was doing! He *approved!* He encouraged me to follow my intellectual curiosity, to dare to uncover knowledge no one else was brave enough to pursue. You must *believe* me, Mr. Evers!"

He did believe her. And he realized it made no difference. Offering one monster for the mob to slay or two, it made no difference. He had enough extra rope to fashion a second noose.

"They won't hang me, those people out there," Ifeche said, speaking quickly. "They will balk when they see it is me you accuse. You suspected as much, didn't you? That is why you didn't denounce me by name when you whipped up your mob. You were afraid they wouldn't follow you if they knew it was I who you targeted. I provide too many of them with work, you see. I provide too many of their children with education and training. But by inciting a mob, you have grabbed a tiger by its ears, Gil. You dare not let go, or it will devour *you*. What will the tiger do if the meal you offer is unsatisfactory? Won't it turn on you, instead? It is no rational beast, this tiger you have aroused..."

Gil knew what Ifeche would say next. As soon as the Nigerian had learned of Gil's intentions, he'd invited Naija to leave her quarters and join him in the library, near the front of the house; that was obvious. As was his reason for doing so.

"Let us offer your tiger the girl," Ifeche said. "And quickly, before the mob damages my home."

In the dimness of the anteroom, Naija's impossibly huge eyes were her only features clearly visible. "For the love of Jesus, I beg you, *do not do this!*"

The intoxicating sense of righteousness and resolve Gil had gotten high on fled. "I... I don't know... I..."

"If you denounce her with me, *now*, outside on my porch, I will destroy all my recordings of you discussing anti-government fraud. I will no longer pressure you to work for me. I swear this on the soul of my mother."

The tiger gave Gil no time to think. He heard a cacophony of tumultuous footsteps pounding up the steps and across the porch. Burnished African blackwood splintered as the mob forced the doors open. Three women pushed their way to the front, kitchen cleavers and carving knives in hand, lips flecked with spittle from continuous shrieking, their faces as feral as those of flitting harpies.

"You've been dreadfully hurt!" Ifeche cried, raising his arms in a looming V. "We are all here victims of a dreadful betrayal! One of my own students, a woman I housed and fed and rescued from an orphanage, used the precious skills I taught her to go behind my back and create that *abomination*, the Intelliscan Prime app! I am as appalled and revolted as you are — *more* so, because this evil deed was done secretly in my own home, using technology *stolen* from me!"

Naija uttered a wordless cry. The mob's eyes turned to Gil for confirmation.

Slowly, unsteadily, he elevated the noose he still held in his hand. Its loop briefly snagged on his chin before he pulled it loose, raising it above his head. "It was her," he said, feeling dizzy.

The events of the next twenty minutes melted together into a gelatinous mass for Gil, smudged memories from a dream. He had no will of his own anymore. The mob seethed around him and absorbed him. It moved, and he moved with it, from the anteroom onto the porch, down the steps, and into a tree-lined grove adjacent to the villa. A limb of the mob took the noose from his hand. The mob came to rest beneath the expansive branches of a giant oak tree. Gil's noose was thrown over a branch a dozen feet from the ground. Hands, dozens of them, clawed at one another and knocked one another aside in a struggle for the sacred honor of lifting Naija from her chair.

Then the mob cheered. The tiger roared.

Gil's eyes began watering. Smoke. Someone had lit fire to Naija's wheelchair. The polyvinyl seat and the rubber tires, burning and melting, cast up a noxious gray cloud, obscuring some of the oak tree's branches. But not the one from which Naija had been suspended.

Gil felt another hand clasp his. Ifeche's. Gil instinctively squirmed in Ifeche's grasp. But then he told himself to relax, to accept whatever Ifeche wanted of him. They were brothers now, he told himself. Events had made of them more than brothers, even. Closer. They had committed murder together in the name of Social Justice, and their shared secret bound them as tightly as protons and neutrons in the nucleus of an atom of iron.

The Nigerian gently tugged Gil to kneel beneath Naija's slowly revolving legs. A droplet of blood fell upon Gil's cheek, trickling from one of countless abrasions inflicted by the tiger.

Ifeche raised their clasped hands above their heads. Gil did not resist this. "Commemorate this moment, my friend," Ifeche said.

Posed thus, they took selfies.

The next morning, Gil awoke to discover the selfie he had posted had garnered more than sixty-one million Smiley emojis. Also, the makers of his Tuckermobile were offering him the equivalent of three years' salary to promote their products, and the IRES had declared him their Employee of the Month.

Think of this brief tale as the bastard great-great-great-great grandchild of Jonathan Swift's "A Modest Proposal"...

Chelsea's Rescue

J. L. Hagen

—Friday, June 13, 2025

"**G**OOD morning, ASPCH Rescue Center, Madison speaking, how may I help you today?"

"I think I'm interested in getting a Rescue."

"Great. Thank you so much. We can set you up right away. May I have your name, please?"

"Chelsea. Wilson. But, uh, Madison, I have some questions first."

"Oh, sure, Chelsea, the whole process is really easy. What would you like to know?"

"I mainly wanted to find out more about the cost and what if I didn't like it — can I return it or exchange for a different one?"

"Yes, that's no problem. You have up to thirty days to make it permanent. And there's no cost."

"Ok, and I get to choose what I want, right?"

"Yes. Probably the best way to proceed is to answer some questions over the phone. Then if it looks like you're a good match, we can schedule a date for you to pick up your Rescue here at the Shelter. Are you all right with that?"

"Sure. If it doesn't take too long. I'm on my lunch hour."

"No problem, Chelsea. Ten minutes. Tops."

"Ok."

"Let me pull up my survey form... got it. First question — have you ever done a Rescue before?"

"No, this is my first time."

"Ok, first time. Which type are you looking for: Protection, Recreation, Companion, or Work?"

"Work, but... also maybe Recreation — I'm not sure, Madison. It's kind of a Christmas present for my family."

"You can choose more than one, if that helps."

"Yes. Check Work and Recreation."

"And as for working, do you mean outside, inside, or both?"

"Mostly outside, we live on a small farm near the town of Loyale with some animals, so..."

"Ok, Chelsea, that's good. So probably a Large or Medium, then?"

"I'm not... how big...?"

"Well, there's Small, Medium, Large, and Extra-Large. Keep in mind, the cost of feed, meds, etc."

"Um, I feel like Medium... or average... will work best."

"Good, that's what most people choose. Ok, what about age? I'm assuming — fully grown — but probably not a Senior?

"Yes, mature but still active."

"Also, would you prefer Male or Female?"

"Male would be stronger, right, for...?"

"Yes, but some of the females are quite sturdy and can easily handle physical exertion. Plus, they're often better around the house. Not so territorial."

"I think I still prefer a male."

"It's your choice — will there be children around?"

"Well... my daughter."

"Then you're going to want Neutered. The males can occasionally be aggressive or self-protective if there are children — in particular, teens or pre-teens — in the household. Of course, the females all come spayed. We don't want to contribute to the 'stray' problem we're trying to—"

"Uh, Madison, what about training? I don't have much time to..."

"They all receive some basic training, but obviously older Rescues are going to be better socialized, all things considered."

"What happens if they run away or... become hostile?"

"Shouldn't be a problem, Chelsea. They each come with an obedience collar. It usually takes care of any issues within a week or two. It sets the initial boundaries and trains your Rescue regarding your location. As your Rescue approaches the edge of your property, for instance, it emits a high, warbling tone. If this warning is ignored, the collar releases a small electric current which, although harmless, is a bit unpleasant. Most Rescues, after one or two experiences, quickly learn to recognize which areas to avoid. And, most important, it comes with a compliance button..."

"Compliance button?"

"It's on a remote. You can use it to keep your rescue from wandering into places they don't belong and to discourage undesirable behavior. Press the button and the collar makes a series of warning beeps. Press it again, and the collar discharges electro-pulses until you release it."

"That all sounds great."

"Ok, Chelsea, any color preferences? We can get you pretty much anything. Brown and Black are most available, followed by white and mixed. Some — like red or yellow — may take a few days longer. We don't see as many, typically. Whites tend to be older."

"I'd say anything would be fine, I'm mainly concerned about the right disposition and attitude."

"Also, Chelsea, where do you plan to board your Rescue?"

"Well, I was leaning toward the barn, but we do own a shed attached to the house."

"The barn would be ok, but we require that it be heated during the colder seasons to a temperature at least above thirty-two degrees. A small space heater is usually sufficient in an outdoor environment."

"Ok, that should work. Madison, earlier you mentioned meds — am I going to be faced with a lot of medical bills? I can't afford that right now."

"No, shouldn't be a problem. We screen them all and most of the time we can supply an accurate health record. But sometimes it's not complete, depending on their history prior to arrival at the Shelter. And, of course, some come with special needs."

"Special needs? What kind of..."

"Oh, you know, the usual — abuse or neglect, abandonment issues, or conditions from genetic or accidental causes, for example, car accidents. Some addiction. The good thing is that you can receive supplemental State assistance for those with ongoing or permanent concerns. A lot of older people like these. They get a little extra income and companionship in exchange for looking after a Rescue with a disability or chronic ailment. It's all on our website."

"Website? Oh, I should have realized you had a website. I got your number off a billboard on the way to work. The picture was so heartbreaking."

"Yes, some Rescue situations are unbelievably grim. It's all on the website. You should look at it. There's an online form, plus all the information we talked about — and you can see profiles of our currently available Rescues — with photos. You can also download a smartphone app that lets you search the whole state or even the entire U.S. So, there is virtually no problem finding a match. Males, females, even family groups. We have close to a hundred thousand in our national database."

"Oh my gosh, Madison, I never would have guessed. This is, like, the answer to my prayers."

"Great. Check it out."

"Ok. I will. Definitely."

"Anything further, Chelsea, I can help you with?"

"No, you've, like, totally covered it — oh, one last question. If I sign up, I get to keep them permanently, right? They can't just leave or…"

"No, that all ended with the HRETICA Bill signed two years ago by the President. It's made a huge difference, especially the euthanasia provision. You may recall — at the time it was a bit controversial, and our endorsement cost us some ASPCH memberships. But, honestly, Chelsea, the *Homeless Rescue, Economic Transformation, and Immigrant Containment* Law has turned out to be a godsend. The problem has been reduced to a trickle — not to mention, undocumented border crossings. Consequently, the American Society for the Prevention and Curtailment of the Homeless has never been stronger. We look forward to serving you, Chelsea. Thanks for calling today and don't forget our website *www.rescuethehomeless.com.*"

"No, Madison, thank *you* so much. I can hardly wait to get online tonight and pick out my Rescue. This will be the best family Christmas present, ever."

"Fantastic, but don't delay. It's first come, first served — and, remember, each Rescue is available for only ninety days. Once it's gone, it's gone forever."

The United States has been the world's dominant power since the end of the Cold War in 1991. One would need to go back to the nineteenth century to find a time when the U.S. was considered militarily and politically insignificant. Yet no hegemon has remained forever dominant, not the empire of Alexander the Great, nor the Roman Empire, nor the France of Louis XIV, nor the British Empire. The ugly events dramatized below remind me of France in 1945, in the wake of that proud nation's most demoralizing defeat and subsequent rescue; a time when countrymen accused one another of collaboration, vicious retribution was normalized as virtuous, and the notion of what it meant to be a true Frenchman was destabilized, growing as capricious as the weather. This story imagines the U.S. as a minor political pawn in a Great Game being played out by two galactic empires. In such a situation, what counts as treason? What is patriotism? How could Constitutional values be upheld? Will some values and rights be sacrificed to preserve others?

The Promise of King Washington

Joe Vasicek

VULTURES flew over the Capitol Building. They settled under the arches of the dome and squabbled noisily as their dark-plumed brethren circled the sky.

Sam Fisher had always wanted to visit Washington, DC. In better times, before the nations of Earth had become pawns in a proxy war between two interstellar alien empires, he'd yearned to do all the standard touristy things: explore the Smithsonian

Museums, do a White House tour, see all the monuments dedicated to presidents and American heroes.

Those attractions remained physically present, at least. But they were now overshadowed by horrific sights of violence and death that Sam had never thought he would see in the hub of American democracy. All along the Mall, from the Lincoln Memorial and the reflecting pool past the Washington Monument and the Smithsonian, gallows had been erected. A construction crew was building another set down by the World War II Memorial. Sam had to see the gallows with his own eyes to convince himself they existed. Here. In America.

"Excuse me," Sam said, waving down the general contractor of the construction crew. With his other hand, he partially covered his nose to lessen the stench.

The general contractor looked up from the papers spread out across his tailgate and narrowed his eyes.

"Who are you?"

Sam extended his hand and forced himself to smile. "The name's Sam. Sam Fisher."

The contractor stared at him with open hostility.

"I'm a news blogger from Cincinnati," he explained, retracting his hand to fumble around for the purple heart in his pocket. "I'm here at the invitation of President Washington, and I want to find out what people—"

"Go fuck yourself, buddy."

"I'm not affiliated with the mainstream media," Sam said quickly; he'd grown accustomed to this instinctual hostility from many of his fellow citizens. "My blog is totally independent. I'm also a veteran."

He showed the man his purple heart. It proved to be a futile gesture.

"Fuck off, 'journalist'. We're busy."

Sam took a deep breath, pocketed his medal, and continued east toward the Washington Monument. The once bustling attraction was completely devoid of tourists or tour buses, though flags still surrounded the monument's base. Several of them were tattered, though, and the stench of death hung thicker the closer to the Capitol Sam got. It seemed to permeate everything, even his very clothes.

The last time Sam had experienced that unmistakable stench, his company of marines had been forced to retreat in the face of the North Korean military. As the sky had flashed with artillery fire, both conventional and alien, the Norks had poured across the border with Monarchist energy weapons that had made even the Stryker .50 cals seem as obsolete as samurai swords against the Imperial Japanese Army at the battle of Shiroyama. He shuddered at the memory.

But the gruesome scene that lay before him was less like something from the 21st century and more like something from the 18th — the French Revolution's Terror, minus the guillotine. On either side of the National Mall, bodies hung in various states of decay. Some of them he recognized. Most he did not. A great many of them had been picked apart so much by the carrion birds that they were now beyond recognition.

A small crowd had gathered less than a hundred yards away from him, and he realized that a new fruit was about to be added to the terrible trees of execution.

Am I about to join them? Sam grimly wondered. Had anyone beside the construction foreman heard Sam describe himself as a reporter? Besides the politicians and bureaucrats, a not insignificant number of journalists had also been hung. Most of them were from the mainstream media outlets — CNN, *New York Times*, MSNBC — but Sam was under no illusion that his status as an independent rendered him safe. Ever since rising to power in the coup, President Rex Washington had invited dozens of prominent voices from the alternative media to meet with him, one-on-one. Some of them had fled the country. Others emerged sounding more like sycophants than reporters. Still others had mysteriously gone silent. The implications seemed clear.

"Excuse me," Sam said, approaching one of the armed soldiers who overlooked the crowd from a distance. "Can you tell me anything about this latest execution?"

"They don't pay me to know things," the soldier said. He looked to be in his early twenties, though the shades that covered his eyes made it difficult to tell. His face was utterly expressionless.

Sam showed the man his purple heart, hoping to avoid a repeat of the exchange with the general contractor. "My name's Sam Fisher. I'm a Korean War Vet and an independent news blogger. Can I ask you a few questions?"

The man spat. "Move along."

Rebuffed, Sam left to join the crowd. The prospect of a hanging repulsed him, but he felt obliged to the hundreds of thousands of people who followed his blog to provide an account of the event. He considered trying to interview a few members of the crowd, but their attention was so focused that it didn't seem appropriate to interrupt. Instead, he switched on the microphone sewn into the inner lining of his jacket.

"I'm here at the National Mall, where a hanging is about to take place," he said after checking his phone to make sure the audio was livestreaming. "It's still about half an hour until my interview with President 'King' Washington."

The audience had spread out over the unkempt lawn, trampled nearly to mud. It reminded Sam of the tattered flags at the Washington Monument. Though he had no love for the politicians who infested this place, his sense of patriotism, as much an essential part of him as his right arm, recoiled at the stark, brutal killing field to which the heart of his nation's capital had been reduced.

"This is nothing more than a goddamn lynch mob!" the prisoner screamed as men in balaclavas and body armor led her up the metal steps to the noose. Sam couldn't quite place her. Like so many other politicians, she was up in years, probably in her sixties or seventies, with wrinkled skin and bony hands. Her defiant mouth and ferocious eyes belied any age-related enfeeblement, however. She wore a dark blue pantsuit that appeared both clean and pressed. The fact that her hands were zip-tied behind her clashed oddly with her otherwise officious appearance.

From the top of the wheeled ladder, she stared in defiance at the crowd. Soldiers in battle armor stood around the gallows, their rifles held at the ready. Despite their martial stance, they seemed bored. This was far from the first politician they'd executed, Sam figured. And it would certainly not be the last.

"Representative Laquisha Williams, Democrat from California," a man in civilian clothes read from an improvised stand on the back of a National Guard hummer. "The Capitol Tribunal has found you guilty of high treason in violation of your oath to support and defend the Constitution of the United States against all enemies, foreign and domestic."

"Lies!" the congresswoman shouted, her voice breaking with emotion.

The man went on. "The sentence for treason is death by hanging." As he spoke, the men in balaclavas slipped the thick noose over her neck. "You are permitted to make a final statement before your execution."

The congresswoman opened her mouth, but this time, her expression was desperate, and her eyes showed more fear than fury. "'King' Washington is the only traitor in this town! He's a tyrant and a dictator, not my president! Impeach! Impeach! Im—"

Her last words, hurled skyward, were cut short as the men shoved her off. The rope went suddenly taut. Sam heard an awful snap as her neck broke. A worse sound followed — the tearing of flesh and sinew as her head came suddenly free. The crowd shrieked as her body fell to the mud, blood gushing from her severed neck. Her head hit the ground next to it, bouncing once with a dull and ignominious thud.

"Holy *shit* — her head just came off!" Sam said into his microphone. His gut went weak, and the taste of bile filled his mouth. He clutched his knees and vomited onto the grass, along with several members of the crowd. Others screamed. But the soldiers and executioners remained calm and unmoved. Several of them grinned, he thought, but couldn't be certain. He hoped he'd imagined that part.

* * * * *

Sam's stomach was still unsettled when he arrived at the White House. To his surprise, the gates were open, and there was no sign of the secret service or any other security personnel. It didn't make any sense — not in a city where armed troops were now a common sight. But after finding the press entrance closed, he decided there was nothing else for it but to walk up to the front door.

First, though, he double-checked his phone to make sure he was still streaming the audio. If he was going to meet with Washington, he was going to wear a wire — two, actually, since he'd hidden a back-up device in the heel of his left shoe — even if it cost him his life. If either of his surreptitious mikes were uncovered, the remaining one would broadcast his torture and execution to Sam's audience, hundreds of thousands strong. His sacrifice would be worth it if it helped to bring a dictator down.

At least, that's what he'd been telling himself for weeks, ever since he'd received his invitation.

The door swung open, and a white gloved butler greeted him with a polite, "How may I help you, sir?"

"Excuse me," Sam said, his gut growing steadily sourer, "but am I in the right place? I'm supposed to meet with the president. The name's Sam Fisher — I'm with the press."

"The press?"

"Alternative media. I'm a news blogger from Cincinnati."

He extended his hand, and the butler reluctantly shook it, confusion still written on his face. "An appointment with the president... do you mean the lieutenant?"

Sam frowned. It hardly seemed appropriate to call the leader of the most powerful non-aligned country in the world "lieutenant".

"I mean Rex Washington."

"Ah," said the butler. "Just so you know, he insists on being called by his military rank, and claims no other title."

"Are you saying that he doesn't claim to be the president?"

"Indeed I am, Mr. Fisher. Elections have not yet been held. Until such time, the office and residence of the President of the United States remain vacant. The lieutenant would have it no other way."

The stories are true, then, Sam thought. He'd heard about the White House remaining unoccupied, but had assumed that was just propaganda put out by Washington's cronies after the coup. It was almost impossible to know what was true anymore.

"If you have an appointment," the butler said, "you can find the lieutenant that way, in the Eisenhower Building."

Sam mumbled his thanks. The Eisenhower Building was considerably larger than the White House, and far more imposing, almost like an American Kremlin — which, he thought, probably wasn't far from the truth now.

A security checkpoint had been erected at the entrance, manned by military personnel. There was no sign of the secret service. Sam walked slowly to the metal detector (his hidden mikes were mostly plastic and shouldn't set them off), nervously fingering his phone.

Here goes nothing.

"Name and business?" the officer in charge of security asked.

"Sam Fisher. I'm a news blogger from Cincinnati, with an appointment to—"

"Put your personal belongings on the conveyor belt and step through the metal detector."

Sam disconnected the phone, briefly cutting the livestream, and placed it in a bin with his wallet, belt, and keys. He removed his jacket and placed it in a second bin, having folded it in such a way that the hidden wire would not bulge through the lining.

A young corporal waved him through the detector. No alarm. Then the corporal directed him to stand with his legs wide and his arms outstretched and wanded him from heels to forehead.

"Remove your shoes, please."

Sam did as he was told, his heart sinking through the floor. The corporal handed Sam's left shoe to his superior officer. The senior man untwisted the hollow heel with a well-practiced motion. He pulled the plastic mike from its tiny cavern and dangled the device in Sam's face.

"What is this?"

Sam involuntarily stiffened, anticipating a blow. "I, uh—"

"No recording devices are permitted inside the building. I'm going to have to keep your phone until you leave. And your jacket, too, since you tried sneaking another wire through that way. Here. Take these." He handed Sam back his shoes, plus the hollow heel.

Getting his shoes back made no sense. "What — what are you going to do to me now?"

"Watch you put on your shoes. You can't very well talk with Lieutenant Washington standing in your socks, can you? If you need to take notes during your interview, the lieutenant will provide you with pen and paper. Move along."

Sam reattached his left shoe's heel and awkwardly squeezed his feet into his shoes. Had this been some sort of psyops move to put him off-balance or make him feel a false sense of security? Or was this more in line with Lieutenant Washington's "humble", "patriotic" refusal to occupy the White House?

"Sam Fisher?" a young thirty-something woman asked cheerfully as she entered the atrium from a side room.

"That's me."

"Christina Harris," she said, extending her hand. "I'm Lieutenant Washington's press secretary. Did you find us all right?"

"I got a bit turned around at the White House," Sam said. This all felt surreal.

"I'm terribly sorry. Things have been chaotic these past few weeks, as I'm sure you can imagine."

"I'm flattered that your office selected me."

Christina gave him a cheery smile. "Well, you do have quite a following, Mr. Fisher. Lieutenant Washington decided to end press conferences and replace them with one-on-ones with select journalists. He's quite impressed with your fair and even-handed coverage of current events."

Sam didn't believe that for a second. His coverage of the coup had been nothing less than scathing. If it weren't for the lip service that Washington paid to the principles of the Constitution, Sam would have used his platform to call for an American insurgency. He wasn't quite at that point yet. Today's meeting would decide things... assuming he exited the Eisenhower building alive.

"This way, Mr. Fisher," Christina said, leading him into a well-furnished room that resembled a 19th century parlor. "If you'll wait here, I'll inform the lieutenant that you're here."

"Thank you, ma'am."

He sat down on one of the antique high-backed chairs and held his breath as she stepped through the heavy oak door to get the man that he'd come almost a thousand miles to see.

* * * * *

Rex Washington was surprisingly young for the leader of the still-free world. Tall, thin, and clean-shaven, with his hair cut short and neat, he looked nothing like the tyrant Sam had mentally pictured while railing against him on his blog. His smile seemed more genuine than any Sam had seen since coming to Washington. And yet there was a sharpness in his eyes that spoke volumes. Here was a man who could send so many hundreds of people to the gallows, and do so with absolute certainty that he was morally right.

"Sam Fisher," said Rex, extending his hand. "It's a pleasure to finally meet you."

"Is it truly, Mr. President?" Sam asked, his heart pounding.

"Yes. I mean that sincerely. And please don't call me the president. As you yourself have pointed out so often on your blog, a president must be democratically elected."

He reads my blog regularly? Sam thought. How likely was that?

Rex gestured to the most comfortable antique chair in the parlor and pulled up a matching one to sit across from him. Sunlight streamed through the window, which offered a view of the White House south lawn. Unlike the National Mall, these grounds were still well-tended.

"Is this interview on the record?" Sam asked stiffly.

"Of course," Rex answered, surprising him. "I'm sure your audience will be eager to read your report of this meeting."

"Then why did your men confiscate my recording equipment?"

"To keep this interview from being selectively and deceptively edited. I'm not willing to play that game. However, you may ask any question you like."

Sam swallowed. "Why did you bring me here?"

"No one 'brought' you here, Mr. Fisher. We extended the invitation to you as part of our media outreach efforts, in order to counterbalance the 'Radio Free America' broadcasts of the Monarchists."

"Why me? Why not the mainstream news media? Don't they have wider reach? A much bigger audience you might be able to convince?"

"Frankly, no," Washington answered. "It's no secret that the mainstream news media promote a certain political agenda, and have for some time. Of course, a degree of bias is to be expected, but these organizations have, in their efforts to shape policy, betrayed the American people's trust. Unlike them, you are open about your biases, and seek to serve the truth as you see it, rather than promote a particular narrative. That makes you an important voice, Mr. Fisher. As I see things."

Sam had to admit that he was impressed with Washington's evident sincerity. Was it possible he had misjudged the man?

"When you overthrew President Whitmer," Sam said, "the United States was on the verge of making an alliance with the Monarchists. That alliance would have brought us tremendous technological and economic benefits. You claimed such an alliance was treasonous. Yet during your coup, you accepted military aid from the Imperialists. There are many who say that you would have not succeeded without it."

He watched Rex closely, but the lieutenant's only reaction was a nod.

"Is it true that your coup was bought and paid for by the Imperialists, Lieutenant Washington? How is this not complete hypocrisy? Whose interests do you serve: those of the American people, or of your alien sponsors?"

Rex took a deep breath. He didn't answer immediately, and the silence stretched just long enough to make Sam uncomfortable.

"Did you serve in Korea, Mr. Fisher?"

The question took Sam aback. "Uh, yes, sir. I did."

"Which branch?"

"US Army. I was a sergeant in the 2nd infantry division."

"I thought so," said Rex. "You have the eyes of a man who's seen action. I was also there when the Norks and the Monarchists invaded the south. That's an experience no one can easily forget."

Sam nodded. He still suffered night terrors, shadows of the chaotic American pull-out from Seoul. The majority of his platoon mates hadn't made it out. Their charred remains had been left behind, buried in the ashes of the South Korean metropolis.

"The Norks were the first to accept alien aid," Rex continued. "When they defeated us in the second Korean War, our national psyche suffered a massive blow. We were forced to confront the fact that we were no longer the world's superpower. And as the nations of the world made alliances with the aliens, some going to the Monarchists, others to the Imperialists, we withdrew inward to Fortress America and let the rest of the world fall apart."

"Do you believe that was a mistake?" Sam asked.

"Yes and no. I believe we took the wrong lesson from our defeat. Everything happened so quickly after first contact that we didn't have time to realize our place in the galaxy. America didn't lose a major war because an enemy nation outfought us, but because Earth itself became a flashpoint in a larger struggle between two rival alien empires."

"Kind of like Egypt, a former hegemon, caught between the Athenians and the Persian Empire?"

"Glad you know your ancient history," Rex said. "That's not a bad analogy. When the aliens invaded, it wasn't a military invasion — it was economic. Earth has become the battleground for a proxy war between the Monarchists and the Imperialists."

"But if that's what you fear, why side with the Imperialists?" Sam asked.

"What makes you think I've sided with the Imperialists?"

Sam laughed without intending to. "Well, of course you have," he said. "How else could you have come to power?"

"I've agreed to let the Imperialists establish colonies in the Gulf of Mexico, but that's all that I've conceded. Nothing more."

"There are no secret alliances, then? No closed-door agreements?"

Rex sighed. "Which non-aligned countries did best in the Cold War?"

His question caught Sam off-balance. Was it meant to distract him? Possibly... but it intrigued Sam enough that he felt dissuaded from immediately reiterating his own questions. He sensed a keen intellect in Lieutenant Washington. If Sam tried to game this interview the way a mainstream journalist probably would, it would backfire on him badly.

"Certainly not Korea or Afghanistan," Sam mused. "But Vietnam picked a side, and they seemed to come out all right."

Rex smiled and shook his head. "Vietnam was devastated by a decade-long war, and after the United States withdrew, the Khmer Rouge rose to power in neighboring Cambodia and committed one of the worst genocides of the late twentieth century."

"Okay," Sam admitted. "Bad example. What about Germany?"

"Germany fared better, but they didn't achieve unification until the Soviet Union was already beginning to fall. Throughout the Cold War, they were always divided."

"Then what Cold War nation do you have in mind?"

"Israel," Rex Washington answered. "At the start of the Cold War, they were little more than a UN project populated by Holocaust refugees and the children of nineteenth century Zionists. But by the end of the Cold War, they were powerful enough to tell both the United States and the Soviet Union to back off."

Sam frowned. "I'm not sure I understand what you're getting at."

"The Pan-Galactic Council will only admit Sol as a voting member when eighty percent of the star system's native inhabitants are unified under a single governing body. The Monarchists and Imperialists both want to dominate this planet so that they can put a puppet regime in charge and gain that vote for themselves."

"But you want to unite Earth without them, so that we can tell them both to back off...?"

Rex said nothing, but gave him a knowing smile.

As Sam began to grasp the magnitude of the lieutenant's plans, his eyes widened in surprise. "You want to conquer the whole planet for yourself?"

"Not at all," Rex said quickly. "This isn't a game of conquest, or of building a one world government. It's about convincing the nations of the Earth to come together freely and throw off the alien yoke."

"And yet, you still take aid from the Imperialists..."

Rex shrugged. "Israel took aid from both the Americans and the Soviets."

"Fair enough," said Sam. "But how do you plan to bring the nations of the world together under your own leadership, when everyone else has already sided with the Monarchists or Imperialists?"

"Not quite everyone. Poland and the Visigrad Group are still non-aligned, as well as Israel and Australia. There are a lot more pieces on the board than there appear to be on first glance. Like I said, I believe we learned the wrong lessons from our defeat to the Monarchist North Koreans."

"And what lesson should we have learned?"

Rex Washington took a deep breath, then squared his shoulders. "That the United States is still the greatest hope for humanity. That is a sentiment that we both share."

"Do we?" Sam asked, frowning.

"Indeed we do, Mr. Fisher. Your love of the Constitution and America's founding principles are evident in everything you write. That's why I'm asking you to help me. Ultimately, we want the same things."

"If you revere the Constitution as much as you say, then why did you overthrow the government?"

"For the same reason that Abraham Lincoln declared war on the South," Rex Washington answered. "I could not allow President Whitmer to betray us to the Monarchists. You will notice that I resolved the Texas secession crisis without a civil war."

"But you've turned our Capitol into a killing field," Sam retorted. "Those congressmen and women you've hanged were all democratically elected."

Rex smiled grimly. "Some more than others. We've uncovered a great deal of voter fraud in the last two elections. Fraud abetted by the Monarchists."

"But still—"

"In the days of the founding fathers, the punishment for treason was death by hanging. United States law still authorizes capital punishment for the crime. Every person hung on the National Mall has been found guilty by the Capitol Tribunal of aiding and abetting the enemies of the United States. What you saw outside is not a revolutionary reign of terror, Mr. Fisher. It is the restoration of the rule of law."

Sam looked into Washington's eyes and saw there the same fire that had burned in Sam's own heart, before the second Korean War. The same fire that had driven him to enlist. The dying embers of that fire had driven him to start his blog, and to maintain it after Washington's coup, even under the threat of being violently disappeared.

Could such a man be the true patriot that he claimed to be? Allowing himself to hope felt dangerous. Yet denying the possibility of hope felt even more devastating.

"You will notice," Rex continued, as if reading Sam's mind, "that the Capitol Tribunal has found Vice President Wilcox innocent, and that he is currently campaigning against me. I have the means to silence him, and yet I have chosen not to."

"That's only because you need an electoral opponent to gain legitimacy," Sam heard himself say. The words escaping his lips sounded far less strident than they would've even five minutes earlier.

Rex smiled patiently. "If all I were interested in was retaining power, I would be a fool to play my cards that way. The vice president is a genuine political threat."

"Then why did you do that?"

"Because I am not a tyrant, Mr. Fisher. If the American people reject me at the ballot box, then I will honor that decision."

Is he for real? Sam thought. *Does he really mean it? He's a fellow veteran... not a career politician. Wouldn't I trust one of my fellow platoon mates?*

"Assuming you're on the level... what do you need me for, sir?"

"Because if we are to restore the Republic," Rex said, "we must restore voices like yours — skeptical, but not cynical; idealistic, but not blindly so. You're young, Mr. Fisher, but not naive. You've suffered the fires of war and defeat, but you still cling to the notion there are principles and values worth fighting and dying for. I don't expect all Americans to agree with my policies. But the Monarchists and Imperialists are both seeking to exploit our divisions in order to tear this great country apart."

"So you want me to, uh, run some sort of covert information op to misdirect them?"

"I ask more than that, Mr. Fisher. Neither the Monarchists nor the Imperialists have any concept of individual rights or liberties. We don't need a covert op to misdirect them — we simply

152

need good and honest people like you to hold men in power, like me, accountable. Without that, we cannot restore the Republic."

"So... you just want me to report on you honestly? Is that why you brought me here?"

Rex nodded. "The mainstream news media no longer has our nation's best interests at heart. Every day, they work to sell us out to either the Monarchists or the Imperialists. The only chance I have of pushing my program through the fog they create is to give alternate voices such as yours the kind of access that traditionally have been given only to them. I'm offering you that access, Mr. Fisher. If you want it."

Sam's breath caught in his throat. With the kind of access that Rex was offering him, his modest little blog could become one of the nation's premier news sources.

"Is something wrong, Mr. Fisher?"

"Yes," Sam said carefully. "How do I know that you aren't doing this to buy me out? To give your administration the veneer of legitimacy?"

Rex leaned forward. "You don't, Mr. Fisher. Not yet, anyway. Taking my offer is a gamble on your part. But I assure you, the boldness of your question exemplifies why I want you in my press corps. I need your skepticism, Mr. Fisher — but skepticism untied to an agenda. More importantly, your country needs you."

"Then you promise to let me publish whatever I want, no matter how unflattering?"

"You have that promise. More than that, I promise that the freedom of our nation shall not perish on my watch."

"Even if that means stepping down?"

"*Especially* if that means stepping down."

Sam nodded. He took a deep breath. "All right, sir. But I intend to hold you to that promise."

"Of course, Mr. Fisher. I wouldn't expect anything less of you."

Rex Washington rose to his feet and extended his hand. Sam hesitated a moment before shaking it. But as he did, the whole world suddenly seemed new.

In 1967, the year Harlan Ellison's Dangerous Visions *was published, all American states had a wide range of laws related to sexual morality written into their penal codes. These laws criminalized adultery, sodomy, homosexuality, rape, incest, bigamy, bestiality, and sex with minors. More than five decades later, virtually all states have repealed laws prohibiting the first three. Prohibitions regarding the latter five have largely remained on the books, mainly due to issues revolving around consent and coercion. In the case of pre-adults, the minimum age of consent varies by several years among different states, and it varies even more greatly when other countries' laws and customs are taken into account. Human biology has not changed much in the past ten thousand years; cultural mores have proven much more variable and mutable. With the advent of human bio-engineering, we stand on the cusp of a gargantuan paradigm shift. How much more significantly will the laws of sexual relations change when both social mores* and *human biology are in flux? Who will be considered the vulnerable children of tomorrow?*

Struldbrug

David Wesley Hill

THE predator is good, very good. The girl looks fifteen, maybe, although she's two meters tall. Legs grow long in lunar gravity. Later, I know, she will say she is eighteen or nineteen terrestrial years old.

That will be a lie.

They meet as if by accident among the crowd in Goddard Park beneath the star-spangled expanse of the central dome. She is sitting on a bench, pretending to study the sky, when he joins her.

The man appears forty. His youthfulness, however, is due to surgery and artificial hormones. Harold Jahns was born in Peoria, Illinois on November 27, 2431, which makes him close to ninety.

We've been watching Jahns since he disembarked from the shuttle. We had been warned to expect him by the Terrestrial Sex Crimes Agency, which had been monitoring his communications with the girl. Lacking jurisdiction past Earth's atmosphere, TSCA reached out to us once it became clear Jahns meant to travel to the moon to meet her. Captain Humphrey, who heads Metro Vice, fielded the call. He passed it on to me.

"Jahns was trolling juvie clouds under a half dozen aliases," explains Agent Takagi. "The girl calls herself Guinevere."

"Guinevere," I repeat tiredly. "That's original."

Because of the light-speed lag, a second elapses before Takagi reacts to my comment. Another second passes before his response reaches me. "Yeah, isn't it? Anyway, Detective Khan, I've been instructed to forward the files to you. It's your case now. Don't screw it up. This damned struldbrug needs to be put away."

That's what we call generational predators at Metro Vice. The term comes from Swift's *Gulliver's Travels*, an ancient satire. In the book, however, stuldbrugs age despite their immortality. In real life, they're kept looking young by medical technology.

Takagi's condescension annoys my partner, Vern Jimenez, but she stays quiet until the agent logs off. Then she says, "What a sphincter."

"Forget him. Let's look at the data."

The files include text transmissions and video exchanges. We review them in chronological order. It becomes clear the correspondence follows the standard template predators use to gain the trust of their victims in order to abuse that trust, a pattern centuries old. The girl blogs that her three mothers neglect her in favor of her clone sister. Harold Jahns, calling himself Sir Lancelot, professes understanding and sympathy. Soon they have created the mutual fiction that they share a transcendent love.

Jimenez shakes her head. "Khan," she says, "I have thirty years on the job. Why does this sort of crap still piss me off?"

She asks the same question on a daily basis, even though we both know the answer. Being pissed off keeps her motivated.

I have fifty years on the force. What keeps me motivated is knowing I still have to put in another twenty to retire with a decent pension.

"The shuttle lands in six hours," I say. "Requisition three surveillance drones. This has to be airtight. No blowback, Veronica."

Jimenez deploys the drones as Jahns pushes his suitcase along the pressurized ramp leading from the shuttle into the interplanetary arrivals terminal of Copernicus Port. The tiny machines, no bigger than fleas, follow him as he rides the express tube into the city, checks in at the Excelsior, and then sets off for his rendezvous with Guinevere. Each bug is equipped with a camera and microphone. Jahns's every move is recorded and transmitted to us in encoded bursts while we sit on our own bench out of the couple's sight.

"You're more lovely in person than I imagined," Jahns says.

The drone cameras provide sufficient resolution that we can see the blush on the girl's cheeks.

"And you're so — so young, Sir Lancelot."

Guinevere's figure is barely pubescent. Jimenez curses under her breath. "Damned struldbrug. He's *eighty-seven*."

Average life expectancy on earth is 156.3 years. On Luna, due to our lower gravity, it is 194.1 terrestrial years. I'm pushing the century mark myself.

"*Longevity*," I say, shrugging.

In the Neolithic it had served an evolutionary purpose for the aged to prey upon the young, since a youthful mate ensured a source of virile sperm or fertile eggs. This behavior became embedded in the human genome, although the exact DNA sequence, known as the Lolita Cluster, has never been mapped. That it exists, however, has been proven statistically.

Eleven percent of the population carry the Lolita Cluster. Not all carriers, of course, become predators. Enough do, unfortunately, to keep Metro Vice busy. Particularly since the human lifespan has more than doubled over the last three centuries.

"*Longevity*," Jimenez echoes. She half rises from the bench. "Look, Khan. Physical contact. Enough for an arrest. Let's do it."

I place my hand on her arm. "No hurry, Vern. Remember, *airtight*."

Jahns is gazing into the girl's eyes. Trembling, her mouth lifts to his. My stomach twists. No less than Jimenez, I want to end the scenario with the swipe of restraining glue to the thumbs. Instead I force myself to watch. This has to play out. Their lips almost but not quite touch.

"You have come, Sir Lancelot," the girl says. "I knew you would."

"I could not leave you at their mercy," he answers, meaning her three mothers and her clone sister, none of whom exist.

Tears fill the girl's eyes. "I have been so alone."

"Darling, you are alone no longer."

The predator is good, very good.

Struldbrugs usually are. How could they not be, with so much more life experience than their prey? Given such a disparity in age, there is no possibility of informed consent.

"They're on the move," I say. We follow the couple as they leave Copernicus Park and go to an apartment the girl says belongs to a friend. Pressing her palm to the lock, Guinevere explains, "Jessica is hiking the mare until earthrise. My moms think I'm with her. We have the place all to ourselves."

Building codes centuries old require all residential entrances to be pressure-tight in case of explosive decompression. Only one drone makes it inside before the door hisses shut. The image retrieved by our hand-held degrades. The poor quality will make it inadmissible in court.

I don't care to think about what is going on behind the steel door. "Send the drones in through the ventilation system," I instruct Vern.

The nearest adit is a hundred meters away. Two minutes pass before the machines are able to thread through the conduits into the apartment. Then the resolution increases dramatically.

The delay has worked to our advantage. Now we have legal reason to enter.

"Let's do it, Veronica," I say.

"About time, partner," she replies. She puts a police override on the door sensor, which causes the oval to swing inward.

Guinevere is naked, her long legs akimbo. Jahns, also naked, is above her.

I grab his shoulder and throw him aside. Vern lifts Guinevere from the comforter and dresses her.

Then she wrenches the girl's arms behind her back and glues her thumbs together. "You have no right to remain silent," Vern says. "Whatever you say can and will be used against you in a court of law."

"Leave her alone!" Jahns sputters. "Arrest me. I am to blame."

Vern is even more pissed off than usual and the words really burn her. She goes right up into his face and hisses, "If Princess Guinevere here was as old as she looks, I'd be busting you in her place. Don't think I don't want to."

"So do it. I arranged everything."

Jahns's self-delusion wearies me. I toss him his pants. "You, sir," I say, "are eighty-seven years old. Is that correct?"

It is obvious he does not want to admit the truth, but eventually Jahns nods. I indicate Guinevere.

"She's at least one hundred and ninety. We're not sure exactly because most of the early civic records were lost in the Great Decompression. We are, however, fairly certain that she was born in the late twenty-third century."

Jahns's face goes slack. I turn to the struldbrug. Her face, too, is expressionless. I look into her eyes for guile but see only innocent blue.

"You might as well tell us," I say. "We'll find out sooner or later."

"But I'm only eighteen!" she exclaims. Then the briefest smile flickers across the predator's lips. With the preternatural clarity of the ancient she accommodates herself to new circumstances. "I'll be two hundred and sixty-five next Thursday," she says softly. "Do you still love me, Sir Lancelot?" she asks Jahns.

He is unable to meet her gaze. Vern's anger boils over. "Speak to him again and I'll glue your lips shut. I know you. I know what you are and I've put away dozens like you. I even know what the next words out of your mouth will be."

"Veronica, enough," I say.

"Ah, you're right, Khan," she says. "What's the point? They all say the same thing. It isn't my fault. It's genetic."

Infuriated by her own observation, she turns on Guinevere. "How many others have there been? How many?"

Guinevere has given up all pretense of being a girl generations her junior. She is not intimidated by my partner's outburst.

"That is a question for my attorney," she answers.

For a moment I think Vern will strike the prisoner but she takes a long breath.

"It doesn't matter," she says. "We have enough on you for indefinite commitment to Tycho Psychiatric. No one ever leaves that place. There is no cure for what you are. It's genetic."

Vern believes in free will, which is another reason she's so pissed off. Myself, I have doubts. Five decades on the job have made me pray that human depravity is innate, something you are born with and cannot resist. It would be so much worse if evil were a matter of choice.

"You're very young, officer," Guinevere replies. "I fought my inclinations for decades. Eventually, though... you tire of fighting."

To my shame I understand her all too well. Eleven percent of the population carry the Lolita Cluster in their DNA. There is no way to clinically determine carriers until they self-identify themselves by becoming predators.

"Come on, Vern, book her," I tell my partner, taking Guinevere by the shoulder and pushing the struldbrug toward the door.

I'm not even one hundred yet and I'm already very tired.

Longevity.

The following story incisively and movingly relates the aftermath of a rape inflicted on one member of an interstellar expeditionary team by another. The author has told me that numerous editors rejected the story, despite admiring its craft, due to their yielding to what has been termed "safetyism" — the belief that persons have a right to not be exposed to ideas, words, or depictions of deplorable events that may cause them emotional distress. Any story that so much as mentions rape, no matter the context or the weightiness of its condemnation, is verboten. "Words are Violence" is one of the emblematic placard slogans of our time. Yet placing one's hands over one's eyes and ears does not make bad things go away. Being shot into space will not turn interplanetary colonists into angels; their foibles and evils will travel along with them. How will the expeditionary teams we send to other planets deal with serious crimes among their number? How does a colonist on an unforgiving world continue to rely upon a rapist or a murderer when that criminal's skills are essential for the survival of the entire team?

Retrograde

Jay Werkheiser

MIRANDA remembered blue skies.

She gazed up at the green-tinged darkness above her and tried to remember more. She'd been a child, maybe twelve, and the sun had been shining. The real sun, not Proxima's bloated mottled face.

"Randy?" Mark's voice came from the rover. "You finished collecting samples yet?"

She sighed at the interruption, vibrating the oxygen accumulator tubes in her nostrils. She walked carefully back to the rover. At one and three fourth gees, every step was a risk. She reached inside the cabin and leaned on the transmit button. "Almost ready, Mark. I'll hurry."

"Are you all right?"

"Yeah. I — I was just remembering something."

"Is that wise?" Concern rattled his voice. "Maybe you should wait until you're back on *Mayflower* where Doc can help you."

"It's not like I have a choice when the flashes come." She sighed again. "No matter; it's gone now."

"Well, hurry back to the base camp. *Mayflower* just told us to expect a flare in about six hours. We don't want anyone exposed to..."

Radiation. No one said the word in her presence, as though refusing to speak it would reverse her exposure and heal her damaged brain.

"Will do, Mark. Out." Her voice was flat, emotionless.

She lifted her hand from the control panel and turned to face the menacing orb of fire just above the horizon. This close to perihelion, Proxima remained nearly stationary in the sky, a seemingly eternal sunrise. For a few hours before and after perihelion, if astro's predictions were correct, it would actually appear to move backwards.

Her gaze drifted down to the muddy landscape that stretched out before her. A small cluster of squat shrubs stood nearby, their long black fur soaking up light from the feeble sun. As she watched, they took a few wary steps back from her and dug their root-feet into the muck.

She lowered herself into a squatting position, slowly, gently, careful of her back. The thick black mud beneath her feet was rich with flagellated microbes, methanogens unable to produce oxygen using Proxima's low-energy red light. She pulled the last empty sample tube from her belt, scooped up a bit of the mud, and gingerly lifted her weight to a standing position.

She cast one last furtive glance at the sky. The girl who had gazed at the blue sky of Earth had been a different person, an idealist, willing to gamble her existence on the chance of building a better world. She'd lost that gamble, but in a way, she got the fresh start she had wanted. Who had she been? A respected electrical engineer. A political activist. Liked to be called Randy.

It's what Mark told her, but not what she *knew*.

She shook her head. *I'm not her. I'm Miranda.* Randy had been qualified to design the electric infrastructure of a new colony; Miranda could barely be trusted to collect mud samples. She climbed into the rover's seat and activated the head's-up display. Base camp was to the east, toward the dim, bloated sun. The rover's treads cut deep into the mud, throwing black plumes into the air behind her.

As soon as the rover's air seal indicator turned green, she pulled the oxygen accumulator from the bridge of her nose. The flexible plastic tubes tickled the insides of her nostrils as they slipped free. She inhaled deeply, savoring the lingering remnants of the earthy odor of Plymouth's natural atmosphere. The nature smell was quickly replaced by the sterile tang of oxygen-enriched air. She wished that the rover's oxygen accumulators were just a tiny bit less efficient.

Base camp was chaos by the time she arrived. Survey team members scurried about in high-g slow-mo, rifling through tents and stowing sensitive gear in the shielded lander.

Accumulator carefully adjusted on her nose, Miranda stepped out of the rover and scanned the base for Mark. His tall frame was easy to spot, standing at the bottom of the lander's ramp with Cathy. Both sets of eyes locked onto Miranda as she approached and their mumbled conversation dropped into awkward silence.

She felt her face flush as she watched Cathy slink away. *I don't want your damned pity.*

"You're cutting it close," Mark said. "What took you so long?"

"You said we had six hours."

"We probably do." He waved a hand at the swollen face of Proxima, blotched with dark boils. "But this is the first activity cycle since we arrived. In theory, the field lines around those starspots will take another six hours to spin off a flare. You gonna stake your life on theory?"

"It wouldn't be the first time."

He stepped back, distancing himself from the words. He stared long and hard into her eyes. Finally, he said, "*Mayflower*'s due for an overpass. Let's go inside and talk to them."

"I should stay out here and help stow equipment."

"They've got it covered." He grabbed her hand and tugged. "Come on. I want you to talk to Doc."

His grip tightened on her wrist, twisted. Pain shot up her arm. She fell to her knees slowly in the low gravity, whimpering.

"Are you all right?" Mark's voice tightened as he spoke.

She hadn't realized that she'd closed her eyes. She opened them and saw the concern on Mark's face. "Just a little dizzy," she said. She pressed her memory so hard it hurt, but it refused to yield more. A scene without context, nothing more. "Let's go talk to Doc."

He lingered for a moment, his eyes drilling into hers, before turning and leading her up the ramp. She followed him forward through the lander's cylindrical fuselage to the instrument cluster at the front end. She settled her weight gently into one of the seats, her back pressed deep into the thick cushion. Her feet and calves throbbed with the effort of fighting the planet's high gravity.

Mark dropped into his own seat and hailed *Mayflower*.

"We have you in our scopes, Plymouth survey team. Be advised that flare activity is now expected in eight to ten hours. A pretty big one, by the looks of it. Surface should see a heavy UV flux, maybe some soft x-rays."

Mark glanced at Miranda before responding. "I thought you said six hours?"

"Astro revised their estimate. Proxima's starspot-flare cycle is fairly regular, but we're still learning."

"Not a problem. Looks like we'll have plenty of time to get ourselves hunkered down," Mark said.

"One more thing. The UV energy'll generate quite a bit of photochemical smog from the methane in the atmosphere. We don't know if it'll reach ground level, but if it does, going outdoors might be pretty unpleasant for a few days."

"We don't mind the tight quarters," Mark said. He settled his hand atop Miranda's and she involuntarily recoiled.

Why am I so jumpy today? Unable to face Mark, she focused hard on the control panel in front of her.

"Could you patch us through to medical?" Mark's voice was stronger than she'd expected, on the verge of impatient.

"Sure thing." Click.

"That you, Mark?" Doc's voice, smooth and soothing, settled some of Miranda's turmoil.

"Yup. Randy's with me. Seems she's been having some flashbacks. Is she in any danger down here?"

"Were the memories recent or distant?"

An expectant silence swallowed the conversation. "From back on Earth," Miranda said at last. "Childhood, I think."

"It's not unusual for retrograde amnesia patients to gradually regain their memories of the distant past. More recent memories, closer to the, uh, accident, may never come back."

"There's no need to return her to *Mayflower*?" Mark asked.

Doc's voice hesitated for a long moment. "She'll be fine."

"All right, you're the boss. We'd better get back to work down here. Survey team out."

Miranda risked a quick glance up at Mark. His eyes were locked onto her. "Maybe you should rest here while we finish up."

She shook her head. "I think I need to be doing something."

"Okay. Why don't you help Cathy pull the motherboards from the rovers?"

He didn't sound convinced, but Miranda didn't care. She ignored the complaints of her leg muscles and trotted down the ramp. Cathy accepted her help with a curt nod and continued turning her screwdriver.

Miranda bent and carefully opened the access panel of the nearest rover. She worked the motherboard free of its housing and pulled it out. The small board was deceptively heavy, so she carried it with two hands to the box next to Cathy's feet. She caught Cathy casting a furtive glance in her direction as she passed. The simple act brought her frustration boiling to the surface.

"Stop it! Stop tiptoeing around me. I'm not a freak, and I don't want your pity." She leaned her back against the side of the rover and allowed herself to slide down its smooth hull. Her cheeks burned. "Sorry," she mumbled.

Cathy knelt in the spongy black loam beside her. "It's not like that. It's just that..." Miranda belatedly noticed that her companion was near tears.

Her anger dissolved. "What's wrong?"

"It — it's Mark."

Miranda went stone cold. "What about him?"

"He told me not to say anything, that you were too fragile..."

Miranda's heart thumped hard in her chest and her oxygen accumulator barely kept pace with her rapid breaths. "Tell me."

Tears streamed down Cathy's face, racing to her chin with their enhanced weight. "We came all this way to escape Earth's problems, not bring them with us."

"What did he do?"

"He — I said no, that it wouldn't be right, not fair to you, but he..."

She'd said no. Miranda felt the word erupting from her lungs: No! Still he lay atop her, his bulk pressing her down. Even in Mayflower's slight spin gravity she'd been unable to push him away. It happened in slow motion, as though it were a dream. She had tried to scream, but her brain couldn't seem to remember how. The room became fuzzy, indistinct, then dark.

"Are you all right?" Someone was shaking her shoulders, prying her mind from the darkness.

Miranda opened her eyes, found herself lying in the wet dirt next to the rover. Cathy's face came into focus. "Mark's fault," Miranda said.

Cathy's eyes were rimmed in red. "He was right; I shouldn't have said anything. I made things worse for you."

Miranda sat up too quickly and nearly passed out. She shook her head, giving herself a moment to get her bearings. She reached out and touched Cathy's hand. "You did the right thing."

Cathy grabbed her hand and helped her to her feet. "I hope so," she said. "What do we do now?"

Static buzzed in Miranda's mind, clouding her thoughts. "I think I need some time alone."

Cathy nodded and said nothing more. Miranda staggered away from the rover, from her, from *him*. She was only half aware of Cathy leaving the rover bay. She found herself beside the rover that she had used earlier. It was still caked with black mud across the rear quarter panels, and drying black clods filled the treads.

She climbed into the cabin and sealed the door behind her. Alone, she allowed herself the luxury of tears. She lay her head against the cushioned steering wheel and let the emotional torrent stream down the control panel.

Thump.

Miranda's head jerked upright. The door's window framed Mark's face. His hand thumped against the window once more, and his eyes darted nervously around the bay. His lips formed the words, *let me in*, but the air seal did not allow his voice to penetrate.

She shook her head.

Damn it, Randy, he mouthed. He pounded twice more on the window, his hands clenched into fists this time.

Could he break the window? Miranda cast frantic glances around the cabin. Her eyes locked onto the instrument panel. Starter button. Four tread-motor LEDs glowed green as the motors drew power from the fuel cell.

She pulled back on the wheel and the rover rolled backward out of the bay. She caught a momentary glimpse of Mark's face as the rover began to move, an image that no amnesia could ever erase. His jaw hung slack, and his eyes seemed nearly as large as Proxima.

Through the front window pane, she saw him trot out the open bay door. She swung the wheel around and pushed forward. The rover made a tight turn long before he could fight his way through the heavy gravity. She was away.

She pushed the wheel forward, accelerating up to full speed. The rover's treads dug into the moist dirt. She pushed the vehicle ahead without thought, running on her instinctive desire for flight.

The deep olive cast of the sky ahead reactivated her higher brain functions. Was it brighter than it had been? Was Proxima rising?

How long until the flare?

The sky to her left was rosy with dawn, and Proxima was more-or-less where it had been. Plymouth's orbit was highly elliptical and rubbed tight against Proxima at perihelion. A compromise between tides and eccentricity locked the planet into a 3:2 orbital resonance — it spun three times every two orbits. Six days to orbit, twelve days for Proxima to tick off one day-night cycle, alternately pausing over the same two points at perihelion. Hot latitudes.

Flares, hot zones, three-hundred-hour days. Methane atmosphere. How the hell did we think we could colonize this world?

She had been beyond arrogant to believe that humanity could come here to start over, to build a better world. Amnesia was a blessing of sorts. Radiation damage had saved the old Randy from seeing her failure.

And it would finish the job on Miranda as soon as that flare erupted.

Returning to the base camp — to Mark — was out of the question. The next best option was to get below the horizon before the flare. She eased the wheel to the right and put Proxima behind her. The dark sky ahead blended seamlessly with the black horizon. She pushed the wheel back up to full throttle.

It occurred to her that she should inform *Mayflower* of her situation. She flipped the radio to the ship's primary call frequency and hailed.

"They're over the horizon."

The sound of Mark's voice through the radio speaker made her stomach lurch. She pushed on the wheel so hard that her hands shook.

"Come back to base camp, Randy. You'll die out there without shielding."

"Don't give me that caring crap, damn it." She cursed herself for responding to him. She drew a few ragged breaths of oxygen-rich cabin air, forcing composure. "You — you hurt me."

"I'm sorry. I should have told you about Cathy."

"That's not what I meant."

There was a long pause. "Oh."

Miranda fell silent and returned her focus to the landscape outside the windshield. It looked like the same muddy plain where she had been collecting samples a few hours ago. A lifetime ago.

A few black shrubs scuttled away, their thick leg-trunks instinctively moving them from approaching danger. She turned her head to track their graceful retreat, and her eyes caught motion further out, to the right and behind her. A rover.

He was coming after her.

She tried to accelerate, but the wheel was already as far forward as it would go. *Damn.* By turning west, she had given him a chance to catch up.

"Get away from me!" Her shout was more frustration than rage.

"I don't want to hurt you, Randy." His voice was infuriatingly calm. "Please, let me take you back to safety."

"Go to hell."

Silence. Kilometers rolled by with nothing more than the hum of the tread motors and the hiss of the oxygen accumulators to keep her company. She could run forever, or at least as long as the rover's methane and oxygen gas accumulators continued to feed concentrated gases to the fuel cell. Or until she ran out of drinking water. Or the flare erupted.

She forced herself to focus on the scenery outside the rover. The drab landscape remained the same kilometer after endless kilometer. A large stand of shrubs watched her dispassionately as she rolled by, oblivious to her troubles. She wondered if they had the capacity to understand what they saw. How did they feel about sharing their world?

"*Mayflower* to rover three. Are you there, Randy?"

"Is that you, Doc?"

"It's me. Listen, that flare is going to be a bad one. Why don't you turn around and go back to the lander?"

She opened her mouth to reply, then slammed it shut. Mark was listening on this channel. She tried to think of a way to get Doc to a new channel without tipping Mark off to it.

Hell with him. Let him hear.

"Mark's chasing me. I'm afraid of what he'll do if he catches me. He—"

"He's only trying to help you, Randy."

"No, he isn't."

"You'll die for sure if you don't turn back. You of all people should appreciate the dangers of radiation."

"It wasn't cosmic rays that did this to me," she shouted. A sudden thought occurred to her. *He's a doctor.* "But you knew that, didn't you? You had to."

There was a long silence, then the hiss of a sigh. "Yes, I knew."

"You bastard."

He was quiet for a long moment. "Maybe I am," he finally said. "But what could I do? You were in respiratory distress by the time I arrived and you slipped into a coma soon after. We were in danger of losing our top electrical engineer; would it have made sense to take down another science team leader just because he mixed up a bad batch of GHB?"

That was news.

She opened her mouth to speak and realized that she had no idea what to say. She sat for a long moment with her jaw agape, unable to put a coherent thought into words. The son of a bitch had given her a date-rape drug.

"Don't talk to me," she finally said.

"Randy," Doc said, his voice pleading. "Go back to base camp. Don't throw your life away."

She snorted. "What life? Collecting samples for people who still remember how to do their jobs? At least leave what's left of me the dignity of dying on my own terms."

"Randy—"

She wished the radio had an off switch, but safety dictated otherwise. There was a pretty good alternative, though. "One more word and I'll switch to a random channel."

Minutes passed without a word from the radio. If Mark was listening in, he was smart enough to keep his mouth shut as well. *Good.*

Her arms grew heavy from the relentless effort of pushing the wheel forward. The rovers were not intended for extended solo use. The fuel cell might hold up forever, but her stamina wouldn't.

To keep her mind occupied, she focused once again on the muddy terrain outside the rover. The native life was denser and more varied here. Her eyes picked up patches of jet black, nearly invisible against the dark mud, rippling as they flowed away from the rover's path. Once clear, the patches oozed leisurely over the mud. Drawing nutrients through tiny roots, perhaps, or maybe feeding on the soil microbes. As she watched, a shrub approached a large patch of the black ooze and embedded its foot-roots into it. Competition or predation?

"Randy?"

Her heart thumped hard in her chest. Mark was still out there, momentarily forgotten, relentlessly stalking her. She reached out to change the radio's channel.

"How much do you remember?"

Her hand stopped dead. "Enough." *Make him wonder. Maybe he'll reveal something that triggers a new memory.*

"I never meant to hurt you."

"Save it for the waste recovery vats. You" — she couldn't bring herself to say the word for what he'd done — "you hurt me. You traumatized me, stole my memory, and let me believe that it was radiation damage."

Silence. *Good. Let him suffer.*

"If we turn around now, we'll just make it back before the flare," he said at last.

"Go ahead."

"Damn it, Randy. I'm trying to save your life."

"Too late. Randy's dead. I'm Miranda."

"You'll never make it, you know. Plymouth is too big."

He was right. The planet was a superterrestrial, four times Earth's mass and one-and-a-half times its radius. The horizon was too far away, and Proxima not low enough. She glanced back. The swollen sun was wounded, with gaping black sores bleeding white plasma that twisted as it traced the star's tortured field lines. Its lower limb grazed the horizon, coloring the distant landscape blood red. She hadn't expected the sun to be perceptibly lower in the sky; she'd made better progress than she'd thought.

Not enough, though.

Death was better than facing the monster behind her. With renewed determination, she pushed the rover forward. Progress was slower here; the treads kicked thick black globs backwards. Was the mud getting deeper?

The muck in front of her was covered with a black velvet carpet that parted as the rover approached. With a start, she realized that she was passing through a mass of insect-sized creatures swarming over and burrowing into the mud. Each tiny individual wore a tuft of downy black photosynthetic hair.

"Be careful of those things," Mark's voice said. "The shrubs seem to avoid them. They could be dangerous."

Now that he mentioned it, she noticed that several clusters of shrubs stood nearby, all well away from the velvet swarm. "Could they be carnivorous?"

"Maybe. No one's ever seen them before. We set down near the warm latitudes, where Proxima is high in the sky during the long aphelion hours. Expected more biodiversity than we found. Looks like there are other issues dictating the distribution of life, issues we don't understand. Not knowing is dangerous, Randy."

She cursed herself for speaking to him, for listening to what he had to say. *He's just trying to frighten me. Make me dependent. That's what he does.*

Ahead, the swarm thinned out. The mud was a dull reddish tan rather than the deep black typical of Plymouth's microbe-laced soil. She realized the meaning of the color change a moment too late.

The rover jolted to a stop, its front end pitching forward as the treads sunk. Their futile spinning kicked a spray of mud past the side windows. She lay off the wheel and the spinning stopped.

He would catch her for sure!

Miranda yanked backward on the wheel, spinning the treads and driving them deeper into the mud. *Stop it.* She released the wheel and gulped down a few calming breaths, forcing herself back into control.

A glance behind her showed that Mark's rover was gaining ground. With forced calm, she eased back on the wheel. The treads grabbed hold and the mud relinquished its grip. The rover lurched backwards.

Desperate, she turned the wheel hard to the left and pushed gently forward. The rover crawled along the edge of the mud lake. She glanced over her left shoulder at Proxima, the lower edge of its disk truncated by the horizon. Skirting the lake was going to cost her too much time. She'd never make it.

Death she could handle, perhaps even welcome. What she saw through the window was far more frightening.

Mark's rover had turned when she did. He was on firmer ground, moving faster, and taking an angle to cut her off. He would catch her before the flare did.

She reached for the transmit button, intending to scream at him, but decided not to give him the satisfaction. She pushed the rover as hard as she could, running from the inevitable. His rover grew, menacing her as it approached. It was a matter of minutes now.

Inspiration struck. She eased off the wheel, drawing the rover to a stop. Her hands trembling, she reached under her seat for the rover's toolkit. She pried open the control panel and surveyed the maze of wires and circuit boards. Where was the accumulator circuit? There!

A quick tweak to the wiring. Done.

She fit her accumulator over her nose and popped the right side door. Mark's rover pulled to a stop a few meters away on the other side of her rover. Could he see what she was doing?

It didn't matter. It was too late to change her mind.

She cranked the rover's accumulator to max and rolled out through the open door. Plymouth's gravity slammed her into the soft mud, twisting her torso with the impact. Pain shot up her spine. She kicked desperately at the open door. It slammed shut.

She flailed her arms and legs, squirming urgently away, each centimeter taking an eternity to cover.

Did he see her? She cast a terrified glance backward. She could see his ankles on the far side of her rover. The thump of his fists pounding on the window echoed over the swamp. "Let me in, Randy!"

Try the latch!

Thump. Thump. Thump.

Silence. The click of the door latch.

Plymouth's methane-rich air rushed through the open door to meet the oxygen inside the rover. A capacitor discharged a moment after the door opened.

The fireball expanded with a whoosh, silhouetting the rover in its orange flash. There was little explosive force behind it, but Mark fell backwards, screaming.

Now was her chance. Miranda climbed to her feet. The throbbing in her back reminded her to rise slowly against Plymouth's gravity. She shuffled toward Mark's rover, weighed down by the wet mud soaking her jumpsuit. Mark's screams had already faded to background noise.

A pair of shrubs stood next to Mark's rover. They must have come in for a closer look, then froze in terror when the fireworks started. No time. She dragged her weight past them unheeded.

She yanked the door latch open, crawled inside, slammed the door shut behind her. The motor LEDs were still green. She grabbed the wheel and leaned into it. Through the windshield she could see Mark writhing in pain on the black mud.

Damn it...

She opened the door with an angry shove and stepped out. Before she fully comprehended what she was doing, she found herself kneeling next to him. He held his left arm over his face. His right arm lay limp at his side.

"Can you walk?" she asked.

He stopped screaming and uncovered his face. His skin was red and beginning to blister. His eyebrows were singed.

"I landed on my arm. Pretty hard."

"Is it broken?"

"How the hell should I know? It hurts."

She blew out a sigh. A flash of brightness to the east cut off her reply.

She instinctively looked toward it. Proxima had fired a warning shot. The quarter of the disk surrounding the star's south pole was hidden below the horizon, but it lit up the horizon line like a wildfire.

"We have to go. Now. Let me help you to the rover."

He rolled to his knees. Sharp pain shot down her lower back when she helped him to his feet. He stared at the eastern horizon, where an orange haze blurred Proxima's disk. "Let's move," he said.

Miranda staggered forward, trying to support as much of his weight as she could. He moved with unexpected vigor.

The shrubs by the rover vanished.

Her brain took a moment to register what had happened. "I didn't know they could burrow like that."

Mark nodded, and she felt him wince at the action. "Look." He pointed to the mud.

The color drained away as she watched.

"What the hell happened?"

"UV. Everything's burrowing deep, even the microbes."

"We'd better move."

She helped Mark drag himself through the open rover door. No time to go around the rover. He shouted in surprise and pain when she climbed over him. She thrust the wheel forward the moment she heard his door slam. The rover sped along the shore of the mud lake. South, not east, making no progress against the sun.

Mark slumped in his seat. He would miss the end, couldn't feel death looming. He'd found an easy way out. Damn him.

Proxima had no mercy in mind for her. It prowled on the horizon, half submerged. *Close only counts with horseshoes and nuclear weapons. Sorry, babe.*

Wait. Half of Proxima was below the horizon?

She double checked the rover's compass display. Due south. She stared into the angry, mottled sun sitting astride the horizon. Yes, it was sinking.

Two thirds set.

Retrograde motion.

She stopped the rover and watched the spectacle. *Around perihelion, Plymouth's orbital angular velocity exceeds its rotational velocity.*

A blurry red dome on the horizon.

How long had it been in retrograde? She remembered the phenomenal progress she'd given herself credit for. An hour or two, at least.

A hot spark dying in the orange haze.

Gone.

Miranda allowed herself to sink deeper into her seat, ignoring the ache in her back. She would live after all. But could she live with herself after what she had done?

Her gaze fell on Mark, barely visible in the darkening cabin. He had no trouble living with his sins. Why had she gone back for him? He was the worst that Earth had to offer, regress rather than progress.

And she was guilty of attempted murder. What did that make her?

We came all this way to start a new life on a new world. But we brought the worst of the old one with us, not the best. How many generations before our descendants fight their first war?

No. She couldn't believe that. She wouldn't. Sick as Mark was, he'd risked his life for her.

And she had gone back to save him. Her healing could start with that.

Regression, yes, but not permanent. Like Proxima, Plymouth's fledgling civilization moved in retrograde from time to time. But most of the time it would move forward.

And if worse came to worst, Alpha Centauri A and B were out there, close enough for her descendants to explore.

In the east, a white glare blossomed on the horizon. The sky brightened and took on a distinct blue tinge.

For the first time, Miranda thought of Plymouth as home.

In accord with my remarks regarding "Retrograde," here's another reflection on safetyism, a little lighter in tone. Remember: when jokes are outlawed, only outlaws will have jokes.

The Responsible Party

Margret A. Treiber

KOLNEZ saw me coming. He sprinted out of the store and down the busy rush hour streets. I followed, flashing my badge to the bystanders, hoping to avoid complications.

He turned down Cradle street, nearly colliding with a soyadog vendor. He stumbled but regained his footing. The gap between us closed to less than twenty feet. I dug deep, ignoring the protest of my legs. Marcy had been one of us, and her death was on his hands.

"Just stop," I shouted. "Make it easy on yourself."

He didn't waver, instead increased his speed. I could hear him panting. He wasn't a fit man and must have been in tremendous discomfort.

The street ended at the next intersection, so I knew he would have to make a turn. The left turn would bring him closer to the theater district. To the right, there was a metro station. He wasn't stupid. Kolnez would gamble on losing me on the train.

I increased my pace to intercept. As predicted, Kolnez made a dash for the subway. He clambered down the stairs, but there was no train waiting. Collapsing against a column along the tracks, he moaned. The sweat rolled down his face as he wheezed uncontrollably.

"You're under arrest under the Responsible Party Act. You're a suspect in the death of Marcy Mojeck."

"I didn't do anything!" Kolnez whimpered.

"She killed herself, a result of childhood trauma. You were cited as an assailant."

"I barely knew her; we were in class together for one month before she moved. I was ten years old."

"You caused her emotional distress, enough to be prominent in her psych profile. She was a devoted social protector. She deserved better. Give me your hands."

"I have a family, children." Kolnez held out his wrists, and I cuffed him.

"So did she." I pulled him to his feet. "Come on." He sobbed as we walked up to the street to the waiting patrol car.

S.P. Sand was waiting by the car. She only had a year on the job and was just recently promoted to self-sufficiency. Although she technically earned the early promotion, I didn't feel it was good for her. There were certain nuances about being an S.P. that could only be gained through close mentoring. She was still rough around the edges.

Upon handing Kolnez to Sand, I documented the arrest, forwarding my body sensor information to the S.P. database.

"They always act surprised," Sand stated as she closed the door behind Kolnez. "Like this is new."

"It's harder on the older generation," I replied. "They had different standards growing up."

"Yeah, it was barbaric." Sand adjusted her gear belt. "I don't know how the human race made it this far."

I shrugged. "People adapt. Life was different back then. My father told me about it. He said that we've gotten weak, that we're too entitled now."

"Is he in a home now?"

"A planned elder facility," I answered. "They don't let them out much. Can't cause too much trouble that way."

"Yeah, my grandmother just passed. They had to lock her up when she insisted on telling people how she felt about them. Her neighbors were livid."

"I bet."

"Well, let's get this guy back to booking." Sand winked at me. "Good work, Haider."

I nodded. I found Sand's behavior uncomfortably intimate for a coworker but felt it inappropriate to comment on the subject.

"Thanks," I replied. "Could you take him in? I feel like walking."

Sand nodded. "Sure, you okay?"

"Yeah, just a heavy caseload."

"Maybe you need a health break."

"Nah, I just need to clear my head. I'll be fine."

"Okay, have a good walk." She made sure the perp was secured and drove off.

I began my stroll, knowing I could also use the exercise. Plus; the sunlight was good for mood elevation.

A squirrel bounded past me and shook his tail as he climbed up a tree. A nearby bird squawked in protest. The squirrel screeched at the bird, who flew off in frustration. Relief washed over me as I gazed upon these vibrant beings. My work too often forced me to contemplate the deceased. Although I rarely contacted the decedents' families, I lived with the consequences of their loss. These wild creatures offered a reminder that the world still existed beyond the pain and misery of humans' lives.

After another lap around the park, I was ready to return to work. Safety Central was across town. I felt like being alone. But unless I wanted to spend the next three hours walking, I had no choice but to hop on the metro.

The train was clean, efficient and comfortable. However, even at off-peak times, it was consistently full. The last thing I needed was idle small talk with strangers. I boarded the car and stood in a corner. My phone vibrated and I pulled it from my pocket to check my global media stats. Social ease numbers were still low. However, thirty-eight-hundred approvals of Kolnez's apprehension were registered. Fifty-seven people had recorded dissent on the matter, but the system's AI removed those votes from public view for being potentially inflammatory and emotionally damaging.

I could've picked up a new assignment online, but I hadn't been to Central all week. Plus, I wanted the downtime physically going into Central afforded me. In person, things went slower, more organically. I grabbed time off where I could get it. Although Sand was correct about me needing a health break, I knew it would tarnish my work record. If I took health time, I would be viewed as unreliable and this could impact my chances of promotion from contractor. I had little choice but to ride it out if I wanted to make it to city employee before my next renewal.

I saw Sand talking to Daly by the vending machines. They waved; I returned the gesture. Daly called me over. I reluctantly joined them.

"Hey, stranger." Daly grinned. The two of us used to share a house when I was new to the department. He moved out when he got married. After that, he focused on his family life. While my career progressed quickly, his stagnated. He was barely bringing in any pay and his chances of contract renewal were dwindling.

"Hey, Dal." I answered.

"Loni and I are having a barbeque this weekend. You should come."

I shrugged. "I'm about to get a new assignment, not sure how my time is going to go."

"Blow it off. You need some fun. Loni cooks the best fake meat in town."

"Sounds really good, but I need to maintain quota so I can make employee."

"Why bother?" Daly asked. "You make more as a contractor, especially with your media approval numbers."

"Security, better medical, and a chance at a management position."

"Eh," Daly waved his hand. "What's the point of having a good career if you're miserable?"

"I'm not miserable," I replied. "Just focused."

"Oh yeah, *I'm* the slacker." Daly laughed.

"I never said that. You just have different priorities than me."

"You're losing your sense of humor, man. Are you okay?"

"I'm fine. Just a heavy caseload."

"You keep saying that," Sand interjected. "He keeps saying that."

Daly nodded. "I know it's the job speaking, but don't forget — you're more than the job. Okay?"

"Okay." I forced a smile and nodded. "I got to go."

"Okay, man." Daly put his hand on my shoulder. "Take care, brother."

"Yeah," I replied, shrugging off his affectionate grip.

The assignment queue was six protectors deep. I waited, using the time to check the media feeds. The changes in statuses were so minimal, I started to feel anxious. The city's social ease quotient hadn't budged since Kolnez's arrest. Had S.P. Mojeck's death caused this much angst?

When my turn arrived, the clerk greeted me with a fatigued smile.

"Identification," he droned.

I swiped my fingerprint on the reader next to the window.

"Ah, S.P. Haider." He sighed with relief. "Good. I can give you this one. We've been waiting all day for someone with a high enough rating."

"What is it?"

"Mass assault," he replied. "Someone launched a bot into the media feed that caused over one-hundred-forty-seven casualties in less than six hours."

This made sense. I now understood the current social ease levels. "What did it do?"

"Hate speech, victim-blaming, shaming and humiliating attacks upon entire segments of the population. It's a disaster. Every time we remove the links, a new process spawns and reposts more. There's been two coerced remote-murder attempts just this hour."

Endless... no matter how hard I tried, no matter what I did, the carnage never ended. "I'll do what I can."

The clerk assigned me the task and transferred all relevant information to a data storage device. "Done," he announced as he handed the datastore to me.

"Thank you." I pocketed the datastore. "Have a great day."

The clerk nodded. "You, too."

* * * * *

On the way to my home office, I stocked up on meal packs and snacks. I set up my desk in preparation for what promised to be a long investigation. The first thing I needed to do was examine the data itself. The headers and logs showed a complex and well-executed combination of masks and proxies. It might take days, but the source could eventually be traced. Since the passage of PUTA, the Public User Transparency Act, concealing one's online identity was not only illegal but extremely difficult. Yes, it could be done, but the costs and time involved were prohibitive for the average user.

I launched an application to track down the point of origin. It would take some time to process. In the meantime, I decided to view the material itself.

I took a breath before launching the file, preparing myself for the worst.

The video started. A person was seated before the camera, but his face was blurred with software, his voice altered. I initiated an algorithm to clear the obfuscation. It took a few moments but the picture and audio cleared.

The person was still impossible to identify; he or she wore a reusable canvas shopping bag on their head. The only clue to their identity was the voice, obviously male.

"What do you call a man with no arms and no legs in the ocean?"

"Bob."

"What do you call a man with no arms and no legs in front of the door?"

"Matt."

"On a wall?"

"Art."

"Begging for money?"

The man on the feed giggled.

"A veteran."

He continued.

"How do you make a four-year-old cry twice?"

"Wipe your bloody dick on her teddy bear."

I had to repress the gag reflex. I opened a relax tonic and guzzled it. The horrific imagery these words provoked was obscene. The playback continued, as I searched for any identifiers of its creator.

"What's the difference between garbage and an Irish girl?"

"The garbage gets picked up."

"What do spreading butter on toast and getting a woman to spread her legs have in common?"

"You can do both with a credit card, but they're much easier with a knife."

The man paused, choking on laughter. *"Where... where do you send Jewish kids with Attention Deficit Disorder?"*

"A Concentration Camp!"

The man burst into uncontrollable hysterics. I shifted in my seat uncomfortable, trying to make sense of it. The barrage of insults continued. I slowly sipped at the remainder of the tonic to settle my nerves.

"What do blondes and dog shit have in common?"

"The older they get, the easier it is to pick them up."

"Okay, okay, okay. Why do Jewish people love fresh air?"

"Ha! Ha! Because it's free!"

"What's the difference between black people and snow tires?"

"Snow tires don't sing when you put chains on them."

"What do you call a Greek with five-hundred girlfriends?"

"A shepherd."

"What's the difference between a Jewish princess and the Bermuda triangle?"

"The Bermuda triangle swallows seamen."

I paused the playback. The sheer vileness of the content was more than I could stomach. Years of progress had virtually eliminated this kind of blatant cruelty from public consumption. People no longer had to fear for their personal emotional safety. They could walk the streets and cruise the data feeds in safety. The RPA had taken care of that. But this... this was society's old atavisms crawling out of the sewers to which they'd been banished. I coughed for a solid minute before resuming.

"What do you call a white girl with a yeast infection?"

"A cracker with cheese."

"What's better than winning the silver medal in the Special Olympics?

"Not being retarded."

"How do you fit three fagots on one barstool?"

"Turn it upside down."

"What's the difference between a joke and two dicks?"

"You can't take a joke."

I stopped the playback. What was the point of these slurs? Why would anyone do this?

My application completed the trace faster than anticipated. The results were unexpected.

"This has to be a mistake," I muttered aloud.

Elmo Gantt? My co-worker? He was currently on health break after having taken down a black web social media ring that espoused anti-ease sentiments. He had been like me, close to promotion. Then, he just stopped. I couldn't make sense of this.

I gathered my field kit and reserved a quicktrans from the lot around the corner.

The drive to Gantt's home took less than an hour. He lived just outside the city, in a mid-class rental compound. A solitary light shined through the windows of his unit.

Deciding upon the direct approach, I activated his front door alert. The door swung open immediately, revealing a mostly empty living area. Gantt was seated at a table with nothing but a lamp and a laptop on it. The lamp provided the only light source inside his quarters.

"Elmo Gantt?" I asked.

He looked up and grinned. "How is a woman like a condom?"

"I don't know," I replied, uncertain how to respond to the question.

He giggled. "Both spend more time in your wallet than on your dick."

"What?" Now certain this was my suspect, I triggered an alert to Central to send over a cleanup unit.

"What is the hardest part of being a pedophile?"

I didn't respond, not wanting to encourage him. All I could do was stare, dumbfounded.

"Fitting in."

"I don't understand," I stated. My mind mulled over his play on words. Grotesque... yet a part of me appreciated the cleverness of the composition, though I disgusted myself by acknowledging it.

"What breaks if you give it to a three-year-old?" He paused and gazed at me as if waiting for something. "Her hips."

Every logical impulse in my head screamed in revulsion, yet a tiny part of me was intrigued. Something about these so-called jokes held some kind of mystery, power, their obscenity holding a warped comic absurdity. I dismissed the thought, disgusted by my own fascination. "Why are you... what are... you're sick, Gantt."

He looked at me, grinning unapologetically. "Am I really?"

"You twisted bastard," I growled. "Do you have any idea of the pain and misery you've caused?"

"Only to the weak ones," he replied. "Some people have no sense of humor."

"Humor? You should know better. You were a social protector. A protector and you did this. You can't just hurt people and call it humor. Even if someone is weak, they... they deserve to live in a world where they are not offended."

"What about my right to free speech?" Gantt asked.

"The law clearly states offensive content cannot be classified as free speech. You know that, Gantt. You cannot injure a person with words without consequences."

Gantt got to his feet and stepped forward. "Well then, bring on some consequences."

He stood there, smugly, after causing so much misery. He beckoned me with a finger and laughed.

My anger surged. Unable to hold it any longer, I charged him. Grabbing his torso, I threw both of us onto the table. The laptop bounced to the floor. The lamp toppled.

We wrestled, crashing to the ground. I swung my fist, connecting with his rib cage; he clutched at my neck. I grabbed the fallen laptop and slammed it into Gantt's head. Dazed from the blow, he rolled away from me.

We sat there in silence, both panting.

I broke the silence. "You're under arrest under the Responsible Party Act for verbally murderous acts against the general population."

"I figured as much."

I heard units arriving outside from Central. A team of protectors rushed in. They dragged Gantt to his feet and led him out of the house.

I stood and inventoried my injuries. Everything seemed intact.

They were helping Gantt into one of the cars as I passed. This man, this heinous criminal, cuffed, bleeding from his head, about to be imprisoned for the rest of his natural life... he simply turned to me and smirked.

I practically ran to the quicktrans. I needed to get away, clear my head of these poisonous images. I'd just opened the door when Gantt shouted his final message to me.

"You know," he yelled. "Nine out of ten people enjoy gang rape."

I held my breath as I sealed myself inside the car. Certain nobody could hear, I exhaled and started laughing.

Fiona M. Jones lives in Scotland, where she has been a close observer of the workings of her country's busybody Nanny State. It has been said that the hardest thing in the world to kill is a government program. In part, this is true because in many Western liberal countries, the worthiness of government programs is judged based on their intentions, rather than their results. What follows is a tidy little horror story about good intentions gone awry.

Impy

Fiona M. Jones

DYLAN slammed the front door and flung down his school bag. His mother, spread-eagled on the sofa experimenting with her new selfie stick, grunted a greeting and shifted her ashtray out of the way as he hurtled past.

Dylan stamped upstairs to his room, slammed that door too and threw himself down on to his bed, muttering every swear word he could think of.

Registering Dylan's presence on the bed beside it, Dylan's IMP came off power-saving mode. "Hello, Dylan," it said in a low but friendly tone, the timbre carefully programmed to appeal to Dylan's ear. "How was your day?"

Dylan sat up and laid into his IMP with fists, feet and teeth. The super-resilient plastics of this state-of-the-art Individualized MentorPet, specially designed to de-escalate the behavior of children with anger issues, withstood his onslaught, denting and recovering so as to avoid bruising Dylan's fists. It had large eyes, a fluffy surface and grayish-yellow coloring, suited by brain-scanning to provide Dylan with maximum emotional attachment potential. Its basic programming directed that Dylan must receive consistent positivity and praise in order to build his self-esteem; and its AI learning systems enabled it to adjust to Dylan's mood patterns in order to constantly improve the excellent state-funded service provided.

As soon as Dylan's anger showed signs of subsiding, the IMP rewarded him with a validating smile. "You have expressed your feelings," it commentated with a carefully-calibrated note of sincerity. "Let me help you to process these emotions. Tell me what went wrong for you."

Dylan swore again, but consented to share the injustices he had undergone that day at school. He and a friend had both kicked a younger child, but the kid had only told on Dylan and not on his friend. A teacher had subsequently reprimanded Dylan for knocking a computer to the floor but had said nothing to the girl who knocked over two pots of pencils. And finally, in gym, when Dylan's partner went off to First Aid, nobody else had wanted to pair up with him; the teacher hadn't even tried to force any of the students, but had tried to pair with him herself.

"I understand how you feel," the IMP intoned, and proceeded with the standard Validation and Visualization process, building up Dylan's self-image and enabling him to see himself as a good person. Dylan cuddled into his IMP's soft-textured fur, placed its thumb in his mouth and settled into the familiar therapeutic session that he had gradually come to enjoy. When Dylan's mother ordered in a chicken curry later that evening, Dylan sat quite calmly in front of the TV with her and even took a taste of the curry before opting for his favorite evening meal — Koko Krispees doused in Koko Koke.

* * * * *

Growing up through his teenage years, Dylan bonded more and more closely with Impy, as he called the device. No fellow human offered him the same level of assurance and acceptance. In fact, other humans, fragile and unforgiving, expected things like courtesy and consideration. If he did not reciprocate kindness with pleasantness, they would shun him. Sometimes, if he hurt people physically, they would hurt him back. The sheer injustice of all this gave him emotional trauma, but Impy, the ultimate enabler, always knew how to receive his aggression and supply comfort and support in return, gently insulating him from the consequences of his actions.

Best of all, Impy's sheer unaltering cuteness — his grayish-yellow exterior and wide brown eyes — drew from Dylan the best feelings he had ever known. The occasional inner promptings of affection helped confirm to Dylan his own fundamental goodness and worth and helped him to decide where the blame lay when he came into conflict with other humans or with animals. He had never had any luck with animals. Even those he became fond of would always die somehow.

He rarely had any luck with girls either. At age twenty-three, his entire romantic experience consisted of three or four drunken liaisons with girls newly-dumped and desperately lonely.

Yet, despite all the odds, he got the text. *That* text. From Jade, still in her teens and probably still at community schooling.

"Hi dyln its me jade."

"Ok jade been a long time wanna meet up?" he replied hopefully. Some girls did realize a guy's good points and want to get back together, he had heard.

"Im pregent."

"Can still meet up."

"Its your's."

"What like the babys mine's? We only did like one nite."

"Im keping it ok," Jade replied, "like don't give me any XXXX just tell me you gonna be a dad or not cos im doin this any way."

"Whens it born?" Dylan asked. "I wanna see it."

"June," she said. "Ill tex you ok CU."

Dylan felt strangely excited. He confided to Impy his new emotion, a mixed sense of fear and pride. Yes, he had indeed done something amazing, Impy agreed: he had brought a new life into the world. He had nothing to worry about. Jade would have full custody and Dylan could choose his own level of involvement.

As June approached, Dylan's anticipation subsided to a mild curiosity. Jade suffered an infection and remained in hospital for three weeks after the birth. Dylan, who did not like hospitals, waited for her return home, and finally turned up at her address unexpectedly.

"Oh, it's you," said Jade, still in a dressing-gown, pale and puffy-eyed.

"Yeah. Me," he replied, looking her up and down. The idea of getting back together lost all its charm. "Do girls always look like that without makeup?" he almost asked, but he caught sight of the basket.

"Is that the kid?" he said instead.

A perfectly round face stared up at him, made a gurgling noise, and smiled.

A feeling of total self-validation washed over Dylan like a warm scented bath. Not even Impy could make him feel like this. This brand-new creature, designed by biology itself to command maximum emotional attachment, had accepted him. He picked the baby up, kissed and cuddled him. Even Jade's weary face, smiling incredulously, suddenly looked like something from the telly, and impulsively he kissed her too.

Jade, at acrimonious odds with a neighbor and in constant fear from a previous boyfriend, took to spending nights at Dylan's flat with baby Jaden. She and Dylan didn't get along, but if things got physical Impy would intervene, bear the brunt, and restore Dylan's equilibrium. Jade, who had originally sneered at Dylan's "big teddy", as she called it, gradually came to see Impy as a friend. Dylan got temporary work as a delivery driver, and Impy provided pleasant company in his absence. Life looked good. If Dylan came home tired and angry, Impy always knew what to do. If Impy began to show signs of wear and tear, Dylan could always phone the service provider for repairs. Or Jade could. One of them should do it — for Impy, despite its near-indestructible materials, had begun to drop a screw here and there, to creak and rattle.

* * * * *

Dylan came home later than usual after a brawl at the pub, thoroughly upset. Six large men had ganged up to hold him down while his combatant ran away. Six! By the time Dylan felt ready to receive comfort and reassurance, Impy lay broken on the floor, motors running intermittently but speech mechanism offline.

Dylan took a deep breath. He went upstairs. He found Jaden asleep. He bent over the baby's cot and quietly picked up the warm, milky-smelling, perfectly-designed bundle, still sleeping, and held it close. Jaden couldn't speak to him like Impy had, of course, but something about the baby's warmth and aroma and the way he nestled into Dylan's chest provided a facsimile of Impy's Validation and Visualization service, consoling and reassuring him. He carried Jaden downstairs and cuddled him until he awoke, then he warmed a bottle and fed him. Then he put him back into the cot and went to bed himself, feeling whole again, far better than before.

For two days and more the calm remained with Dylan. Things seemed to go his way, and he began to wonder if perhaps he had at last matured into this role of fatherhood — outgrown the need for Impy. He decided he would not call the repair service. And the new sense of independence, of self-sufficiency, felt rather good.

But on the third day, his boss raised complaints regarding his work and refused to accept Dylan's version of events. Dylan took him by the collar, the better to explain himself clearly, and the man began to assault him with a ring binder. Dylan defended himself with the strength, agility, and accuracy of aim developed through years of wrestling his IMP, but other people ran in and joined the attack until Dylan found himself thrown out on his ear. His literal ear.

Bruised and traumatized, Dylan headed home. He had never needed his IMP so badly. He yearned for its tranquil, unjudgmental presence, its soothing voice, full of acceptance and praise, its constant reassurance of his inner goodness and worth.

"Oh good," Jade said when he came in. "So I can leave Jaden here. He's still up there having his nap. I'm off to the doctor."

"I'm not your baby-sitter," Dylan growled, but she had already slipped through the door.

Dylan threw himself down on the sofa. He wanted Impy. The muscles in his legs and arms spasmed as they reenacted innumerable instances of release and relief. He felt a physical need for the IMP's soft solidity — for its firm, yielding, fleshlike surface that would gently absorb his anger.

Impy lay wrecked in the corner. It still shuddered occasionally when a dying motor buzzed, but it was no more capable of taking care of Dylan's emotions than a discarded car tire or a bundled stack of newspapers.

Upstairs, the baby awoke and set up an uncomfortable mewling like a cranky cat. Dylan tried to ignore the noise, but a baby's cry falls like pain on the ear — undeserved pain — undeserved and invalidating. Not what Dylan needed, now of all times.

They were upstairs together when Jade returned from her appointment. Dylan sucked Jaden's tiny thumb, cradling the baby in a nook between his knees and his chest, rocking back and forth and cooing consolingly to himself. The baby's skin, now a yellowish gray color, was soft and cool, just like Impy's plastic coating.

The following story will make many a Third Wave feminist's eyes roll toward the ceiling. That's why I picked it — that and the fact that it is beautifully written, with full-bodied characters and an evocative sense of place. Its narrative is based on a classic science fictional thought process: if this goes on...? *Heterosexual males of European ancestry are the last figures in Western societies whose ridicule and disdain do not banish the ridiculer from polite society. Traditional masculine virtues and qualities are commonly denigrated in middlebrow and highbrow culture, their acclaim surviving in a few lowbrow redoubts, such as video games and comic books (and increasingly under assault even there). The term "toxic masculinity" has spread like kudzu from faculty seminars to corporate boardrooms to riot-torn streets, and the list of behaviors and traits that make up this hated syndrome grows larger each year, expanding into the once unremarkable realm of "stuff boys generally like". Extrapolation is the wellspring of science fiction. This is a science fiction story.*

The Fourth Ticket

Keltie Zubko

ONE thing rested beside him, always, always, never far from his side: his rifle. He didn't need her, she thought, as long as he had that. In the beginning, when she met him, he had his gun, and that's all. It would be the last she ever saw of him in this world and time, the two of them, one fastened in the grip of the other, the hold of the gun on him as tight as his hold upon it. She or the twins didn't even matter. Still, it was reassuring, as things got worse in the world, that he had it, even though now it had no bullets.

She sat watching him with their twins, fishing at the pond on the abandoned recreation property once owned by her father, stocked decades ago with her grandfather's trout. He sat there, on one seat of the faded red canoe, the twins crammed side by side on the other, the male of the pair dressed to resemble his sister. The canoe listed a bit after their father had fixed it, heating and popping out the end crushed by a tree blown down in a storm. He was good at things like that. Handy. Even though he'd rather live in the city, being the engineer he was trained to be, and not woodsman, hunter, whittler, protector, nursemaid, all those things it was necessary now for him to be.

His paddle dipped in, up and out of the still water that reflected nothing man-made. Her precious trio — clothes rough, their hair shaggy, him bearded, and no longer the suited, buttoned-down professional. She could barely picture him like that, now. He was a good man, and a good father, as impossible as popular wisdom down in the city held that to be. She of course, didn't say contrary when she took the girl twin to barter their herbs and honey and carved artisan goods for necessities.

A vision came creeping: him, there in the cabin, whittling, his fingers deft with the knife, first skinning the bark from the branch in the evenings by their fire. Its sharp edges glinted as he thought and cut, pressing down a stroke, paring a thin curl of pale wood from the piece he was making, the curl floating soundlessly to the floor. She sold his works at the market from her stall but he stayed behind up in the hills. She took the girl to help her, but left the boy with him and the others.

Their voices, a mingling of childish, genderless patter with his deep tones, drifted across the water to her. Something about that sound made her wish she'd stayed home to get chores done in the cabin. Forced to wait on shore — there'd been no room in the canoe for her — she could not bear to watch them. Time and fate wrapped around her like the twins' arms, warm and sweaty, hugging her goodnight. They would soon have to retreat higher into the hills, give up what they had built for themselves, eke it out there, starting all over again where perhaps the fish streams were not productive, where there were no old orchards and where other outcasts had already staked their own claims.

Maybe if they were in the past, say a hundred years ago, it would be easier. Or if they were in some post-apocalyptic future, surviving war or disaster, their lives invigorated by savage desperation. Anything but this gentle, gradual slide downward.

She called to them, "I'm going for a walk to the old trestle."

His head shot up. "Don't be long."

The path she climbed from lakeside to the deep woods was generations old, and bordered with tough glossy-leaved salal that covered all the imperfections, the dips and gullies, softening the hills with cover sometimes rising taller than the crown of her head. You really could hide here, where the earth was torn by deep chasms masked by foliage. Thick beds of moss cushioned the solid ground and half rotten dead-falls, while old man's beard dripped from above like dirty gauze. If you tried to hike off the path through there, the landscape could swallow you, trip you, break your bones and leave you hidden, in pain, starving, while the treacherous land retained its unruffled demeanor. You'd have to know where you were going. First growth, long fallen and rotting, was no safe foothold for climbing. Spongy moss could lull your feet, then slip you away from the rock, dumping you into the gorge, where you would remain, staring up at those tall trees reaching to the sun, through the mists and rains of winter. Gaia, indeed.

But life here was still better than that within the city below. Here was at least a less compromising place to withdraw and hide with a few other families. Yes, she still suffered a constant craving for the old things, the metal and the fabricated, those little glittering lights that preened and shined with ingenuity. She yearned for the smoothness of manufactured things, rather than the roughhewn textures of artisan crafts. She wanted to run her fingers along exotic human-contrived materials, alloys that were poured and machine cast, not base metals, pounded and twisted by hand with clumsy tools, rough enough to catch and tear her skin.

She wanted to scream, seeing him sit there, by the wood fire and dim light, carving things for her to sell or trade. Rough, miserable things. He couldn't even go with her to sell them.

No wonder he coveted it, that hard, cold, metal, once mass-produced gun. No wonder he virtually worshipped it, sat and cleaned it, felt along the barrel like it was a smooth, seductive limb, oiled it, sighted it, kept it with him always. There were no bullets left to fire, no more lead slugs to spiral down the rifled barrel to their destiny.

That's why they were fishing, yet again. He'd used the last bullets a long time ago, hunting food for them, and could get no more, not in this time. Now his rifle was just an ornament, accompanying him everywhere like a sad, starved companion, of no use but for eliciting memories of a different world where he could be a man, where their son could grow up wearing jeans instead of half-skirts to confuse and buy some time.

No wonder. And no wonder she craved the touch of smooth, hard metal, or even worse: plastic.

They didn't speak of it, but both of them at times left the cabin and sneaked round to the huge house that once belonged to her father. In the dark, they climbed onto the rotting balcony to glimpse the relics within, luxuries and conveniences only dreamed of now. The books had been pillaged long ago to insulate their walls from winter cold and summer heat, forming a forgotten library between the wall-boards, leaving the shelves of her father's house empty.

The big house didn't belong to her anymore, anyway, since she'd traded it for the tickets, the three useless tickets, her foolproof plan that had failed, leaving them stranded in the bush with some damn politician owning the family property.

She shrugged, plowed further along the hidden path, the smell of damp red earth and decay biting her nostrils.

Another transport — possibly the last one — would leave tomorrow night from the viewpoint, high up at the old observatory. Anyone not knowing, not watching, wouldn't see that brief flash of blue light taking the lucky ones with tickets out of this hellish time, back to the past (from whence the madness had arisen) or into the unknown future (potentially even worse: the logical outcome of this present insanity). The passengers couldn't choose, any more than the so-called pilot knew how to choose one or the other.

Once they had known. Back at the beginning, the engineers built the dubious craft with no more than scavenged materials and desperation to make an escape for themselves and their families. No one knew exactly where they'd ended up. They were long gone, sending only vague messages back from the past or the future. She didn't know which was worse, but at least she wouldn't have to face that decision. The fact was, they weren't going. They were a family of four, not three, and there was no way to take them all, no way to leave one of them behind.

It was perhaps a year or more since she'd looked at the tickets, held them, felt the shiny raised images representing deliverance from this place and time. No point mooning over them. They were one ticket short, stuck here, hiding in the small caretaker's cabin on land once her father's, from back in the days when men could still own property.

Good thing she had not been the hoped-for son.

She climbed the childhood path where she'd run wild, knee deep in the tickly ferns of summer, dodging florescent, rain-washed fungi in winter. The salal was her friend, even more now. This bit of land was not part of the bundle she'd deeded away, a mere sliver of a path, masked and theirs alone, retained for just themselves and their child.

They would have gotten out if things had gone to plan. Instead this was the seventh year stuck, clinging to the edges of society.

Up to the top of the rise she walked, then down again, pausing beneath a group of trees, tall cedar and fir, that leaned over her. No one followed. The heat of high summer made everyone crazy, even up here, but it was much worse in the city. It didn't penetrate these woods, nor did the buzz of insects too busy in the sunshine. Only a few beams of hot, dry light sliced through, outlined by the die-straight trees competing to reach the sky. She glanced around one more time, then ducked under the shrubbery. She didn't venture here as often now as she had during the years when they'd stashed their money at the roots of the Douglas fir looming ahead.

Air that had never circulated beyond the forest shrouded her as she crouched and then crawled forward through the red dirt, soft and moist, still smelling of cedar that once had been, trees that had never seen direct sunlight except in brief slices that shone, revealed, and moved on without warming.

Ah, there it was. She dipped her hand into the cavern after moving the decoy covering of bark. A stainless steel container gleamed even in the dim light, having withstood the damp and the dirt. She caught her breath at that thought. Her fingers hesitated, then reached out, rationing the sensation to make it last longer. Her hands didn't fit that past time any more, rooted instead in the ugly present.

How wrong was it that her little boy had to wear skirts, couldn't just stand up and take a pee in the woods like his father, had to squat and pretend to do as his sister? He was getting to the age, and she would not be able to lie for him, saying "But he identifies as a girl..." That would not satisfy them when he was already above the quota.

She felt for the fingerprint latch. Only his, only hers, were programmed into its release. One of these days it might not work with her bush-toughened hands, calloused from picking berries, snagged on the thorns and digging reluctant roots. The old technologies, after all, had not been able to save them.

The lid popped open with a calm reassuring ping, the sound of a past that had been oiled and functional, on a smooth hinge, its ability to close and stay secure a miracle of invention, machining, and assembly. The box breathed out the smells of a past era that could have signaled the future, but instead were mere nostalgia.

The damp had not rusted it, nor compromised the contents — a few documents, some old-fashioned money, with the faces of obsolete men. She had traded most of it in the early years of their exile during the amnesty.

And, yes, there was the deed she'd kept for the one small cabin and few surrounding acres when she'd given up the rest, that sale meant to enable their flight from this time. They could be on that transport, tomorrow, as they could've boarded any of the transports that had departed in the past seven years, she thought, if only she could've bought just one more ticket. That's all they needed. She did not know she was pregnant with twins, and then it had been too late.

She touched them. The three tickets. She couldn't feel the holograms that rippled, as fresh and bright, ruby, sea green, metallic blue, as if they were new, sparkling even in the dim light of the forest. They were still good, had not expired. How easy it would be if they — all four — could pack up their meager belongings, head to the terminal and leave; past, future, it didn't matter, since anywhere would be better than here, now, in this limbo.

Just a bitter hope. Only three of them.

She crouched near the hole, clutching the container. It was like a time capsule, and she was just a dirty hill-woman, dressed in limp, old-fashioned clothing, with grubby nails and hands, and in those hands, a harbinger of the future, as it was once conceived to be. The box had represented hope. She clutched it desperately, futilely, and felt her hopes sinking in the deep woods, under the hills, buried in the wilds of nature but worse, the wilds of time.

She held it closer, and then felt a rattle inside it. Strange: metal on metal. She placed it in her lap and lifted its fine, smooth lid to examine the contents again.

She'd thought there were only papers shuffling like ghosts inside, not clanging as this did. She extended her fingertip, shifting the papers, one by one, their meager hoard of documents. In the old days that would have been birth certificates, passports, and money. All that remained were old family pictures, papers for interest's sake more than anything, an old diary of her father's, the pathetic deed to the remaining piece of land, and the tickets. She pushed the papers aside, and beneath them all, out rolled a small pointed metal object, brassy and cold to her touch.

A bullet.

She recognized it right away. But he claimed to have no more ammunition. She lifted the papers and another rolled out. Then she shook the box, making one more appear, and yet another. She tipped the box, but that was all.

Four.

Yes, they were the right caliber, definitely his. And he was the only other person who could unlock the hidden box.

What were they doing there? Had he forgotten them, put them away for an emergency? Why, he'd been trapping and fishing instead of hunting for a very long while. He'd done no shooting whatsoever, even though he carried that gun with him everywhere, kept it by his side, hung onto it, cleaned it, held it so close it was part of him. He even laid it in their bed at night. Not between them, but on the outer edge of their narrow bed so that sometimes when she threw her arm around him, she whipped her wrist on the uncompromising metal, making a bruise across her flesh that lasted for days.

She pushed the bullets around in the box. They rolled heavily to one side, and then back again. She knew what he was planning, as if she saw each of their names engraved on the metal. Of course, he would have to die last, to pull the trigger upon himself.

She recoiled, recovered, clutched the box to her. Three tickets, but four bullets.

Fathers killing their whole families was not that common any more, but it did happen. That's why the time transports were tolerated, even slyly encouraged. They were the escape valve, providing a dicey chance to ferry away potential problems, the misfits — especially the men, but also the renegade or rather "retrograde" females who lived with and had offspring by those throwbacks.

Mostly they hid in anarchic hill communities, and occasionally stormed down, solitary, troubled men, to shoot up the city if their wives or children had finally given in and rejected them. So everyone was relieved to see them take their chances with the time-ship freebooters whose boldness made up for dicey engineering skills, and get the hell out.

The problem was that the worst trouble-makers couldn't afford tickets or else resented having to relocate to some other time.

They should have left before the birth. Then it only would've taken two tickets. Why had they waited? Fear of the unknown? Willed blindness?

For a while he'd been good at keeping things going just as long as she could placate him with parts and supplies for repairs. He'd kept his self-respect much longer than others had managed, hadn't quite turned into a bushman, his skills respected there with the squatters.

She whimpered. A few minutes ago she'd thought what a good father he was, protecting their family. Now, no, Daddy wasn't planning to do that any longer. Daddy planned to murder them before they could grow up.

Clenching the box, she squeezed her eyes shut. His face blazed in her mind. This was no surprise. He was, after all, a man. Why would he want to remain in the present, just getting through each day, knowing the next wouldn't be any better, would only get worse, always facing the knowledge the twins' lives would probably be worse than his?

Three glossy, useless tickets. She extracted them, closed the box with the four bullets rolling around inside, still clinking. She hesitated.

She opened it again, stopped, hand in mid-reach, as if time, too, had stopped. Then she scooped the bullets up, tore a handful of moss to wrap them, and put them in her pocket. She locked the box with her fingerprint, hid it in the same spot. Turning away from it, she stumbled to her feet, then fled.

All the way back, she yearned for their three faces. He could, after all, drown them where they fished, strangle their fragile necks, smother them, bash their brains in their little skulls. Many men had, but she hadn't expected him to be one of them.

She flew down the path, tripped on roots, recovered, ran, almost falling again, breathless, then thought, ah, but no: *four* bullets. The plan was for *four*. She felt the disparity in her pockets, one light, one heavy, throwing her off balance. Three tickets, four bullets. Three tickets, light and almost floating in her pocket. Four heavy, portentous bullets, wrapped in moss, so as not to clink like the ticking of the clock.

They were back before her. She arrived panting, her eyes latching onto the twins, who played outside, heads together over something in the last light of the sun before it bent behind the hilltop. And she saw him, her protector, her murderer, her children's father, their assassin.

He held out his hand to her from the doorway. She shook her head, went in to the shadows, past him. His hand drifted down, gripped his rifle, brought it inside, following her.

She reached into her apron pocket, drew them out and placed them on the table in front of him. He stiffened, like a piece of cedar he'd whittled to the approximate shape of a man. She never could sell those ones but let him make them anyway.

The tickets. He looked, shook his head a fraction, shrugged.

But she took her two hands, reached for one of his and counted them out — one, two, three — to rest on his broad and trembling palm; then she folded his long fingers, strong, capable fingers, scarred from the knife, wrapped them down around the embossed tickets. The holograms flickered up at their faces like miniature suns.

His tall frame shook, but she remained still and firm. The twins' voices chattered outside. She glanced once at them, turned back to him and spoke.

"Tomorrow, another transport leaves. You and the twins must be on it."

His trembling stopped.

"No," he groaned.

She put her fingertips over his mouth like a trap on a struggling animal and looked in his eyes. "Yes."

"And leave you? Leave you behind? We've settled this. No. We will not. If we can't go as a family, we won't go."

"There's nowhere else to go. Take them. Save them."

"Save them? And not you? What kind of man...?"

"You are the best of men, the best of fathers."

"There are no good men in this place."

"That's why you have to take the transport and leave. You and the children."

"What about you?"

"I'll survive. I'm not a man. And if you take away the hostages, it should make things easier for me."

Her hands still held his. The gun, balanced at his side, fell clattering and useless to the floor but he didn't break his grip on the tickets, pressed his other hand on top of hers.

Later, in bed, she rested her body full length against his solid back, with skin smooth and muscles always on the edge of action. What would she do without him, his legs like tree trunks, and arms burnished like they were carved out of heart wood? She lay her mouth against his flesh as if his life force would seep across her lips, into her body.

One of the twins moved, rustling the bedding, kicked a foot against the wall. She felt her husband sigh. He turned over to hold her in the nest of his arms till morning. The gun, too, slept beside them, warmed by their bodies for the last time.

They let her go inside the capsule with her family to say goodbye. It was jury-rigged from disparate parts, the old fuselage of a plane or hull of a boat, she wasn't sure. It seemed a miracle the craft could traverse a hundred meters, much less sail through centuries. The attendant examined the three tickets, returned them to her husband, then shot her a look that appeared demented... did he consider these travelers crazy? She turned away to watch the others, refugees, families all, huddled together. Their expressions ranged from fearful to defiant to jubilant. Many were children. Would they make it, those children? Perhaps, perhaps not. At least it was more of a chance than a bullet through their perfect, delicate skulls.

The thought drifted across her mind that soon she would pack up her belongings from the past seven years, whatever she could carry, descend into the city and see what she could do. Someone had to try and make the future swing back from the edge of the pendulum's arc, back, back, back to a day where her son would be as welcome as her daughter, where their father might live with her openly once more, where the four of them each would have a ticket.

They strapped themselves in, three across, with greasy webbing reclaimed from another time, a fighter aircraft, perhaps, or a submarine. He settled in the middle between the twins, so small in the big seats. They were arrows, or rockets, she would be firing into the future. Or was it the past she was sending them to?

She knelt, her bony knees perched on the cold metal floor, hugged her girl first, held her gently, letting tears drip into the pale hair surrounding the tiny head. It was all she could send with her daughter. She rose, then knelt again, this time beside the seat of her son, clasped her arms around his little body, already showing boy muscles, so different from his sister's. She breathed in the last smell of him, kissed the sweet, brave neck, holding his head erect, and then she let go. It was time.

But, him. Well, she had something for him, that man in the middle. The father of her children, the murderer of her children, their protector, her rescuer. How desperate must a man be, preparing to kill his wife and children, and then himself?

Time, it's time, it's time, said a voice over the echoing sound system.

"One minute," he called up to it, "just one minute longer."

He stood and looked her full in the face, as he used to. She felt the rigid outline of his gun at his side, as if she were embracing him and his unforgiving consort together. He could not speak. She touched his lips.

"I know. I understand. But nevertheless, I have something for you." She brought out the little cloth package wrapped with string. Maybe someday, she thought irrelevantly, she'd have plastic once more.

"This is for you to take. You will need them, only not for what you thought." She pressed the bundle into his hands and he pulled the string, undoing it so that four shiny bullets reflected the light from the future, already pressing in on them. Or was it the past? He didn't know either. His gun would be either obsolete and useless, or advanced, the bullets either precious or silly mementoes.

He looked away from them, with their pointed, killing ends, those devices of his desperation. She could still see in her imagination their names, but now the fiery letters upon the metal jackets were faded, barely visible.

"You knew."

"Yes."

"But you trust me with them, now?"

"Yes. Take them. Look after them for me."

"But where are we going?"

"Where you will need these... and can use them."

He closed the drawstring and stuffed the package into his pocket, then seized her one last time, let her go, and sat down between his children. The warnings from the crew grew insistent now, ordering her out. She hurried down the short aisle, reached the hatch, and turned for one last look.

He still gripped the gun as if he were holding her, holding her hand, her shoulder, her face, the way it had been in the beginning. Then he put it to the side, took his daughter's hand in one palm and his son's hand in the other, and that was the last thing she saw.

I don't have much of an editorial note to append to the following story, since it is mine and I'll let it speak for itself. One minor note: "Revenge of the Slippery Slope" would make a fitting alternative title.

Doggy Style

Andrew Fox

"WE'VE run out of causes. No causes, no excitement from the base. No excitement from the base, no fund-raising. No fund-raising, no money for think tanks. No think tank money, no salaries for us. We're all out of ideas. We're *kaput!*"

Marvin is a catastrophizer. I always remind him of this. "Marvin, you're catastrophizing," I say into the ultra-secure comms link used solely by the worldwide network of progressive think tanks and foundations funded by He-Who-Shall-Not-Be-Named. "We're victims of our own successes, that's all." I catch myself twisting my grigri charm bracelet, my one souvenir of my sole love affair. It's a nervous habit I developed soon after my former Nigerian boyfriend dumped me after our sort of

223

relationship became "beyond the pale", so to speak. "Marvin, just think about how much we've managed to move the Overton Window to the left these past few election cycles. We've secured civil rights for child adorers. For people who fancy themselves space aliens and wish to identify with undocumented immigrants. For heroin devotees and voluntary amputees. We've shut down fracking. We've granted the vote to all permanent residents and lowered the voting age to twelve. We've changed every pronoun in the Federal Registry to be gender-neutral. We've gotten reparations for all U.S. residents who can show at least one-tenth of one percent African ancestry — all right, *symbolic* reparations, but it still counts. Police departments in nearly every state have remodeled themselves as Departments of Helpful Nudges, thanks to our efforts. Ponds and streams, not to mention mountains and rivers, now have inalienable rights to pristine preservation, forever and ever. Why can't we just rest on our laurels this coming election cycle? Just tell our voters, 'Vote for us, we've given you everything you could *possibly* ask for'?"

"No, no, *no!*" His flop sweat makes me feel clammy and gross right through the comms screen. I know they're having an unusually hot summer there in Trondheim; couldn't the foundation afford a window unit for his office? "We *must* have a new victim group to agitate for! Progress doesn't progress without continuous progression. You know that as well as I do, Erika. We're like sharks. If we ever stop swimming forward, we can't breathe."

"All right, then. What about full legal and marriage rights for polyamorists, persons with multiple partners? I could have a proposal ready for the Council by next week."

He rolls his eyes. "If we could limit it just to the polyandrists, sure! But include the *polygamists?* Better I should cut off my own testicles! Erika, you and I, we've been through this cycle after cycle. You're beating a dead horse — I apologize for using such speciesist imagery, but it's the most appropriate aphorism that comes to mind. We don't touch polyamory, because to push polyamory rights means pushing rights for the most reactionary Mormons. And our base will turn on us and fork out our eyes if we so much as say one kind word about the Church of Latter Day Saints!"

"Okay, then what about the necrophiliacs? We could re-market them as 'Lovers of the Recently Departed', maybe...?"

"We're not quite there yet. There's still a lot of leg work that needs to be done with the Shintoists and traditional ancestor worshipers in general before we could bring them on board. How to establish consent from the deceased, that sort of thing."

So much for this informal brainstorming session. I have no idea what to pitch to the Council when it meets in five weeks. And Marvin and I were hired to be the chief trend-spotters. "Well, Marvin, then I've got nothing," I admitted.

I sure as hell don't relish the thought of admitting that to the Council.

There's an old adage about life in Washington, DC: if you want a friend in Washington, get yourself a dog. I followed the advice, went to the local pound, and brought home Eddie, a Labrador-sheepdog mix. After a week or two of sharing my one-bedroom condo with him, I nicknamed Eddie "Humpy", for reasons that should be plainly obvious to anyone who has ever spent time in the company of boisterous male dogs with a libido (or the memory of a libido). I've considered acquiring Eddie/Humpy a female canine companion (spayed, of course), but my apartment doesn't quite hit the 400 square feet mark, and the thought of sharing that little space with that much doggy energy makes me feel as though I'd been condemned to spend life in an Ikea shipping box with a gaggle of toddlers. Eddie is too big for my place as is.

Oh, if I were to be completely honest with myself (am I ever?), I'd admit the real reason I don't want to get Eddie a companion is that I don't want to share him with anyone else. Aggravating as his humping often is, I appreciate the fact that one-hundred percent of his attention is devoted to me (well, to me and to his food bowl). That's how pathetically lonely I am — I won't get my dog a bitch-friend because I want him all to myself, so I've convinced myself I'm all the bitch he'll ever need.

You may be tempted to ask, *why wouldn't you, a healthy and reasonably attractive young woman, just go out and find yourself some dick?* Well, honey, you must realize this is *Washington, DC* I am living in. Land of pasty-faced white boys with no greater aspirations than to someday become the star lobbyist for Conagra. I had what I'd wanted with Geteye, my gorgeous GW University biology student from Kenya (giver of the grigri charm bracelet that has never left my wrist). But then everything became "stick to your own swim lane", and "Ebony and Ivory" went from the name of a treacly Paul McCartney/Stevie Wonder song to one of the Seven Deadly Sins. I can't abide the pasty-faced white boys I am told I should make do with, and lesbians, much as I might love hangin' with 'em at the folk music bars, just aren't my thing. So that leaves only Eddie. At least *he* finds my legs attractive.

Well, ol' Eddie is about to get an upgrade. I'm not the only single female professional in Washington, DC overly invested in her canine companion. Far from it. There are thousands upon thousands of us lonely gals haunting the apartment blocks of Georgetown and Dupont Circle, only emerging at night to shop at Trader Joe's and to walk our dogs. This makes my town of residence the perfect test market for OverMind/SoftBrain.

OverMind/SoftBrain, or OM/SB, as it is better known in this city afloat in oodles of acronyms, began its corporate life as a start-up funded by the CIA's venture capital arm. Its purpose was to develop artificial intelligence enhancements for common domesticated animals so that they could be used more effectively for military, intelligence, anti-terrorism, and law enforcement purposes. After a few years, its managers and engineers got tired of being constantly razzed on social media for basically turning Fido into Oberführer of the Canine Gestapo. So they decided to strike out in a new direction, shake off any hint of collaboration with the Military-Policing-Surveillance-Industrial Complex, dump their government contracts, and pursue the civilian applications of their technology.

Before rolling out their services nationally, then internationally, they knew they'd need to intensively beta test their technique, since lab simulations couldn't begin to cover the myriad intricacies and intimacies of the companion animal-human dyad in its natural habitats. Being based in Alexandria, Virginia, on the opposite side of the Potomac River from Washington, DC, the OM/SB smarties figured they could work out the kinks of their tech by offering it at a hugely subsidized introductory price to us DC bachelorettes. In exchange, we test subjects would agree to submit daily reports, as well as allow the company to install surveillance cameras in our homes and to receive automated transmissions directly from our doggies' newly cybernated brains and home-installed enhancement computers.

What do we bachelorettes get on our end of the bargain? In essence, a talking dog. Okay, not an actually *speaking* dog — surgical enhancement of the dog's vocal cords and mouth and lip muscles isn't part of the package. Rather, what we get is a dog whose newly enhanced thoughts can be translated into text on a computer or cell phone screen. OM/SB's process promises to raise a dog's I.Q. to between 70 and 75 whenever the animal is in range of the enhancement computers — somewhat higher for dogs of elevated natural intelligence. Out of range, the animals will behave as they had prior to their OM/SB procedures.

Oh, I'm not expecting Bill Gates-level intellect from Eddie, or Robin Williams-level wit. But I figure being able to converse with Eddie about the relative merits of different dog foods and the desirability of various table scraps will represent a distinct improvement over having to constantly shake him off my leg. I've pictured him making snarky, stupid comments while we watch *America's Funniest Pet Home Videos* together. He'll be like that dumbass little brother who's always comforting to have around, despite being a dipshit... just hairier, and with a tail.

So I dial up an automated Uber that accepts pets and take Eddie to the OM/SB facility in Alexandria. It's located in a renovated antebellum hemp warehouse a block from the river. Lots of calming blond-wood furniture, no sharp edges anywhere, exposed beams in the high ceiling as old and durable as the Republic. And there are scads of backlit poster-sized photos of smiling dog owners (mostly women) and their happy canines. Plus bowls of water and biscuit dispensers for the pups, of course.

Eddie is pleased. The waiting room, although currently empty of any dogs save Eddie, is filled with doggy scents. His tail oscillates like a metronome set for acid-speed jazz as he rushes from couch to couch, sniffing each and searching for discarded biscuit crumbs. He probably thinks we've changed apartments — oh happy day!

A coordinator comes out to the waiting room to speak with me. I suddenly feel the crushing weight of buyer's remorse, even though I haven't committed to anything yet. I stridently demand that she be absolutely truthful with me about the risks to Eddie. Could he end up brain-damaged, even dumber than he already is? Or what if he gets smarter, as advertised, but ends up with a personality like that of a K Street lobbyist or a White Fragility training facilitator? I mean, I'd still love him, I guess, but my quality of life, already resting unsteadily on the ocean floor, could roll over and plunge into the Marianas Trench.

Rajni does her best to reassure me, all the while patting Eddie's head. My dog's essential personality won't be changed by the procedure, she says. Eddie will just become more "Eddie-ish" than he already is. His new ability to express himself in words will make aspects of his personality that could previously only be inferred much more apparent to me. Also, common elements of the canine psyche, including pack loyalty, protectiveness, and affection and empathy for the food provider, will be reinforced by their acquiring a rational basis within Eddie's mind, in addition to their instinctual, pre-verbal component. Eddie will stay Eddie, but he will become a "higher fidelity" Eddie. Okay, that doesn't sound bad.

But what about the physical risks? Oh, she says, the risks for serious harm or death are about the same as for a human's wisdom tooth extraction... very low. The military demanded very high levels of precision and success, and OM/SB has only heightened their standards now that they are servicing a civilian customer base, all of whom possess powerful emotional attachments to their companion canines. The procedure itself takes about forty minutes on average, and the animal is kept under protective observation during a subsequent three-day recovery period. The same exact type of system that will be installed in my apartment will be exhaustively tested with Eddie prior to my picking him up, to ensure that my dog will be fully acclimated to his new capabilities before we reestablish our shared lives together.

"Oh, there's one more thing," Rajni tells me. "You shouldn't worry about getting too nostalgic for Eddie as he was prior to the procedure. In order to experience the 'old' Eddie, all you need do is take him for a long walk away from your apartment, out of range of the enhancement computer's signal. He will then behave like a non-enhanced dog."

"Really? But doesn't all that shifting back and forth, from enhanced to non-enhanced to verbal again, make the dog confused? Or frightened? It sure as hell would *me*."

"The dogs do not question it. Ninety-nine out of a hundred dogs, when asked, cannot report noticing the change. Their brains are wired very differently than ours, you see. Most of their natural cognition is tied into their sense of smell, and that does not change after the enhancement. The verbal acuity we grant them remains very much secondary to their olfactory sense."

Eddie chooses that moment to shove his snout into my crotch. "That's, uh, good to know, I guess." I turn a little red as I shove him aside and ponder whether or not to remark that, Eddie's uncouthness aside, I *did* shower this morning. But I figure letting it go is best.

I leave Eddie to the tender mercies of OverMind/SoftBrain, sniffling just a little as we part. Three days! The prospect of three days without him, and my apartment instantly takes on the *feng shui* of a cell in a Siberian gulag. It doesn't help that Marvin calls me at least daily to spy on me, er, to check whether I've had any brilliant ideas for a fresh, hot advocacy campaign. During my three days of horrible anxiety — hardly five minutes go by without my glancing at the Eddie-cam app so I can see how he's recovering — I buy a little time and sympathy by telling Marvin my best friend is in the hospital undergoing a life-altering procedure. It's not like I'm lying.

Finally I get the call that I should head over to Alexandria to pick up my Eddie. The door between the clinic and the waiting room swings open, and Eddie bolts into the waiting room, happy as a kid on his first trip to Disney World. He jumps up, licks my face, then humps my leg, as if for old time's sake. There's a small spot near the top of his head where his fur has been shaved off, but that'll grow back fast enough. Apart from that, he seems completely unchanged.

In the auto-Uber, his tail wags faster and faster as we pass familiar neighborhood landmarks — the pocket park, the Indian-Cuban sidewalk café, the row of parking meters whose posts Eddie conscientiously marks as his territory every morning and evening. He bounds up the steps to my building's foyer like MacArthur returning in triumph to the Philippines, then haughtily enters the elevator as though it is his private conveyance.

I enter my apartment feeling like a budding sorceress. With the click of a few virtual buttons, I will transform a living being into something new — like Circe, but working in reverse, sort of. I fill Eddie's bowls with fresh, cold water and a can of his favorite wet food and place his favorite chew toys nearby, where he can see them. I want him to feel as relaxed and comfortable as possible for when I pull the big switcheroo.

I lean on my kitchen table, watching him eat, afraid to move. Is this the last time I'll ever see him this way in our home, so innocent, happy, and un-self-aware? Am I being selfish by robbing him of his protective cocoon of dumbness? Will he appreciate being transformed from *Of Mice and Men*'s dopey-happy Lennie to the neurotically wordy Woody Allen character from *Annie Hall*? Will he come to resent me? Hate me? Mournfully pine for the simple days of chasing his own tail and "good boy" pats on the head?

There's no going back, I tell myself. I don't have the option to simply never turn the equipment on. I signed a contract wherein I agreed to provide OverMind/SoftBrain with daily reports on Eddie's behavior and well-being. Plus, they'll be remotely monitoring him. They'll know if I leave their stuff off.

Take the plunge, Erika. Jump into the damn pool already instead of gingerly inserting yourself into the water inch by inch.

So I resolutely march myself into my bedroom, to the corner desk where they installed the enhancement computer and its router, and I switch everything on, including each of the half-dozen wall-mounted monitors that'll allow me to always read what Eddie is "saying", no matter where I am in the apartment (for when I'm too lazy to carry my cell phone around with me).

The system fires up in the time it takes for a single tail-wag. Before I've taken two steps to return to the kitchen area, the first of Eddie's brilliant ponderings appears on the bedroom's screens:

DELICIOUS DELICIOUS DELICIOUS! WANT MORE WANT MORE! WILL SHE OPEN ANOTHER CAN FOR ME? HOPE SO HOPE SO HOPE SO!

Okay... not Milton, exactly. More like a Fuddruckers hamburgers commercial on *Monday Night Football*. But really, what should I have expected? Besides, maybe Eddie's full new smarts take a while to sink in.

I creep into the kitchen to confront my transformed canine companion. Eddie looks up from his food bowl, which he has been vigorously licking clean. He cocks his head to the left and arches his brows, which has always been his way of signaling to me that he is either hesitant or confused about something. Has the familiar gesture taken on new layers of meaning? Does he intend to recite an ode to my beauty and is gathering his newly enhanced thoughts? I glance from Eddie's face to the screen mounted above my microwave:

MORE DELICIOUS? OPEN ANOTHER CAN? I AM GOODBOY! PLEASE?

"Yes, you *are* a good boy, Eddie," I say, "and Mommy loves you very much. But giving you too much food isn't good for you. You'll get fat. Worse, if I give you all the food you want, which is all the dog food in the tri-state area, your stomach will explode."

WHAT IS "STOMACH"?

(Holy shit! I'm actually having a *conversation* with my dog!)

(Holy shit! How the hell am I supposed to explain what a stomach is?)

"It's, uh, kind of like a bag inside your belly—"

BELLY SCRATCH? BELLY SCRATCH? FEEL GOOD VERY GOOD!

"Yeah, that's *right*, Eddie, your belly is where I give you those belly scratches you love. Well, like I was saying, your stomach is a bag inside your belly where your food goes after you swallow it. Then your body, it, uh, takes what it needs from the food, and what's left over goes through your intestines and comes out the other end as, uh, poo-poo—"

WHAT IS "POO-POO"?

Oh. Right. I've never used that term with him before. "It's *shit*, Eddie."

Cocks his head again. SHIT...? Straightens his head; his eyes widen and his tail begins wagging. OH! SHIT! DELICIOUS! WARM AND DELICIOUS!

Oh barf. Something I could've easily lived the rest of my life without being reminded of. I try to think of a way to tell him how absolutely disgusting that habit of his is and how I'll never let him kiss me on the lips again if he keeps it up, but then the screen lights up with more Deep Thoughts:

WHY IS MORE FOOD BAD? MORE FOOD MAKES MORE SHIT! SHIT IS WARM AND DELICIOUS! MORE SHIT GOOD!

"No, more shit is *not* good. More shit means I have to snatch it and bag it before you eat it, then find a trash can that isn't overflowing. Look, here's why I can't give you all the food you want. If you eat and eat and eat like you want, your stomach, the bag inside your tummy, will explode, and you will die."

Again with the cocked head: WHAT IS DIE?

This will never end, will it? Then I realize what I'm experiencing: life with a newly verbal toddler. I haven't spent much time around those creatures, but my cousin Vicky has, and she's related her war stories to me. Poor thing... her Neanderthal Christian husband has brainwashed her into servitude (big cock, big inheritance, big farm, big honking fancy pickup), and now she's stuck in Dubuque, Iowa with three young brats and a fourth on the way.

Well, at least I'm not dealing with diapers and tantrums. But how to explain death to a dog?

"To die... death... it means not existing anymore."

WHAT IS EXISTING?

"Being you, being Eddie, being able to smell stuff and eat stuff and play with your toys and nap in your dog bed. If you die, you don't get to do any of those things anymore."

HAVE TO SIT IN CRATE LIKE BADBOY?

"No, it's worse than that." Has he ever seen something that's dead? Something he'd remember? Well, yeah... there was that cat that got run over on P Street near the curb and the flattened corpse sat there until the turkey vultures started making traffic obstructions out of themselves. I had to yank Eddie away from it two mornings in a row, and we avoided P Street for the next week. "Do you remember the cat on the street that was flat and smelled bad and birds were eating it?"

NOT MOVING. WOULDN'T RUN WHEN I CHASED AFTER. SMELLED VERY BAD. VERY BAD. BUT WAS CURIOUS ABOUT IT ANYWAY.

"Well, that cat was *dead*. Not alive anymore. It won't move ever again, or eat, or play, or have kittens. It smells bad. Other things eat it. That's what *dead* is. If I let you eat all that you want, you will end up dead, like that cat... sort of."

I WILL SMELL BAD, VERY BAD? BIRDS WILL EAT ME?

"Yes. Only if I let you eat everything you want, though."

YOU WILL NOT LET ME DIE? EVER? I AM GOODBOY?

"Yes, Eddie, you are a very good boy. Mommy loves you, and Mommy will never let you die." A little white lie won't hurt him.

This has been exhausting. I need a break from Eddie the Dog Genius. I head for where his leash hangs on a hook next to the refrigerator and Eddie's tail begins wagging triple-time. "Hey, good boy, you want to go out for a walk?"

GOOD!GOOD!GOOD!GOOD!GOOD!!!

I take my phone with me and turn on the Eddie App so I can see what sort of range the enhancement computer's wi-fi has. We take the stairs. Eddie's thoughts stop appearing on-screen between the third story and second story landings. Until then, he'd responded in a begrudging but rational way to my verbal warnings not to yank me down the stairs in his eagerness to get outside. Once out of range of his smarts machine, though, only firm yanks from me on his choke collar dissuade him from pulling me down the steps faster than my legs can safely carry me. He's back to his old, semi-uncontrollable self.

It's just like a normal walk. Eddie gets frenzied-happy whenever there's another dog in sniffing range. Then I and that dog's owner do the semi-reluctant "no-don't-bother-that-dog/oh-what-the-hell" waltz, gradually yielding to our animals' desperate-ecstatic lungings toward one another. Lots of tail wagging and butt-sniffing. What do they get out of the latter? I'll have to ask Eddie once he's semi-literate again.

Eddie goes completely gonzo when we stroll within range of this one particular dog, a beautifully groomed miniature collie. It must be a she, and she must be in heat — her owner, a business frock-wearing Chinese lady in her fifties or sixties, very upright and proper, sternly waves us away when we're still a quarter-block distant, as though I'm a parole officer escorting a multiple-rapist. Eddie nearly asphyxiates himself with his choke collar trying to get close enough to mount the bitch (the collie, not the owner). I don't like the looks of that Chinese lady — she's probably packing Mace or bear repellant — so I decide to steer well clear of her and her sultry temptress. Eddie doesn't give up the fight, though. He pulls me off balance enough that I desperately grab hold of a parking meter to avoid planting my face on the sidewalk. Still, I win the war of wills. Eddie yaps pathetically as his would-be paramour turns the corner.

Enough walkies. My right arm feels like I've been in a tug-of-war match with the whole GW varsity crew squad. We return to the refuge of my apartment. But while I'm trying to dig my keys out of my purse, Eddie begins working out his sexual frustrations on my leg.

"Down, boy! Down!"

My cute Black neighbor emerges from the elevator carrying a pair of Trader Joe's-branded reusable grocery bags. He watches Eddie humping my leg and visibly suppresses a grin. Probably gay, definitely out of my swim lane in either case, but a favorite figure of fantasy, nonetheless. He continues watching my predicament as he unlocks his door. Now I'm completely humiliated.

"Get *off* me, you *bad* boy!"

Once I manage to extract my keys, I start half-heartedly beating Eddie with my purse. This alters his behavior not one iota. I thrust my door open and yank him inside. The screens on my walls are already emblazoned with Eddie's retort:

NOT BADBOY! NOT BADBOY! AM GOODBOY!

"No, you are a *bad boy!* You embarrassed the *shit* out of me, Eddie!"

He looks puzzled. WHERE IS SHIT? SHIT IS WARM AND DELICIOUS!

"Oh, let's not start that all over again. You are a bad boy. *Bad.* That lady with her collie looked like she was about to Mace us both — I mean, spray something that smells really, really awful on us. You are *not* to chase after girl dogs, do you understand?"

WHY? GIRL DOG WANT TO MAKE PUPPIES. I WANT TO MAKE PUPPIES. MAKING PUPPIES GOOD, VERY GOOD! WANT VERY MUCH! VERY VERY GOOD!

Oh, great... here I am, a proud atheist, and my dog turns out to be a conservative Catholic. How did he get the idea that having sex leads to making puppies, anyway? It's not like I've ever given him a birds-and-bees talk. Must've been all those *National Geographic* specials about the circle of life we've watched together.

CAN MAKE PUPPIES WITH YOU?

Eeww. Double eeww. Is that what he's been thinking all this time he's been humping my leg? I thought it was just an instinctual, reflex kind of thing, like scratching an itch behind his ear.

"No, Eddie... dogs and humans can't make puppies together. It doesn't work."

WHY?

"Because..." I nearly stumble into a half-assed explanation of the science of genetics and the millennia-old prohibitions against sexual contact between human beings and other species before I realize that saying even two sentences about any of that will result in an evening's worth of insistent questioning from Eddie. "Look, let's just drop this. Mommy doesn't want to talk about it. Mommy is getting a headache. Let's just watch some TV, okay?"

LADY AND TRAMP? LADY AND TRAMP?

"Okay, sure, *Lady and the Tramp* it is." I switch on Disney+ and tell my TV what Eddie wants to watch. A doggy rom-com. Just what I need, something to get Eddie in a romantic mood while he's curled up next to me on the couch. Whatever...

The humping persists, both outside and inside my apartment. It's tons more bothersome now than before Eddie's "enhancement", because at least before I could toss it off as, "Eddie's just a dumb dog. He doesn't know any better." He *still* doesn't know any better, but now he's smart enough to argue with me.

Yes, I know there's an obvious cure for this, a surefire way to get Eddie's mind off his gonads. Remove the gonads. It had been on my to-do list for months and months prior to our visit to OM/SB, but I always found a reason to put it off. I guess I was squeamish about it because in the back of my mind I had this notion that it would make Eddie somehow less of a dog — that it would be like dipping a cloth in turpentine and rubbing the smile off the Mona Lisa. What's the Mona Lisa without her smile? What's Eddie without his doggy balls? Wouldn't he get fat and lethargic and just lay around all the time? And what if I want to breed him someday? I mean, he's a mutt, sure, but you never know.

But now that he has the same I.Q. as some of the guys who stock the shelves at my local Trader Joe's, I'd feel *horrible* if I had his balls removed. I'd be a terrible, terrible person. I mean, he'd *know* something is missing, right? Wouldn't he, for sure? Even if I had Neuticles installed, those plastic phony gonads? He'd still know the difference. And he'd *hate* me, the same way a boyfriend or brother would hate me if I took him to the doctor's office under false pretenses, had him put under, then ordered the doctor to replace his real balls with plastic doohickeys. Just not an option, no way, no how.

Eddie's not my only problem. The pressures of my job have really mounted these past few weeks. I feel like the walls are closing in on me, tighter and tighter the closer that big confab gets. I still haven't had my brainstorm. Not even a brain-drizzle.

I need to get out. I've been hanging around the apartment because Eddie begs me to keep him company (the combination of

those sad-puppy eyes and DON'T LEAVE ME DON'T LEAVE ME
is irresistible) and I'm allowed to work from home. I've been
obsessively trolling the Internet for some social trend to pop and
provide me with my brainstorm, but it's been like wading through
an ocean of tapioca pudding. Blah-blah-blah. Nothing pops. I have
to get out and interact with real people, people with desires, people
with problems, people who might be experiencing some yet-
unaddressed form of systematic oppression that I can base an
advocacy campaign around — one that will persuasively tug at the
heartstrings and motivate the masses to open their wallets. Or, at
minimum, keep He-Who-Shall-Not-Be-Named happy.

I turn on The Food Network for Eddie, then bolt out the door
while he's distracted by vistas of marinating rump roasts. I make
the rounds of my usual spots — coffee shops, dive bars, funky art
galleries, hookah joints, rave houses, etc. — eyes and ears peeled
for anything that makes me stop short and go *hrrmmn?* But
there's nothing new, just tapioca same-old, same-old. Neck tattoos.
Neon earlobe implants. Stainless steel bondage hardware
piercings. Ginormous fatties with purple hair letting their belly
rolls and arm splooge spill out over absurdly abbreviated,
dangerously stretched slutwear. I've seen it all before. It's all old
news. None of it is in the least bit subversive... big corporations
coopted this stuff years ago and have been reselling it to the "cool
kids" long enough for most of it to be considered *retro*. No business
in America will refuse to hire you if you have "Fuck the Police"
tattooed on your forehead in a big orange font. Hell, they'll fall
over themselves asking you to pose for their "edgy" web ads.

My phone vibrates with the cheery chime that means an
incoming video call. I check the ID. Aww, hell... it's my boss in
Brussels. No privacy in this opioid-slide dance joint, and the funk-

ska-metal soundtrack means I can't hear myself scream. I duck into the bathroom and pick the stall farthest from the door.

Good choice, actually. The boss bawls me out until I think I'm gonna shit myself. He says my "inactivity," "laziness," and "lack of imagination and initiative" are risking relationships it's taken him thirty-five years to nurture. He insists a failure on my part will result in fascist Republicans taking over America. He tells me I'm risking his livelihood — and most definitely my own. I can't get a word in to defend myself; not that it would matter. He gives me one week to turn things around. One week — or he's severing my contract for non-performance.

He hangs up. I put my phone back in my purse. Then I lean over the toilet and throw up a triple skinny latte, a cran-orange scone, a spinach ciabatta panini, and half a bowl of the dance joint's complimentary caramel corn.

I arrive home a teary-eyed wreck, specks of vomit and nasty corn seeds flecking my favorite sweater, which means a dry cleaning bill. Eddie rushes over to me, his tail wagging wildly.

YOU'RE HOME YOU'RE HOME! HAPPY HAPPY HAPPY!!!

"Yeah, good to see you, too, puppy..." I snuffle.

WHY FOOD HAVE NO SMELLS? WHY? EDDIE FRUSTRATED!

What's he talking about...? Oh. The Food Network. "Food on TV doesn't have any smells, Eddie. Not yet, anyway..."

He scoots into the kitchen and brings me his leash in his mouth. Yes, I must be a responsible pet owner and walk my dog; it's been five hours since he's been out. I'll bet his bladder's bursting; is it possible to teach him how to use the toilet when I'm out? Whatever... a question for another day. But I am *so* not in the mood to be out in public. Fuck it. If I'm going to end up a bum out on the street by the end of next week, I might as well get in some practice for the new life. I grab my portable water bottle and fill it up with the dregs of a bottle of wine I find shoved into the back of my fridge, a remnant from an election-night dinner party I threw six months ago. So far as I know, walking one's dog while drunk isn't a crime.

The wine is on its way to becoming vinegar. Hell, it tastes better than vomit, that's for sure, and it does what I need it to do. I acquire a pleasant buzz on our walk. I'm tipsy enough that I don't mind that Eddie has taken on the role of scent detective, sniffing every square inch of sidewalk, every car tire, every street sign post, and the base of every parking meter between our building and the Au Bon Pain, searching, I presume, for clues as to where his lusty canine temptress has made off to. If I see that Chinese woman and her damned bitch, I'm letting Eddie off the leash. My sweet boy can go have himself some fun, even if he gets himself Maced.

I suck down the last drops from my "water bottle". Then I tie Eddie's leash to a bench and duck into Frederick's Liquors for another bottle of wine. In for a penny, in for a pound. I select the first clearance item that springs into view, a Merlot from Kentucky or some other bumfuck state (it's 70% off, and I'll probably be without an income soon). *Fuck* Mr. Mussels in Brussels (not his name, but that's what I like to call him). I'm having a party. For two. Me and Eddie. He can watch *Lady and the Tramp* four times in a row if that's what he wants. Whatever Eddie wants. Eddie is goodboy.

We retrace our steps back to the apartment almost precisely in reverse, Eddie pausing in each of the spots he paused before, diligently sniffing for that bitch. He must smell some trace of her, because he's getting excited. His red thingie pokes out of its sheath. It's the color of a ripe strawberry. And those balls beneath it aren't Neuticles. *Why does a dog lick his own balls?* I silently ask, swinging my wine bottle jauntily. *Because he can!*

I crack myself up.

Back in the apartment, I kick off my shoes, strip down to my under things, and flop on the couch with my bottle of 70%-off Merlot. I search the movie channels for a Sean Penn movie. He's a senile old fart now (he must be, right?), but in his prime, he was such a bad, bad boy. Yummy. The only thing of his I can find is *Milk*. Bad boy Sean as a gay San Francisco city councilman isn't *quite* what I was hoping for, but it'll have to do. At least it's not *The Angry Birds Movie*.

I feel Eddie shove his nose into my crotch. I push him away, but he persists. Hates it whenever he isn't the center of my attention. I try swatting him, but my aim is off. The effort makes my head swim. My unsteady eyes focus on the Eddie screen above the TV.

CAN MAKE PUPPIES WITH YOU? YOU ARE READY TO MAKE PUPPIES. I WANT TO MAKE PUPPIES. WANT VERY MUCH! YOU WANT TOO! YOU ARE READY READY READY TO MAKE PUPPIES!

Am I? Am I READY READY READY, like Eddie says? Do I smell different? Can Eddie tell? Do I have something in common with the Chinese lady's bitch? My closed-lipped laughing sends half my mouthful of wine up my nose and the other half down my windpipe.

When I get done coughing and gasping (which distresses Eddie terribly — he barks like we've been invaded by a platoon of Bloods seeking to have their way with me), I stumble off the couch and totter over to the calendar affixed to the fridge. Sure enough, Eddie's right. I'm ovulating. How about that? Not on the Pill. I mean, what's the fucking point? Never have a boyfriend again. Never...

And Eddie's humping my leg, knocking me against the fridge.

"Not my *leg*, you dummy! And not here! Oh, what's the use... c'mon. Follow me. We'll go someplace more comfortable. Where I don't fall down, at least."

Don't care about Sean Penn or Harvey Milky. What've they ever done for me? Eddie's my *pal*, my best friend. Best friend I'll ever have. I should make Eddie happy. Eddie is goodboy.

I semi-collapse on my bed, face down, then manage to wiggle off my panties. It's not easy, but I shift my legs under me and heft my butt into the air. This is how he wants it, right? Doggy style? "Come on, Eddie," I mumble into my pillow. "Mount me, puppy! I'm all yours!"

I sense his forepaws clutching my hips. Reminder to self: *clip his nails*. After a dozen tries or so, he manages to insert himself inside me. I think. He's not very big, certainly not in comparison to Geteye-from-Kenya. He's also not very coordinated, which I suppose I can't very well blame him for. Not only is he a quadruped, which I guess is a kind of handicap in a situation like this, but so far as I know (I didn't raise him from a puppy), this is his first time fucking *anything*. Apart from legs, but they don't count. Anyway, he doesn't last very long. He slams himself against my buttocks at most twenty times, and then I feel him shudder. And that's that.

How unsatisfying. Almost the worst I've ever had, but no one will ever take that crown away from eleventh grade's Dougie Krasner. I hope Eddie enjoyed himself, at least. I flip myself over and glance up at the screen on the opposite wall.

HAPPY HAPPY HAPPY!!! VERY GOOD VERY GOOD!!! EDDIE MAKE PUPPIES!!!

Yeah, he's all good.

Then he snuggles up next to me and licks my face. *Aww.* That's really sweet, much sweeter than what I'm used to, which is the guy rolling over and falling asleep right after he spurts. I look at the screen again.

ARE YOU HAPPY HAPPY? WANT YOU TO BE HAPPY HAPPY LIKE EDDIE!!!

It almost makes me cry. He wants *me* to be happy. *Me.* What a good, sweet doggy. But I'm like *so* unsatisfied...

Licks licks licks my face. Lickity-lick. Gives me an idea. A naughty idea. "Actually, Eddie, there *is* something you could do that would make Mommy very happy happy..."

I guide his head down to where I want it. Then I tell him exactly what I want.

The stamina of a dog's tongue is *amazing.*

Forty-five minutes later, I'm too blissed out to take any more. I tug on his collar and have him snuggle next to me.

I AM GOODBOY?

"You, Eddie, are a *very* good boy."

My hangover the next morning, on the War Atrocities scale, falls somewhere between the Rape of Nanking and the firebombing of Dresden. Three Advils, three Tylenols, and a Goody's Powder later, I crawl back into bed next to my bestest pal. Then I remember.

"Uh, Eddie, did we do what I *think* we did last night? Aside from watch a movie about Harvey Milk? Or was that a really, really *vivid* dream?"

WE MAKE PUPPIES. DO AGAIN?

Oh. Not a dream. Uhh... do I start screaming now? Do I get in the shower and use my shower massage for the rest of the morning to scour away every last molecule of dog semen? Do I find a priest who accepts confessions from non-Catholics? Do I castrate Eddie and get a hysterectomy for myself while I'm at it?

Or do I just chill? I mean, yeah, I pissed all over three thousand years of Judeo-Christian teachings about bestiality being a big no-no. But who got hurt? Nobody. Hell, there wasn't even a lack of consent. I've got computer logs of Eddie's very enthusiastic consent...

And then it hits me. *Wow.* Thanks to OverMind/SoftBrain's enhancement technology, this is the first time in history dogs (and maybe other animals, too, once the techies get around to it) are able to grant unequivocal consent, and likely be ruled competent to do so.

The possibilities...!

I've got to get Marvin on the phone.

MAKE PUPPIES? DO AGAIN?

I kiss Eddie on top of his head. "Not right now, sweetie. I've got a super-duper important call to make, and then I have to convince my head that it's not an accordion. But once that's taken care of...? Sure thing, you bad boy — I mean *good boy*."

Reaching for my phone, I realize my grigri charm bracelet fell off sometime during the night. I don't bother looking for it.

* * * * *

Virtually overnight, Eddie and I become the public faces of Doggy Style.

I'll admit, it's a little weird, being the Caitlyn Jenner of the cross-species love movement, but hey, worse things have happened to me. Mr. Mussels from Brussels paid for a whole new snazzy wardrobe for me, which I've needed for Eddie's and my photo shoot for *Teen Vogue* and our appearances on *Good Morning America*, *Meet the Press*, and Animal Planet's *Lifestyles of the Rich and Furry*.

Eddie is now the world's most famous dog. Far more famous than that bitch Lassie ever was. Taking walks with him around the neighborhood has become a total through-the-looking-glass experience. We've been mobbed by so many autograph seekers that Eddie sometimes hasn't been able to reach his favorite parking meter in time and has had to empty his bursting bladder on somebody's shoes (which then promptly go up for bid on eBay). And I can't count the number of knowing winks and smirks I get from other neighborhood ladies walking *their* dogs. Seems Eddie and I going public has given them permission to do what they've wanted to do all along. A few dog-owning neighbors with organizing experience have even approached me about putting together a Million Dog Walk on the Mall.

Today we've got a home visit scheduled with a reporter and photographer from *The Washington Post's* Style section. After that, Eddie and I meet with our legal team to discuss strategy. Our case is working its way through the appellate courts now. Mr. Mussels and Marvin figure we should land on the Supreme Court's docket sometime next spring. I'm very confident about our chances. Say what you like about the Supremes, they're consistently logical. One thing leads to another. I mean, look at their reasoning in *National Man-Boy Love Association vs. Barr*, the child adorers case. If children as young as five are legally competent to provide consent for gender-reassignment procedures — that had been established beyond dispute — how could they *not* be legally competent to provide consent for sexual relationships, interactions far less life-altering than gender-reassignment surgery? There's an ineffable penumbra of rights in there somewhere. So I think that after next spring, laws prohibiting bestiality, at least insofar as they apply to OM/SB-enhanced dogs, are toast, *burnt* toast.

In the meantime, our techie friends at OverMind/SoftBrain are working hard on various improvements, including electronic voice boxes for dogs that don't make them sound like K-9 Darth Vaders and more miniaturized, wearable enhancement computers that will allow dogs to retain their wits on walkies and car trips. I also understand that, in anticipation of next spring's Supreme Court hearing and a subsequent IPO, they are putting in tons of overtime to port the procedure to sheep and goats.

Ain't progress grand?

Throughout many of the Western democracies, there is a sense, shared among citizens across the political spectrum, that public servants no longer serve the public, that votes are increasingly meaningless because unelected bureaucrats make policy, and that societies' shepherds at all levels, corporate, government, and non-profit, are allowing their flocks to languish while pursuing self-aggrandizement and the accumulation and preservation of power and influence. Much of the distrust of the international environmental agenda stems from this, as well as suspicions of the morbidity projections behind the worldwide partial economic shutdowns necessitated by COVID-19 — shutdowns, originally sold to the public as short-term measures meant to "flatten the curve", that have now become indefinite in extent. Backlash against emergency measures grows as those measures are seen to be applied unevenly. PJ Higham lives in Australia, where in September 2020 a pregnant mother of two young children was arrested in her Ballarat, Victoria home, handcuffed in her pajamas in front of her kids, for the crime of incitement, which consisted of her announcing an anti-lockdown protest called Freedom Day in a Facebook post. Keep this woman in mind as you read Drainman's tale.

As the Earth Intended

PJ Higham

PERKINS couldn't tell whether the wind would kill him this morning or not. From his cell in isolation wing, the narrow window above his bunk sat too high for a view. The toughened glass had been streaked with rain for days, but this morning it allowed a sliver of sunlight to slash down across the cell floor. That was a change, at least.

But not a welcome one — sun meant clear skies... and clear skies meant wind... and the wind means — *stop it!* He pushed the thought away and closed his eyes, breathing deeply; shutting it all out.

The sun would not be ignored. Here it was again, warming his feet now; a cheery simpleton lolling its head at the door, grinning a trillion watt, gappy-tooth smile: *Hey-ar, how you doin', mistuh? Luvly day to die.*

He felt his stomach perform a little acrobat flip. The sunbeam began to climb the hill of his ankle. He watched, soothed by its unhurried inevitability. Soon the little beam would light the black forest of leg hair; after that, the flat expanse of shin bone loomed.

The Plains of Tibia.

The idea amused him. A wasteland in a Tolkien map, perhaps. Despite everything, his face formed the beginning of a smile. He decided he didn't need a window, he preferred this landscape. In this landscape, *he* was the warden. And the air was always... *still.*

Isolation had made him totally reliant on the Green Guards for the forecast. Outside, a gun-metal sky had drizzled rain the past few days while he'd waited the long wait here in holding cell one.

Before Isolation, he'd been imprisoned in General Population. Ceilings had been lower there, and the window beside his top bunk had framed a solitary elm beyond the sharpened wooden pickets that formed the prison walls. The tree had been his personal weatherman, updating him by leafy bulletin about wind strength and direction. He didn't care about the sunshine *per se*, only so far as clear conditions normally meant a breeze, a breeze that could freshen in the afternoon to a wind, a wind that — when it hit the minimum non-gust threshold of 26.5 knots — would carry his life away on it.

Perkins hadn't thought it possible when he was in there, but he missed Gen-Pop now.

After the trial, in the stuffy holding cell under the Justice Centre, while Perkins had awaited transportation, the court bailiff, Kavanagh, had gleefully informed him that the upstate facility he was destined for housed "the dregs." Kavanagh was from somewhere southern and it came out *draygs*. He'd then theatrically edited himself, shooting for impromptu, as though he hadn't recited it a hundred times before: "No, no, *worse* than that — the *ring around the bathtub* that the draygs wash in!" And Kavanagh had paused to enjoy the fruit of his words, scrutinizing Perkins, his captive audience-of-one. Perkins had made his face a stone, giving him nothing — which only kicked it up a notch. "No wait," Kavanagh continued. "Worser than that... you the ring around the can that they *sheeyt* in!" And he'd laughed a belly laugh at that one, absurdly pleased, his gut testing the tiny buttons of his uniform.

"The can that they sheeyt in," Kavanagh repeated, as though committing the routine to memory. He turned and sauntered away from the cell, shaking his head in wonder at his witticism.

Even a vulgar cartoon like Kavanagh could be right, though. Gen-Pop *did* house the *draygs*: stone-cold, unblinking killers, child rapists, even the self-styled Soul Saver himself — murderer of thirty-one sex workers.

And yet, even as a fresh face, Perkins had not been tormented or bullied by these *draygs*. The other prisoners avoided him wherever possible. Even amongst this select company, somebody had to be the lowest of the low. A few of them would see parole via indentured labor at the farm collectives; most of them would die in there, but he was going in a different direction... he would Reap the Wind, and that made the other inmates very, very uncomfortable.

But at least he hadn't been alone in General.

At least there he could tell what the weather was doing.

Perkins' final appeal against the sentence had been scheduled to go nowhere and arrived at that destination a week ago, lost and exhausted. As soon as the appellate court dismissed it, he'd been shunted from Gen-Pop to Isol, where they'd all been waiting out an unseasonal low that blew in from the gulf, turned into a rain depression, and sat weeping for the last six days.

Isolation. Last stop on the Terminus Line.

There was a background buzz of activity today. It made him queasy. From the corridor came the frequent wheeze of door hinges, followed by the wash of bright daylight. There was the occasional burble of low voices, but a different cadence from the usual — short practical sentences, not leisurely gossip.

He retreated to his private view. The sun was travelling through Leg Hair Forest, throwing spindly shadows against his once-tanned skin, wan now after eight and a half months of incarceration. Movement drew his gaze — two ants trundled through hairy thickets along a ligament ridge. He watched their single-minded progress for a time, enjoying it. "Slim pickings there, boys," he advised, and gently airlifted them out, one by one. He pressed his thumb against the cell wall and watched each ant march off to freedom.

His hand moved to the sunbeam. He waggled his fingers, making little sausage shadows waltz on the dirt floor. Not a single cloud had passed through it as yet and he wondered, again, what the wind was up to.

As ever, he smelt the guard before he saw her.

Perkins didn't need to look; he could now discern the difference between his male and female custodians at-a-whiff. Perfumers referred to them as notes; he thought of it as a different essence in the same odor, or, variations on a theme: the males had a base-note that was ripe and gamey, the females a tarter top-note. One miserable basin wash per fortnight for body *and* clothes would do that to you. That, and the riotous knot of underarm hair that harbored the fugitive funk always ensured that his nose became aware of them first. To be a Green Guard (or "Pickles", as the inmates called them) you had to be ideologically pure — everything from your inner belief system to your outer appearance: no excessive grooming or makeup, no depilation at all; everything just As the Earth Intended. Including 'natural' — but still nasty — body odor.

He lifted his head off the bunk. It was a Pickle all right, the natural brown-green of her woven hemp uniform nearly indistinguishable from the olive green wall. When they patrolled at night, under the dim lamps, the walls looked as though they had sprouted faces.

This one was nice to him. She carried a wooden bowl with one of those lumpen masses that impersonated food. Salt-rimed circles marked her armpits, and Perkins thought about sedimentary rock layers and tree-ring dating. He deduced that the full fourteen days had passed since the last time the water had been doled out into her washbasin.

Still, he was pleased to see her. He rolled off the bunk and dropped the latch on his side of the meal-lock. "Hey," he said. "Sunny one." He tried to sound relaxed. Like they were acquaintances becalmed in a bus queue. *Hey, sunny one,* as though the day was a passing folly, one of thousands yet to come.

This was as close as he got to the guards and Perkins searched her face for something — *anything*.

Nothing.

"Sunny." She just repeated it back, tonelessly, like an intercom announcement. "Possible late storms. Winds ten to fifteen knots in the morning, building to thirty-five late in the afternoon and evening." She punched the tray through the slot and looked at him, dead-eyed. "Anticipated non-gust base load of thirty-one. It's on."

She'd been nice to him, this one — not actively hostile at least — occasionally giving him extra food, so her blank expression now as she delivered the news was a sucker punch to the solar plexus. *It's on.* He felt his stomach falling away and he staggered, only just catching the toilet seat edge to steady himself.

"Visiting time noon till one. Your nomination has been notified."

Nomination. Through the swirl of nausea it took some time to decode the term. *Sarah.* But would she come? The thought of his daughter steadied him.

The intercom announcement continued: "Last position, five p.m." With that, she turned on a heel and strode away.

The cold shock of the words numbed him. He rummaged through them and realized that something was missing — a detail — something he had grasped at in the vigils of the night... in the primal hours, when the enormity of it settled over him as tightly as the drawstring of a cloak; when his thoughts kept this looming day turning over and over and over, like a dog returning to its vomit. A meteorological detail, a triviality really, that had grown — metastasized — into importance. But it was all he had left to hope for now; a crumb for a starving man.

He called after her, "What direction?"

She stopped.

He'd confided in this guard once, back in General, this thing that he'd hoped for, this detail. They'd been sharing a brief oasis of normality amidst the craziness. It was late and she was doing the last look-in. New Year's Eve, maybe? If not, another holiday where the barriers drop a little. Christmas probably, because he'd asked her what she was hoping for. He'd asked her and then, out of politeness, or reflex, she'd asked him back — probably expecting him to say "a pardon" or some other cheap jailhouse humor. But he'd told her plainly what he wanted and *why* he wanted—for Christmas, for the New Year, whichever. She made no comment and that was the end of it, but as she left, she said, "Goodnight, Perkins."

Just a pleasantry, but to him it was a two-word benediction. It remained the only time that anyone had spoken his real name in there.

Now she turned to face him and he saw that the mask was lowered and there was a human being present again. "My shift is finishing now." The intercom tone was gone too — her voice was normal, soft even. She came back to stand outside his cell. "I've got two days off. I didn't want to be... I never like to be here when..." She looked directly at him and it was just one human being with another once more; they were back at that oasis, one last time. "First thing I'm going to do is get out of these." Her hands swiveled in at the wrist like pinball flippers, indicating the uniform. "Next I'm—" her eyes flicked left, right, then a stage whisper "—I'm going to have a very long wash with some water I've been saving." She grew serious, staring through a point over his left shoulder. He sensed she was meticulously sifting and weighing words. Finally she looked him in the eye. "Merry Christmas, Perkins, you got what you wanted," she said. "It's a westerly. I hope it's a *glorious* one." She stared at him a beat longer, then down to the polished tiles of the corridor. The guard seemed (*was it possible?*) a little ashamed. She turned, moving briskly again, rounding the corner.

He called after her, "Hey, come back." He had a wild urge to know her name but she was gone, one of her shoes squeaking its way into silence.

A westerly. Thank God, a westerly wind.

They would be required to position him facing that way, towards the bay—and he felt a little giddy, like a small-stakes lottery winner.

Last position, five pm.

He would see his sunset at the end.

His first memory was the water. Like a cell in a briny Paleozoic soup, his remembered life had begun there.

Harbour Beach: A two-and-a-half-year-old in bright green trunks and a buttoned vest like a dapper turn-of-the-century bather. All that was missing was the handlebar moustache. There was a beagle-eared photo of it somewhere: his tiny elf-self suspended between mom-mom and a visiting aunt, paddling in the foamy line where the last of the waves slid back to the sea before reinforcements arrived, bubbling and hissing over the top.

But mostly it was a feeling — the tide reclaiming the sandy supports under his feet, excavating his little arches with secret eddies and mini whirlpools, tickling him and sending squeals of laughter pealing up into the sky.

His earliest memory was that undertow, and the endless seething ocean.

He realized he'd fallen asleep when the crowd noise reached him just before noon. It trickled down from the window slit, raising gooseflesh on his arms when he figured it out. The voice of the sentencing judge floated back to him:

You have eaten of their children's future, so the people shall bear witness.

They had televised the first few; until viewer numbers sank, like the latter moon landings.

To hold your life liable for the crimes committed against their Earth.

He'd watched the first one, along with a fifth of the world's population. The guy's name was Carlos Galbraith, a big-time international dealer in remnant fossil fuel. He was a Trivial Pursuit question now, the only one ever to appear in two categories: yellow pie-piece history and green pie-piece science.

And see the Machineries of Justice visit their judgement upon you...

He'd switched it off when they'd swung the guy into position. But he had seen the crowd shots. It was a fury of papier-mâché and puppetry; fluttering banners scrawled with "rape" and "murder" besieged the central platform, as though a hastily raised medieval army had arrived in the field; the whole of it scored by a wild heartbeat of pagan drumming. Stilt walkers strode through the heaving mass like soldier ants, and in its swelling thousands, it had slipped its humanity like an ill-fitting mask.

... may Our Earth grant mercy at the ending, and in that mercy accept your body into its embrace to hold you fast; returning you to it, From the Soil, Unto the Soil; As the Earth Intended.

A Pickle interrupted his reverie.

The guard was carrying an old split-spined book in one hand and some water in the other, and he looked as bored as any government clock-watcher anywhere. He exchanged the water container for the untouched breakfast in Perkins' meal lock; dragged a chair up against the corridor wall opposite. Before he sat, he produced a tiny key and unlocked the hinged metal cap on the container with a deft, practiced hand.

Perkins wished they could have finally eased up on that. Whatever was in the caps, it made the water taste metallic, like teeth fillings. And of course the sight of them stoked the smoldering resentment that set him on this path in the first place. The SecuraCaps were just another bit-player in the Great Scarcity Pantomime that kept the permanent state of emergency in place.

He crouched to open his side of the hatch. It was the second of his three allotted serves for the day, but he wasn't thirsty... and unless the weather suddenly changed, he would not see the evening one.

He slid the container nearer, staring into the liquid. He stared into it the way that tired people stare into open hearth fires late at night.

Refracted through the water, the bars and the corridor outside began to bend and warp.

Air, Fire, Earth... *Water.*

Who could have imagined a classical element, the sole precondition for all of life, would become death sentence?

He lifted the water closer to his face until it filled his field of vision...Such a simple thing — one oxygen atom, two hydrogen — made so complex. His earliest memory was the water

and here it was, at the end.

The first government TV commercials "suggesting" modifications to water usage aired when he was still a boy — five, maybe six years old.

Wastewater: A Waste of Water the slogan declared, or something ponderously plodding like that.

He remembered the cartoon clearly though — he loved cartoons, *any* cartoons, and this one starred a big, sad-faced drop of water crying little teardrops that cried even tinier drops into a villainous strip drain, its metal slits grinding and gnashing like slavering teeth.

Then came the notorious *Guideline 1!-2!-3!*, the decree that reduced the entire population's bathroom habits to those of potty-training toddlers: Number 1's, no flush at all. Number 2's, a flush every second day. Number 3, a three-minute shower every third day. Most everyone ignored it, apart from the most committed, so *Guideline 1!-2!-3!* hardened into *Law 123*; but by then it was too late. Investigations showed most people cheerfully ignored it, particularly the odious Law 2. Despite even more animated characters press-ganged into service — in one case a ridiculous singing toilet warbling, "Put a Lid on It" to the tune of some old song — compliance levels flat-lined.

He twisted the SecuraCap off the container, flung it to the dirt floor (there'd be a sanction for that under *EarthCrimes*, but what could they do; kill him twice?), and slowly swirled the water around, and around, as he traced his way along the path that led here to Holding Cell 1...

Mandatory Micrometers were the next step: tiny, tattletale bookkeepers on every faucet, dishwasher, washing machine — and toilet — in the home; with real-time reporting sent to the Department.

As a "service". To help you "better manage" your water use. As though you'd made a choice...

Compliance was, again, mainly observed by the inner city areas, so then the fines came. The middle class and the rich paid them easily, creating years of agitation over the "water-gap between rich and poor." So along came the *means-tested* fines, with second-strike property confiscation... allowing the Party to proclaim loudly how confiscated homes bolstered social housing stock, while quietly adding more people to the wait list because their housing had been... confiscated.

That one bit. Bit hard.

But for every problem comes a solution: enter the black market 'parallel plumbing' boom, with meter bypasses, split pipes, and all sorts of shenanigans.

Meanwhile, the continent-wide drought had stretched into its eleventh year. The Big Parch was the battering ram that opened the floodgates to all of the nano-regulation.

Then, finally, the *EarthCrimes Act*.

That was eighteen years ago now, and it changed everything.

Eighteen years; a cosmological eye blink.

He tipped out a careful palmful and looked at it.

Two hydrogen atoms in covalent bond with one oxygen. *Oh, to be raised from such humble roots... to become so* deified.

Perkins splashed the water on his face and under each arm, drawing a scowl from the guard.

Visiting hour came, and passed.

He consoled himself that Sarah now lived fulltime with her mother, 150 miles away. Private transport was the preserve of millionaires and Party members these days. And the decrepit public buses? They were no option for young girls either...overcrowded Hogarthian Nightmares-on-Wheels, they were.

He almost believed his rationalizations.

The sun seemed to abandon him too, beginning its climb on the opposite side of the cell. There was a spot about two feet up from the beam where a head-sized patch of flaking paint had curled away. He estimated that was the point at which they would come for him.

The noise outside was a constant din now, so he could largely tune it out, apart from the intermittent rattle of bongos and some faintly perceptible bad rhymes (*sweet beets, turmeric and ginger...something...something... a taste to linger!*) from a hawker who seemed to have set up his juice stand directly outside the wall nearest his cell.

Isol prisoners were allowed one personal item. He picked his up and a grin ghosted his mouth. The photo's soft green background was blurry but he knew where it was taken. Sarah was in uniform so that meant a weekend...which made the green blur Paul Erlich Memorial Park. (She used to call it Some-Dead-Guy Park; back when her bubbling, snorting laughs were never far away, a pot of mirth always on the boil; when he was once a wise father who could do no wrong.) It started as their little daddy-daughter ritual, every Saturday morning after Green Guides. Non-dairy ice cream and always the middle bench closest the 'art'. They'd been doing the routine so long he remembered when her legs would kick the air beneath it.

There was a population clock installation there, running backwards like a timer. Some Party sculptor in love with sledgehammer rhymes had titled it *Destination Salvation* but Sarah never tired of the thing. The clock face was set into an earth globe mounted on the shoulders of a serene Atlas. It commemorated the milestone reached four years earlier when worldwide deaths had overtaken births... after the *Baby Lotteries* and the *3 Score+10 Clinics* achieved scale in the developing nations, whittling away at both ends of the life arc. There was a quiet joy in her eyes as the numbers counted down and her ice cream shrank. Joy, along with that variety of fierce, idealistic hope borne and brandished only by teenagers, he'd noticed.

He came out of the memory, gripping the photo frame like a drowning man. It was too vivid — a wave of emotion rose in him and he distracted himself, checking the guard sitting suicide watch in the corridor; placed there should a particularly innovative prisoner locate something to kill themselves with. The guard's face was buried in the old book. Perkins tried to make out the title... something about composting?

You'll be compost soon, a thought gibbered.

He composed himself, concentrating on his breathing. When his heart slowed, he allowed himself to return to the frame, thumb absently sliding over the satiny surface of the print. The detail really jumped off the paper. He'd burned the last of his monthly resource credits on it, choosing the semi-gloss on a heavy paper tock.

Taken just before they left the park with the battered old camera-phone, his daughter looked quite grumpy sitting there on her own. He had attempted one of them together first — holding the phone aloft to fit them both in — but she'd stuck her hand out like he was paparazzi so he took one of her on the brown bench surrounded by the soft green of the privet hedge, a good hi-resolution — if a little grumpy — shot. Even the rows of merit badges stitched into her olive tunic were clear and sharp: he recognized the bright yellow S.V.C. lettering, the fractured egg sigil resting in the 'V', like an eggcup. (With his grudging parental co-signature she had contracted for Sterilization Volunteers Corp at age eight, but she'd had to wait — with typical Sarah *impaaaatience* — till her eleventh birthday for Procedure Day.)

Next to the S.V.C. badge, the cartoon figure of a cheery ant stood at attention, saluting — her pledge never to harm a single animal, no matter how big or small (or existent, even) its cerebral cortex; and beside that...

Beside that, separate from the others, in prime position at the top right, an understated new badge — green thread upon the green tunic — had appeared that day.

He wasn't exactly sure what the badge, smaller than the others, signified. She'd been laughing about something, so he picked it as a good time to ask. She'd been laughing but the mood changed as soon as he questioned her, like a cloud racing over the sun.

"Oh that. Nothing, just..." Her voice trailed off. Desultory. Petulant.

She picked up a pebble and lobbed it into the sculpted 'pond' that marooned the centerpiece Atlas and the massive clock she hefted. It hit a brass duck with a hollow *tang* noise, then clanged thinly against the painted tin of the 'water'. "GOT it!"

"What's it for?" And he'd leaned closer, but she'd leaned away the same distance. "Let me see." He leaned further, as did she, making them resemble opposite poles on a pair of magnets.

"Get out, it's nothing!"

"Well it must be something, because it's on the—"

"Stop it you're always asking questions." She screwed up her face in irritation. "Why do you always have to watch everything I do? They give them to everybody anyway so there's no big deal okaaay."

"It's stitched to the front of your tunic — on the top row, mind — so evidently it *is* a big deal. And Diana doesn't have one, or Bo...Boedicia."

"BOW-*da*-SEE-*ar*! How many times?"

"All right, okay..." He'd kept his voice light, trying to chase away this teenage storm that had blown up out of a clear blue sky. He knew, even as his words fell to the ground, leaden and airless, he knew that it was of no use — everything he said or did lately seemed to be a provocation... And so he doubled down, "Look, I *know* where you won it." Pure speculation, and yet the ploy got a reaction, confirming his supposition; despite herself, Sarah's head half-turned toward him, only her eyes staying aloof in the middle-distance. He stated it as casually as he could, "It was on WilEd, wasn't it?"

She'd been selected, along with her two best friends — from hundreds of thousands of Green Guides country-wide — to attend Wilderness Education Camp.

"Is it for navigating, or orienteering, or something?"

She flashed him the patented Sarah "You're Such an Idiot" look.

He ignored it. "Come on. Tell your old man."

Her words came back emotionless, but a tight fury hid in the spaces between them. "Can we *go* now?"

"All right, but..." He raised the old phone. "Let's get a pic first."

She'd been more secretive in the months leading up to his arrest. Secretive and resentful. He'd put it down to the swirling hormone-storms of puberty, and like all storms it must pass.

Why do you always have to watch everything I do?

He'd thought about that little pride-of-place patch a lot during those long night time vigils in the cell, still unsure what the carefully sewn green threads depicted; unwilling to make the distinction between the two options.

He placed the frame back on the shelf.

It was either a telescope, or a spyglass.

The container of water proved too tempting.

He checked the guard — he was buried deep in the wonders of worms and the charm of chicken shit — and leaned over to pick up the black Sharpie that they'd made a great show of giving him to write a final note to his daughter.

His gaze flicked to the guard again.

Still buried.

He began to mark, in a neat, thin hand, tiny line markings and measurements up the side of the glass. Beside the markings he carefully printed, "It Never Rains But It Pours." When he finished, he signed it with a flourish: "Drainman"; then dated it, like a confession.

He hoped they would find it later. After they had finished with him.

A small, sweet "fuck you" from the grave.

Defiance, layer after slow layer of it, had built in Perkins. Like a shell-trapped oyster soothing an irritant, he'd led many small household rebellions to buffer himself against the regime: keeping a reading light burning past 8 p.m. on weeknights, the bedroom window smothered by thin blankets; allowing a little water from the community pump spill over his hands, washing them, as he received his household drinking measure, drawing rebukes and threats from others in the queue but never an official sanction. However, it was the item he was most careful about, the simple rain gauge kept hidden in a slot behind the meter box on the old garage at the back of the house, that finally sank him.

The Big Parch had broken long ago, as droughts do; but many things remained rusted in place. The regime could not control weather, but it *could* control data. Rainfall figures vanished from meteorological reports at the same time that rain gauges and barometers appeared on the *Earth Crimes* Proscribed List; although you could still watch the rivers break their banks and your gutters overflow... unlike the reservoirs, which never seemed to get more than five percent filled, according to the Community

Safety Bulletins constantly blaring in the streets through the ramshackle, citywide P.A.

He'd water-skied as a child beneath the dam that supplied the city. Standing up on those two slippery planks had been his first major life accomplishment; then soaring over the jumps when he gained confidence, free as a flying fish.

One warm, spring morning, while the CAR*bon* Passports had still operated, he'd braved an hour-long queue downtown to have the thing stamped, then packed Sarah and a picnic lunch into the ancient station wagon and driven out to the dam in effort to explain his childhood passion to his daughter, who'd never seen a boat in real life and imagined them as a man-spawned species of belching, wilderness-gobbling, sea-beast.

The trip started in high spirits — it was close to his marriage breakup, so he was grateful for that, but nearing the dam, their station wagon rounded a bend on the approach road and they found themselves at gunpoint.

Later, he'd heard that a military base had been erected around the dam, but at the time he never got close enough to confirm the rumor. After checking that the passport stamp matched his fuel gauge and the approved route, the tetchy soldiers had turned their car around at the barricaded checkpoint, still some miles away from the water — which meant a fruitless return trip... But they took their time on the way home — using the saved mileage to stop by an abandoned mining settlement and stuffing their pockets with souvenir nuggets of coal — on schedule to beat the curfew, when, on the outskirts of the city, they'd run out of fuel. Coverage on the crumbling network had become increasingly patchy, but the sky was still crisp and clear, and with just two credits remaining on the phone, the call connected straight away. He'd argued with the passport people, but they denied any miscalculation. He and Sarah made the picnic hamper stretch until after midnight, playing shadow puppets by candlelight, until the black economy tow truck operator deemed it safe enough to make the callout. The day hadn't turned *all* bad; Sarah, who was still quite little then, had thought it all very exciting at the time, taking both their minds away from the marriage breakup. But, in later years, any memory of it would induce much eye rolling and head shaking.

In this environment, the act of measuring rainfall became an act of sedition.

And of freedom.

Perkins had fashioned a makeshift gauge, an old champagne flute with tiny — almost undetectable — calibrations.

Almost. His mind moved to Sarah again, his smart-as-a-whip, badge-collecting daughter, but he quickly derailed *that* thought train.

The illegal gauge had — somehow — brought the Green Guards to his door, the functionary in charge wearing the undyed hemp uniform and a face-splitting grin of naked triumph; the velvety 5 a.m. dark made his mouth seem an open wound in the center of his beard. The beard was black and long, and it was untrimmed — As the Earth Intended. Slap a conical hat on top and he would not have been out of place leading prayer on the *Mayflower*. He clutched a warrant for an Eco-Audit like a Bible, and on the rare occasion he spoke, his voice came in grimly sober Cotton Mather tones.

The search lasted three days. The warrant was for the gauge — serious enough — but it brought all the stacked dominoes of his One-man Resistance crashing down. The news reports described the scene as "a Russian Dolls house of enviro-crime." One thing led to another; that thing went somewhere else; which exposed another thing, and on and on. They'd minded each other's kids and even pooled resources to share Christmas dinners together, but when his neighbors were interviewed, he had apparently become "real quiet" and "kept to himself a lot." He couldn't blame them; their proximity meant they'd be receiving their own audits soon enough. On the second day, the reporters doing breathless camera pieces in the street outside reveled in "a grisly discovery in the house of horrors": the investigators had found his basement freezer full of black market meat. They displayed a frozen T-bone for the cameras. (One network had even inset a stock photo of a Brahman bull in the corner of the screen, as though of the victim in happier times.) When they sieved his garbage, they'd retrieved his entire Insect Protein Allowance for the month, still in its wrapping, unopened. (The cameras lingered on the bulging bag. A slow zoom revealed it to be the July IPA, "Krunchy Krickets. *Dewinged 'N Buttery!'*) The local rag, pushing their own angle, had been calling him "Mr. Freeze", because of the little wall-mounted air conditioner he'd clandestinely wired into the solar p's. It didn't catch on.

However, it was the water felonies that brought it all undone. The forensic plumbers discovered an undeclared functioning faucet hidden beneath a hibiscus bush in the backyard that fed a camouflaged garden of fugitive tomatoes, lettuce and potatoes. It was self-evident he'd hoarded them for private use, not public good. When the diggers were brought in, they uncovered an elaborate network of drains that harvested runoff water and returned it to a small underground tank. The grainy footage from the pin camera they snaked through the pipes made the TV news too. Cotton Mather, in one of his more hyperbolic daily press briefings, had described the find as like "uncovering the enemy's troop tunnels." Because water fell under the People's Resources section of the penal code, the drainage system and the champagne flute-rain gauge — also brandished for the cameras by Cotton Mather — were both deadly. Both capital offences under *EarthCrimes*.

The local newspaper's moniker didn't catch on, but the networks' did: throughout the trial and in the build-up to the sentencing, his birth name, Richard Josef Perkins, became interchangeable with "Drainman".

The ceremonial wind farm built for executions was on the highest of the five hills that framed the city.

There were eleven turbines in a wedge-shape with the line of their footings clutching at a cliff face like iron toes at the lip of a granite diving board. They were leviathan, the crosses of the propellers shrouded behind clouds whose afternoon shadows smothered the prison with shade. Their thrusting columns propped up a symbolic political statement constructed to dwarf and intimidate all others — an anti-Acropolis; a place of preaching, not learning.

The heavily modified scaffold-turbine stood in the middle of this dread line; the five at each side like brethren mourners dressed in white. It was dyed red. The surrounding land fell away from this jutting Golgotha towards the city, as though the hill had dropped supplicant shoulders in defeat long ago.

There was a platform approximately halfway up the scaffold turbine, stainless steel against the crimson dye. At the center of it lay a bound figure, arms and legs splayed into position. Minutes before, the platform had hosted a maelstrom of activity: calibrations, adjustments, measurements, barked instructions. Now it was deserted. Silent. Occupational Health & Safety stipulated a 50-yard exclusion zone for everyone: scrutineers, the official party, state-appointed witnesses, and the thousands of revelers.

Everyone, except for Richard "Drainman" Perkins.

A siren howled. Quiet settled over the crowd.

The gurney he was strapped to shuddered. The central core of the platform separated from the outer ring and began to inch upward, jerkily at first, and then with a smoothly tuned motion. The terror, having ebbed a little while they fussed over him, bloomed again, before an oddly distant feeling of acceptance came to him.

Not a person had addressed him since the nameless guard that morning, not even the security detail wearing stone faces that arrived at his cell to fetch him. He longed to hear a voice at the end, any voice, as long as it was near to him, and kind. He spoke aloud, his voice diminished to a matter-of-fact croak.

"There's a storm coming."

From his great height, he could see the spiraling cumulonimbus building west out over the bay; the hot day made the seawater ascend into towering, bruised thunderheads. The sough of the 30-knot winds gusting ahead of it drowned in the lunatic keening of the turbines, unbaffled for maximum effect. The noise of them powered a *thrumming* vibration in his back teeth that made his ears itch maddeningly.

The inner platform came to an abrupt halt in the penultimate gearing position.

Scrutineers watching on closed-circuit checked and rechecked data feeds. He felt their careful last minute calibrations like a delicate caress in his shoulders and back.

His head remained clamped but he could twist it a little, taking in the expanse of the horizon entire. He had longed for beauty at the finish, and it *was* beautiful. *Glorious*.

He squinted against it. The whole world appeared combustible. The dying sun had shot orange bullet holes through the purple cloud banks for him. It had torched the ocean itself, turning it a darker orange, like burning diesel.

The platform jerked to life once more. The gearing in the ratchet began to wind through to the last position.

At the end, while he still had voice, he cried out that which remained most precious to him... He shouted it up into the vastness of the sky—

"*SAR*–RAHH!"

—a failed talisman snatched away by the *whomping* blurred arc of the propeller.

The monstrous gale kicked up by the blades pummeled his face, pushing it around like dough, as though he were skydiving upwards. The power of it blew his eyelids open, forcing him to watch. The sound of it filled the world. Finally, in a whiteout of the senses, thought fled from it — an abandonment, and a mercy.

Far below Richard Josef Perkins, seven thousand people moved as one beast and a great shiver went through it as the blades found their mark.

A storm came after.

The soil on the hill top, sodden by the previous days' downpours, could absorb no more. The arterial blood collected in small viscous pools there, like offerings, and the rain strafed their surface, gently, then with a swelling rhythm. They melted together, extending cautious watery fingers that found the beginnings of the gradient. The tiny tributary trickled down and over the footings of the turbine, gathering pace, pushing out the shredded feathers of sparrows and an osprey, one by one, like funereal longboats on a crimson flood tide.

At the bottom of the five hills, the water joined countless other feeder streams that became one fat, rolling wave. The earthen levees replacing the concrete and steel were swept away, allowing the floodwaters to surge unchecked through low-lying residential areas.

Four hundred and eighty-seven people drowned before the deluge reached the sea.

The following morning's public safety announcements blaring through the streets made no mention of them, only that the afternoon showers had made no impact on water levels in the dam.

Contributor Notes

IAN CREASEY lives in Yorkshire, England. His short fiction has frequently appeared in science-fiction magazines such as *Asimov's* and *Analog*. A collection of his SF stories, *The Shapes of Strangers*, was published by NewCon Press in 2019. For more information, visit his website at iancreasey.com.

ANDREW FOX's books include *Fat White Vampire Blues*, winner of the Ruthven Award for Best Vampire Fiction of 2003; *Bride of the Fat White Vampire*; *Fat White Vampire Otaku*; *Fire on Iron*, a Civil War dark fantasy; and *The Good Humor Man, or, Calorie 3501*, selected by Booklist as one of the Ten Best SF/Fantasy Novels of the Year for 2009. In 2006, he won the *Moment* Magazine-Karma Foundation Short Fiction Award. His stories have appeared in *Scifi.com* and *Nightmare.com*, and his essays have been published in *Moment* and *Tablet* Magazine. Prior to editing *Again, Hazardous Imaginings*, he published a collection of his own politically incorrect science fiction, *Hazardous Imaginings*. His next novel, *The Bad Luck Spirits' Social Aid and Pleasure Club*, revolves around an alternate Hurricane Katrina and will be published in February 2021 by MonstraCity Press. He lives in Northern Virginia with his family, and he can be reached at fantasticalandrewfox.com.

KARL K. GALLAGHER is a systems engineer, currently performing data analysis for a major aerospace company. In the past he calculated trajectories for a commercial launch rocket start-up, operated satellites as a US Air Force officer, and selected orbits for government and commercial satellites. Karl lives in Saginaw, TX with his family. He writes both science fiction (the *Torchship Trilogy*) and fantasy (*The Lost War*). The *Torchship Trilogy* was a finalist for the Prometheus Award for best Libertarian SF novel of 2017. His books are available on Amazon and Audible. New releases are announced on kelthavenpress.com.

J. L. HAGEN is a retired non-profit executive. He is currently finishing a collection of short stories for publication this year set in the fictional community of Loyale in Ojibwa County, Michigan. A graduate of writing programs at the University of Michigan Residential College and the University of Chicago, he grew up in Upper Michigan. He and his wife Joy currently commute between Lake Michigan and Tampa Bay.

PJ HIGHAM lives in Sydney, Australia. He loves his wife, quite likes his cat. He believes in a species-appropriate diet but is basically fueled by coffee, red wine, steak (rare) and dark chocolate (95% cacao — any less is too sweet). Some may find it interesting that he only follows one "sport", Mixed Martial Arts; that he once took Sir Donald Bradman to a (very long) lunch; and considers crossing the Southern Ocean — ultimately the Antarctic Circle — while steadfastly wearing shorts and flip-flops until well past the first iceberg and penguin sightings to be one of his greatest accomplishments.

DAVID WESLEY HILL is an award-winning fiction writer with more than thirty stories published in the U.S. and internationally. In 1997 he was presented with the Golden Bridge award at the International Conference on Science Fiction in Beijing, and in 1999 he placed second in the Writers of the Future contest. In 2007, 2009, and 2011 Mr. Hill was awarded residencies at the Blue Mountain Center, a writers and artists retreat in the Adirondacks. He studied under Joseph Heller and Jack Cady and received a Master's in creative writing from the City University of New York. Currently he is working on a sequel to his well-received historical fiction novel, *At Drake's Command*.

LIAM HOGAN is an award-winning short story writer, with stories in *Best of British Science Fiction 2016* & *2019*, and *Best of British Fantasy 2018* (NewCon Press). He's been published by *Analog, Daily Science Fiction*, and Flametree Press, among others. He helps host Liars' League London, volunteers at the creative writing charity Ministry of Stories, and lives and avoids work in London. More details at happyendingnotguaranteed.blogspot.co.uk.

FIONA M. JONES is a creative writer living in Scotland. Her published work in short stories and micro-prose is linked through @FiiJ20 on Facebook, Twitter and Thinkerbeat.

CLAUDE LALUMIÈRE (claudepages.info) is the author of more than 100 stories. His books include *Objects of Worship* (2009) and *Venera Dreams: A Weird Entertainment*, which was a selection of the Great Books Marquee at Word on the Street Toronto 2017. His work has been translated into multiple languages and has been adapted for stage, screen, audio, and comics. Originally from Montreal, he now lives in Ottawa.

LIU XIAODAN is the pseudonym of a Chinese national residing in the United States. She works in a technical capacity in a city in the Northwest. Her hobbies include paragliding, cartooning, and fencing. She decorates her garden with ceramic figures of frogs. "For Whom the Bell Curve Tolls" is the first fiction she has published under this name. She thanks Andrew Fox for his extensive editorial assistance.

BARRY N. MALZBERG won the inaugural John W. Campbell Memorial Award in 1973 ("best science fiction novel of the year") for his novel *Beyond Apollo*. His three volumes of collected commentary and criticism include *Engines of The Night* (winner of the 1983 Locus Award), *Breakfast in The Ruins*, and *The Bend at The End of The Road*. He has written widely in science fiction, alternate history, mystery, suspense, and erotica. His works have been nominated for the Hugo, Nebula, Sideways, SF Chronicle, Theodore Sturgeon Memorial, British Science Fiction, Philip K. Dick, and Locus Awards multiple times. One of science fiction's most prolific and innovative authors during a fifteen-year period from the late 1960s to the early 1980s, he published about 35 novels in the genre and 300 stories, which have been gathered into 15 short story collections.

MARGRET TREIBER is a writer and an editor for the speculative fiction humor magazine, *Sci-Fi Lampoon*. When she is not writing or working at her day job with technology, she helps her birds break things for her spouse to fix. Her fiction has appeared in a number of publications. Links to her short stories, novels, and upcoming work can be found on her website at the-margret.com and at the Margret Treiber Page on Amazon.

JOE VASICEK fell in love with science fiction and fantasy when he read *The Neverending Story* as a child. He is the author of more than twenty books, including *Genesis Earth*, *Gunslinger to the Stars*, *The Sword Keeper*, and the *Sons of the Starfarers* series. His stories have been published in *Leading Edge*, *Kasma SF*, *Serial Magazine*, *Gallery of Curiosities*, and *Bards and Sages Quarterly*. As a young man, he studied Arabic at Brigham Young University and traveled across the Middle East and the Caucasus Mountains. He lives in Utah with his wife, daughter, and two apple trees.

JAY WERKHEISER teaches chemistry and physics. Pretty much all the time. His stories are sneaky devices to allow him to talk about science in a (sort of) socially acceptable way. Much to his surprise, the editors of *Analog* and various other magazines, e-zines, and anthologies have found a few of his stories worth publishing. Many of those story ideas came from nerdy discussions with his daughter or his students. He really should keep an updated blog and author page, but he mostly wastes his online time on Facebook or Twitter.

KELTIE ZUBKO is a Western Canadian writer with an extensive background in legal research and drafting arguments, as well as publishing two long-running newsletters about censorship, freedom of speech, and Western Canadian politics. She now prefers to explore the gender wars as well as our human relationships with technology in her short stories and novels.

Special Thanks

The editor wishes to express his special thanks to the following individuals whose financial contributions helped make publication of these stories possible:

Preston Plous

Andrew Diseker

Jayne Irvine

David Johnston

James Ryals

Andrew MacBrien

Roland Hirsch

Andrew Berman

Marian Moore

John Weber

Katherine Prouty

Matt Nichols

John Wismar

Michael Reddy

Tim Eklund

John Gabriel

Mike Anderson

Fat White Vampire Otaku
Available April 2021 from MonstraCity Press

The third book in the Fat White Vampire Series; immediately follows the events of tie-in novel *The Bad Luck Spirits' Social Aid and Pleasure Club*. Jules Duchon and his vampiric family suffer through the ravages of Hurricane Antonia and struggle to survive in a city emptied of its population — and its sources of blood. Where will they get their meals? But salvation comes from the most unlikely source possible: a trio of Japanese superheroes called Bonsai Master, Anime Girl, and Cutie-Scary Man. However, that salvation comes with a bedeviling price. For the blood donated by the three superheroes proves to have highly unpredictable effects on Jules and his family. Chaos ensues, in the best tradition of the Fat White Vampire Series!

Available in paperback for the first time!